RED TEA

MEG MEZESKE

CITY OWL
PRESS

RED TEA
By: Meg Mezeske

CITY OWL PRESS
www.cityowlpress.com

Cover Design by Mibl Art. All stock photos licensed appropriately.

Edited by Amanda Roberts.

For information on subsidiary rights, please contact the publisher at info@cityowlpress.com.

Print Edition ISBN: 978-1-944728-83-0

Digital Edition ISBN: 978-1-944728-84-7

Printed in the United States of America

To my parents
(contingent on purchase)

ONE

JORDAN ALWAYS TALKED TO TAXI DRIVERS. SOMETHING ABOUT such a brief, anonymous encounter made them eager to talk about anything. Even things they wouldn't, or shouldn't, share otherwise.

Still, she was taken aback. Perhaps she had just misunderstood. Her Japanese was imperfect, after all.

"Pardon?" Jordan leaned forward to better catch the driver's response above the breeze whipping in the window, which was already sultry despite the early morning.

"It's too bad about that boy dying," he repeated loudly, then swiveled to look at her when she didn't reply. A puff of cigarette smoke and a surprised grunt burst from his lips when he saw her confused expression. "You didn't know?"

"No, I didn't... Who died?" Jordan asked with careful enunciation, swallowing her discomfort.

"One of the students at your school." He said "your school" so matter-of-factly. As though she weren't about to arrive for her very first day of work. As though she were already a fixture there. "He died just the other week. Everyone around here is pretty broken up about it."

"Can I ask what happened?"

This time, the driver didn't turn to look at her, peering at her through the rear-view mirror instead. His eyes narrowed with thought before they returned to the road.

"Word is he killed himself." The driver's voice didn't betray any emotion, but he shook his head and exhaled a long sigh of smoke.

"I—I'm sorry," Jordan said, both with sympathy and regret for asking. Like a reflex, thoughts of her brother surfaced, and she felt a familiar pang deep in her stomach. She tried to push his face from her mind, focusing intently out the window for something else to latch onto.

Jordan watched the homes and shops of Ogawa roll by. Most were either streaked with green algae or mottled with rust. She wondered if all of Japan's little riverside hamlets were like this: crumbling, wet, oppressively muggy. Even the air felt thick and heavy, and the other cars trudged past as though suspended in gelatin.

The driver spoke up again, his affable tone restored. "There it is!" he said and pointed out the window.

Jordan saw a three-story building rise into view and was glad for the distraction. The school looked more recently built and its floor-to-ceiling windows were spotless. It shone in the yolky morning light like a soap bubble. As the taxi slowed to a stop, Jordan watched students file in its huge front doors, greeting each other as they entered.

Only when the driver politely cleared his throat did Jordan realize she had been staring, rooted to her seat. She handed over her fare and grabbed up her jacket and bag as she scrambled out of the taxi.

The students around her stopped and looked on with interest as she neared. They tried to hide their excitement, shielding their whispers and smiles behind their hands, yet none mustered up the courage to approach her.

Nervous, Jordan patted her hair and skirt. She had taken a taxi instead of bicycling the short distance from her apartment so that she'd look impeccable for her first appearance. It had been a good idea, but now that she had arrived, it did little to boost her confidence. Between the conversation with the driver and the students' penetrating looks, anxiousness clutched at her.

With a deep breath, Jordan straightened and marched toward the school. A gangly girl standing at the door finally let out a squeak of a greeting.

"Good morning, *sensei*."

"Good morning," Jordan said a little too quickly and tried to make up for it with a broad smile. She brushed past the girl and her friend as they dissolved into titters.

Jordan walked into a wide entryway that held rows of shoe compartments and an umbrella bin housing a few torn and rusting occupants. She found an empty cubby for her shoes, which she slipped off and replaced with a pair of indoor slippers from a nearby shelf. At least she had been in Japan long enough not to embarrass herself with improper shoe etiquette. But, she realized with a sinking feeling, she had no idea where to report to. She cast her gaze about until a student finally took pity and pointed her to the stairs.

As she walked up, the teenagers made way and fanned out like frightened sparrows. Jordan tried to smile at whoever would catch her eye, feeling like a new student herself instead of an instructor.

The stairs ended outside of a large room that bore a helpful sign marking it as the teachers' lounge. With a shaky breath, Jordan grabbed the handle of its sliding door and bowed at the waist as she entered.

"Excuse me," she said as formally as she knew how. She straightened from the bow and announced herself to no one in particular. "My name is Jordan Howard, and I'm your new assistant language instructor." She could've kicked herself for her voice rising in question.

From some desks near the door, a handful of people stood up smoothly and bowed in return. Among them was a middle-aged man with wings of dark hair encircling his bald head.

"Jordan-*sensei*, good morning!" he said with enthusiasm and straightened his glasses to get a better look at her. "I'm Principal Kikuchi. We're so pleased to have you join Ogawa High School."

"Nice to meet you," Jordan said and bowed again for good measure.

The principal offered another formal pleasantry she didn't quite catch before he gestured to an older woman. If Jordan had to guess, she was nearing seventy.

"This is Vice Principal Umiko Nakamura."

Jordan was surprised at how tall the vice principal stood. Ms. Nakamura gave only the barest indication of a bow, remaining at almost her full height. Her mouth was small and pinched, emphasized by her unsmiling, tight-lipped expression. The only cheery thing about the woman was her incongruously pink jacket and skirt.

"Nice to meet you," Ms. Nakamura said as flatly as if she were giving the time, and she looked Jordan up and down. Jordan swallowed and listened attentively as the introductions continued from teacher to teacher, bowing and nodding like a marionette, until at last, a bell rang.

Jordan drained her second cup of green tea, rolled the glass between her palms, and surveyed the teachers' room. Besides her, only the frail lunch lady remained. All the other teachers had filed out to their home-rooms and the principal had retired to his office when the first bell of the day had sounded.

As she waited for the other teachers to return, she organized her stack of three textbooks, one for each grade level. "First grade" was the equivalent of an American high school sophomore class, and so on.

Jordan tapped her foot against the floor, unsure of how to occupy herself. She stared out the large window in front of her, which framed a corner of the baseball diamond, a wing of the school that mirrored where Jordan sat, and low, green hills in the distance.

The entire length of Ogawa trickled along and abutted such hills. The small town was bound on one side by these stubby, broccoli-like trees and by a long, twisting river on the other.

Though not yet nine o'clock, the air was stifling. Not a single cloud smudged the sky, and Jordan felt herself sweat more with every passing minute. Already, she could feel her blouse sticking between her shoulder blades, and a bead of sweat snaked from the back of her knee down her calf.

She stood to find a washroom for freshening up and jumped when a loud chime lanced through the intercom. A moment later, students began to file through the halls, filling the recent silence with muffled conversations and footsteps.

Ms. Nakamura slid open the door and moved to her desk without even a glance in Jordan's direction, soon followed by a trickle of teachers. A short woman with round, close-cropped hair made a beeline from the door toward Jordan. She smiled broadly and held out her hand.

"Good morning! I'm Chiaki Okubo, the English instructor," she said in brisk, near-perfect English as she shook Jordan's hand. "I'm sorry I didn't introduce myself earlier but I was already late for homeroom announcements. Are you ready? We only have a few minutes."

Jordan was pleased and surprised by such an informal introduction. Mrs. Okubo merely seemed anxious for an answer.

"I'm as ready as I'll ever be," Jordan said with a smile.

"Okay! Bring your third-grade textbook. I'll be back in a moment." Without waiting for a response, she strode off. Jordan grabbed the top textbook from the stack and stood patiently for no more than a minute. When Mrs. Okubo returned, she cradled a tower of books, sheaves of loose assignments, and a pencil case in her short arms. "Let's go."

Jordan had to hurry to keep pace with the small woman as she exited the teachers' lounge and made her way up a staircase. Mrs. Okubo spoke again after a few steps, unfazed by her burden and quick pace.

"So, what do you think about Japan? It must be very different from your home."

"It's very different, yes, but I like it so far," Jordan said.

"Think you can handle a whole year? How long have you been here?"

"This is only my third day." Jordan raised her voice to be heard over the slapping of her shoes against the echoing stairs. "I spent the first day getting from Tokyo to here and yesterday sorting out my paperwork. My alien registration card, bank card, all that."

"So, this is your first time at Ogawa High School?" She seemed curious but pushed ahead without waiting for details from Jordan. "Well, the students are very excited to meet you."

As if on cue, Jordan saw necks craning as she passed each class-room. Heads turned in concert with her passing steps, as though the students' noses were connected to her by long threads. She smiled and nodded, assuming someone would notice, and returned her attention to the petite English instructor.

"I'm eager to meet them, too."

"You'll meet the first- and third-grade classes today. Second-graders tomorrow. But don't worry about that too much. You can give the same introduction for each class." An odd grin quirked her lips. "You're our first female assistant language instructor. You may even be the first foreign woman some of these students have met."

Jordan's stomach was already painfully tight, and Mrs. Okubo's words settled in her gut like burrs. Unsure of anything to say that didn't reveal her nervousness, Jordan simply nodded.

"Well, here we are." Mrs. Okubo stepped in front of a closed door underneath a placard that read *san-nensei, ni-gumi*: third grade, second class. There was a porthole window on the door, and Jordan could see the dark silhouettes of at least three students crowding behind the frosted glass. The sun at their backs made their faces indistinguishable. She heard low laughter and shushing as Mrs. Okubo continued.

"Introduce yourself—tell them a little about your hometown, your family—and we'll take it from there. Okay!" She said the last bit more loudly, probably as a warning to the students, and slid open the door. Jordan stepped inside and took a deep breath.

All the students sat at their desks, giving no indication of having spied against the window only moments before. Most had their hands clasped on their desks or in their laps, some grinning or leaning toward their friends with whispers on their lips. Jordan overheard hushed remarks between a pair of girls and couldn't help but smile.

"She's so pretty—and tall!"

"I'm jealous! I want her blond hair."

They jumped and returned their attention to the front of the classroom when Mrs. Okubo dropped her stack of books against her desk.

"Good morning, class."

"Good morning, Okubo-*sensei*," the class intoned with practiced unison. Mrs. Okubo looked at Jordan, and she took that as her cue.

"Good morning, everyone." Jordan scanned the room, meeting the eyes of whoever would catch her gaze for more than a moment.

"Good morning, Jordan-*sensei*." Many students stammered and tripped over her name. Some laughed at their friends or repeated her name to themselves to get a feel for the sounds on their tongues.

"Everyone, as you know, this is our new assistant language instructor, Ms. Jordan Howard," Mrs. Okubo said with slow, clear precision. "Now it's time to introduce yourselves—the American way!" She grabbed Jordan's hand and shook it to demonstrate, which lead to another round of murmurings. "Kenji, please come here to introduce yourself."

A handsome boy at the front of a row—hair styled to look tousled—pointed at himself incredulously then looked behind him, as though searching for another Kenji. This earned a few laughs, especially from a tall classmate who gave him a friendly shove out of his seat. Kenji sauntered to the front of the room and took Jordan's outstretched hand.

"My name is Kenji." His handshake was firm but hurried and he smiled with warmth. "Nice to meet you."

"Nice to meet you too."

As Kenji returned to his desk, a few boys gave him teasing congratulations. Even some calls of "teacher's pet" could be heard as the next student rose from her seat.

This continued for a few minutes, some students were hesitant and timid. Others laughed and made a show of the handshake. Jordan struggled to remember each student's name but soon became lost. She looked to their nametags pinned to their shirts for assistance, but they were written in the Chinese-based *kanji* character system, of which Jordan only knew a scant few.

The girls all wore white short-sleeved shirts with maroon ascots. Their long skirts were grey-and-maroon plaid, paired with knee-high black socks. At least, most of them were dressed to uniform.

One sullen girl who mumbled through her greeting—Emi—had unbuttoned the top of her shirt, exposing a hint of cleavage, and hiked up her skirt to the middle of her pale thighs. Her friends tried to emulate her style but introduced themselves far more politely. These girls began to chat among themselves as soon as they returned to their seats.

The boys wore similarly conservative uniforms: black slacks and white button-down shirts. Their neckties bore the same grey-and-maroon plaid as the girls' skirts. Some had loosened their ties because of the heat or removed them altogether; whether this was a breach of school conduct, Jordan couldn't be sure.

Finally, only one student remained—the tall boy who had been joshing with Kenji. All long limbs and lanky movements, he shuffled toward Jordan with a lopsided grin. Standing so close, she was even more surprised by his height, though she supposed he was one of the oldest students. She held out her hand.

"My name is Ryusuke," he said haltingly and bowed. "Nice to meet you."

"Nice to meet you, Ryusuke," Jordan said and bobbed her outstretched hand, which he failed to take. He bowed again after a moment of hesitation. A few students laughed.

"Shake her hand," Mrs. Okubo said in English, but her instructions only further confused him and he looked anxious.

"*Akushu!*" Kenji supplied.

Ryusuke smiled with relief, his face flushing. He sheepishly looked toward the class, and with great emphasis, wiped his palms on his slacks. Everyone laughed at this, Jordan included, and he enveloped her hand in his. He shook it firmly and turned away.

"He was very excited to meet you," Mrs. Okubo said to Jordan as the boy returned to his seat, then she addressed the whole class. "Well done, everyone. Now let's all listen as Jordan-*sensei* tells us about herself and where she's from."

"Well, for starters, I'm twenty-two years old and just graduated from college. I have a very big family," Jordan said and made a sweeping motion with her arms to indicate a long line. "I have two sisters and two...uh, one brother. I'm the youngest." She forced a smile to gloss over the fumble and looked at the floor, allowing herself a moment to recover. Mrs. Okubo glanced in Jordan's direction when she didn't continue right away.

"I heard you're from Las Vegas. Is that right?" Mrs. Okubo prompted.

"Yes, I am," Jordan said quickly and raised her head, taking care to project her voice.

"Oh! Like in James Bond," one boy said and mimed shooting a gun with his hands clasped together. Others nodded in sudden understanding.

"Um, something like that," Jordan said gamely and continued. As she spoke, she tried to take in each student. Some nodded with excitement, while others listened politely as the sun climbed up the window.

"You survived your first class," Mrs. Okubo said when they arrived at the teachers' room.

"Barely." Jordan smirked to show she was joking. Actually, she felt remarkably at ease. If every student was so open and friendly, she imagined her time in Ogawa High School wouldn't be as intimidating as she had feared.

"We have about ten minutes before the next class, so please take your seat for a moment," Mrs. Okubo said but had no intention of taking a break herself. She scurried off and disappeared among the other teachers milling near their desks and filing in and out of the copier room.

As Jordan took her seat, she was happy to find a cold glass of green tea placed on her desk. She drank the tea gratefully in a few gulps, parched by the heat and from speaking throughout the entire class.

A female teacher seated close by glanced in Jordan's direction at the sound of her chair scraping the floor, but she returned her attention to a student instead of greeting Jordan.

The student was a gawky boy. He looked younger than the students Jordan had just met—a second-grader, judging by the color of his nametag—and he seemed upset. His eyes were red, and his voice quavered as he spoke. Jordan knew it would be impolite to eavesdrop, yet she couldn't help but train her ears on him.

"...he keeps insisting that Yuki didn't do it," the boy said between hiccuping gulps of breath. "I just—I wonder if he's right."

"He's upset. After all, he lost his brother." The teacher didn't sound sure of her own words, and her voice wasn't much steadier than his. "Denial is common after a death. I know it's hard to understand, but..."

Jordan shifted her focus elsewhere and reprimanded herself for listening in on such a private conversation. Selfishly, she also regretted that her snooping had poked at her own deep, gnawing aches.

Before long, the boy excused himself and left, his head drooping with the weight of his thoughts.

With a sigh, the teacher shook her head and stared at her clasped hands. A minute passed before she remembered Jordan's presence, but once she did, she perked up and turned in her chair to face her.

"You must be Jordan-*sensei*," she said in Japanese. "My name is Reiko Tatsuya."

"Nice to meet you," Jordan said and bowed as best she could while seated. Ms. Tatsuya also bowed her small frame, thin and bird-like, and readjusted her glasses after they slipped down her sharp nose. "What subject do you teach, Tatsuya-*sensei*?"

"Mathematics," she said. Her lips stretched over her jutting teeth in an odd sort of smile. Then she lowered her eyes. "It's not as exciting as English, I'm sure."

"I wouldn't say that. Your students must like you very much if they come to visit you in the teachers' room."

"Oh, you mean that boy just now? Akira?" Ms. Tatsuya's large glasses made her look bewildered and wide-eyed. "Akira was Yuki's best friend. I asked him to see me since he's having such a hard time of it."

"I'm sorry, but I don't know who you're talking about," Jordan said, feeling discouraged. She tried to piece together the bits of conversation she had just overheard but couldn't place them in some larger picture.

"Yuki? He died about a week ago." Ms. Tatsuya's eyes teared up behind her glasses. "I'm sorry. I thought you knew."

"Oh! I had heard something... I just didn't know the student's name. I'm sorry." Jordan could tell the diminutive woman was upset, and she didn't relish wading into others' personal tragedies. She would have let the matter lie, but Ms. Tatsuya picked it up after a beat.

"He committed suicide," she said, her voice becoming a pitiful wail.

"I'm so sorry." Jordan felt her throat constrict around the words.

"Yuki wasn't just Akira's best friend. He was probably his only friend. They were both in my homeroom class." She sniffled but restrained herself from crying, eyes shining and red. "I can't believe Yuki would kill himself. He had so many plans. He never..."

Jordan nodded and waited for Ms. Tatsuya to continue, but the other woman stared at the handkerchief she had pulled from her pocket and turned away. Mumbling to herself, Ms. Tatsuya picked up and set down a handful of papers, only to grab at them again a moment later, forgetting all about their conversation.

"Ready?"

Jordan jumped at the brusque voice behind her, not hearing Mrs. Okubo approach. "Yes!" Jordan grabbed her textbook and darted out of her seat, grateful for the excuse to leave. "I'll see you soon, Tatsuya-sensei. Umm, it was nice to meet you."

"Hmm? Oh, yes, the pleasure's all mine," Ms. Tatsuya said as though she were just waking up, her distracted gaze never leaving her desk.

"She's an odd duck, that one," Mrs. Okubo whispered once they were out of earshot of Ms. Tatsuya. "Just come to me if you have any questions, okay?"

Jordan nodded and followed Mrs. Okubo out of the teachers' room. As she slid the door shut behind them, she spared one last glance at the mathematics teacher, who stared out the window silently.

Jordan exchanged her indoor slippers for the flats in her cubby, purse and jacket in hand. Jordan was alone in the entryway at the foot of the stairs. Either most students had returned home at the close of the school day or they were attending their many after-school clubs.

Jordan felt a bit uncomfortable heading home when the faculty room was still packed with teachers poring over assignments. But as far as she knew, she had no further duties for the day and would only be wasting time by pretending to look busy at her desk.

She decided it was best not to concern herself with the other teachers' responsibilities as she stepped out the door. She was tired and had had a long day, after all.

Her apartment was a short distance away, and she planned to walk home instead of calling a cab. It was still bright out, and the oppressive midday heat had mellowed.

As she passed the covered bicycle port and made for the road, she heard a voice calling her name. Turning back, Jordan saw two figures loping toward her at a brisk pace. A moment later, she recognized the boys from her first class that morning: Kenji and Ryusuke.

"Jordan-*sensei*," Kenji said with gusto. Despite Kenji's youthful features, Jordan could tell he would grow up to be quite handsome. He was favored with a straight, bright smile and eyelashes so dark they seemed painted on. "Would you like to watch our baseball team practice?"

A quick glance showed he was dressed for it, wearing a nondescript jersey with the sleeves rolled up, baseball pants, and high socks paired with cleats.

His tall friend was dressed the same, glove in hand, and stood beside him, smiling. Jordan could feel beads of sweat stippling her neck after only a few moments outdoors, and she longed for some rest after an exhausting first day. But she suspected the boys would be disappointed if she declined, and she was flattered.

"I'd love to, Kenji," she said in English. At the confused expression that crossed Ryusuke's face, she added in Japanese, "Sure, let's go."

"Please follow me," Kenji said, and Ryusuke's smile broadened.

Jordan took a seat on the concrete risers as Kenji and Ryusuke returned to the field. A few of the other boys looked to the stands and waved. Jordan waved back. She glanced around for an instructor, but it appeared as though the students had organized themselves.

They formed small clusters in the fields, tossing balls in practiced drills. Jordan watched attentively for a few minutes, but the warm sun still hanging high above began to lull her.

Kenji left his group and barked an order to the rest of his teammates. Some of the players trotted to the diamond. One began to don catcher's gear, and three took places in the outfield. Jordan decided Kenji must be team captain, if he was leading the group.

Kenji spoke to Ryusuke as he passed, prompting the tall boy to stop and say something playful back. Kenji pushed him and grinned. From her place in the risers, Jordan heard Kenji say, "You are such an idiot."

Ryusuke ambled to the pitcher's mound, and Kenji joined the line near the batter's box. Soon, Ryusuke began pitching to his teammates— rather expertly, Jordan noticed. He had seemed oafish before, a little too tall for his own skin, but on the mound, he was fluid and imposing. He threw each pitch with obvious force and power, and very few balls floated past him to the outfield. Kenji came to the plate and was struck out in three pitches.

"Home run!" Ryusuke teased. "We'll never win with that swing, Captain."

Kenji handed off his bat and headed for the mound.

"Yeah, well, pitchers don't have to be good hitters, right?" Kenji said and motioned to Ryusuke, who gave him his glove before jogging toward the plate.

The drill continued at a steady but relaxed pace. Kenji and Ryusuke took turns on the pitcher's mound with two other boys, and the outfielders switched out to bat. Jordan watched the balls arc through the air, as though plowing furrows through the humid dampness. They skirted the sky like tiny sails at sea, and the trees' shadows barred the field as the sun drew to the horizon.

It was dusk by the time baseball practice ended. After saying goodbye to the team, Jordan began to make her way home. She walked the same narrow road her taxi had followed that morning, passing a fire station with an almost comically large statue of a fire extinguisher out front. This was followed by rows of houses with yellow lights in their windows.

After a few minutes, she came to the largest, and only, major roadway through town. The north-south highway ran the entire length of Ogawa, primarily used by commuter vehicles and shipping trucks passing through on their way to larger cities. Jordan had yet to explore all of Ogawa, but of what she had seen, she could count every stoplight on one hand, and all of them along this single roadway.

Jordan crossed the highway via an underpass and made her way toward a Lawson store just off the road. The convenience store's blue-and-white sign cast a pale light across its parking lot. Jordan pushed open the door and felt a sweep of conditioned air across her flushed face.

Though she had done little but stand and shake hands all day, Jordan was exhausted and hungry, now that the nervous tension began to loosen its grip on her stomach. She passed aisles of snack foods on her way to the refrigerators along the back wall.

Jordan skipped over the sandwiches, from egg salad to *yaki soba* noodles piled in torpedo rolls. She selected two *onigiri*: triangular mounds of rice the size of her fist. One was filled with flaked bonito and the other with cod roe, both wrapped in sheaths of seaweed.

She also grabbed bottled oolong tea and melon *pan*, a sweet roll crowned with a lattice of sugary crystals. The store was empty, so Jordan went straight to the register, which was manned by a teenage girl.

The girl smiled politely from behind sleek, dark hair that draped her face, but she showed no other sign of recognition. Not one of her students, then. Jordan offered a greeting and placed a handful of yen and her point card in a tray near the register.

As she waited for the girl to complete her transaction, Jordan's eyes fell on a stand of newspapers. The shelf contained the national *Mainichi Shimbun* newspaper and a local publication bearing Ogawa's symbol in the header.

The front page's lead story featured a record-breaking strawberry grown by a local farmer in his greenhouse. Jordan took another glance at the photo of the grinning man, holding a huge fleshy strawberry the size of an apple, and added the newspaper to her purchase. Though she knew she'd be unable to read many of the *kanji* characters, she hoped she could glean enough information to make small talk around the school.

She thanked the young clerk and stepped outside. The sky had become inky with only a shrinking swath of blushed light along the horizon. The path to Jordan's apartment was sparsely lit, so she quickened her pace while she could still make out the deep, treacherous gutters that lined each sidewalk.

She passed a pharmacy and a grocery store before walking down a narrow side street that hedged in a few dozen houses. When Jordan emerged onto a larger road, she could see her apartment building.

Beside the building was a fallow rice paddy that sprouted with thin, pale weeds. Jordan skirted the edge of the dry paddy and walked in its soft dirt to avoid the shoulder of the dark road. The soft chirping of frogs emanated from the vacant paddy and the lush, water-drenched fields that stretched along the opposite side of the road.

Jordan entered the apartment building's stairwell and climbed the steps to its second floor. Her apartment was flanked by two identical spaces that mirrored those below. She had yet to meet any of the building's other occupants, who either kept to themselves or held different schedules than hers. Jordan saw only two cars in the parking lot and could barely make out the sounds of a television behind her neighbor's door.

As she entered her own apartment, she took off her shoes in the recessed entryway and placed them in her shoe shelf. She had no indoor slippers, enjoying instead the feel of the warm wooden floor beneath her bare feet. The entryway opened up into the kitchen, which was connected to the living room past sliding glass doors.

Jordan had been more than pleasantly surprised by the amount of space when she had moved in just the day before. She had imagined she might have to live like a sardine in a tin or squeeze into a pod-like room, as popularized by hotels in Tokyo.

Instead, she had a furnished kitchen with a small table and two chairs, a living space with a television, a three-tatami bedroom, and separate toilet and bath rooms. It wasn't much smaller than the loft in Las Vegas she had just moved from.

Jordan was still getting used to calling the apartment "home," and its interior gave little indication of who lived there. The furnishings had accumulated over the last decade, as the assistant language instructors before her had come and gone. They had created a hodgepodge of personal aesthetics, from a vintage bookshelf to zebra-striped couch cushions.

Advised by her Japanese Exchange and Teaching Program counselor to bring just two large suitcases' worth of belongings, Jordan had packed only clothes, personal necessities, and a few teaching aids—nothing to distinguish the place as her own yet.

She dropped her purse and jacket in a pile on the kitchen table and fished a bonito *onigiri* and the oolong tea out of their plastic bag. Jordan sat down with a sigh and nibbled the crisp, salty seaweed on the *onigiri*, unfolding the newspaper with her other hand.

The publication was thin, especially for a weekly edition, and she thumbed through the local and national news sections in no time, only understanding a portion of the content. Jordan turned to the recreation section and saw a photo of Ogawa High School's baseball and *kendo* teams posed in solemn groups. She recognized Kenji, Ryusuke, and most of the other boys from that afternoon, though it was odd to see them so unsmiling.

The article was positive, either boasting of the baseball team's record or their promise for the season. She couldn't be sure without consulting a dictionary, so she flipped to the next section. Birth announcements and obituaries.

Below the photos of plump, soft-cheeked babies, an image in the obituaries caught Jordan's eye: a serious teenage boy with wire-thin glasses. A *kanji* character below the photo read "Yuki," and Jordan's pulse tripped as she scrambled for her phone to bring up Google Translate.

Yuki Watanabe, age 15. Survived by his mother and father, Shiori and Hiroshi Watanabe, and younger brother, Shun. Yuki loved science and hoped to one day become a chemist. He will be sorrowfully missed by his family and his friends at Ogawa High School. Memorial services will be held on September 4 at the Yamashita Funeral Home.

Jordan remembered Akira from that morning, Yuki's best friend, and she felt a pang. Familiar feelings of grief began to curl their cold fingers around her neck, her wrists.

Jordan closed the paper quickly and finished the second *onigiri*. Minutes passed with her doing nothing but staring at a few grains of rice that had fallen on the table. Finally, she heaved herself from the chair and went to the writing desk in the corner of the living room. Only an unadorned photo album sat on the desk—the single nonessential Jordan had allowed in her overstuffed suitcases.

She touched the cover of the album, hesitating for a moment before letting it fall back to expose its glossy leaves. From the book, her own face looked back, her mouth open with laughter and cheeks blushed by the sun. On either side of her stood her four siblings with their arms thrown over one another's shoulders. Both of her sisters and one brother were dark brunets—the other brother fair-haired like Jordan—but the upturned noses and high cheekbones they all shared gave them away as family.

Jordan's brief smile crumbled as she touched a finger to the photograph of her brother Aiden. The young man was grinning just as widely as Jordan, straw-blond hair shining with imbued sunlight. They weren't the closest in age, but they were most alike in personality. Or had been, she corrected herself.

Jordan admitted that she had envied Aiden and his willingness to act on his urge to roam, whereas she had so recently pulled up anchor that she could still see the shore. When she was just beginning high school, Aiden had forgone college and instead hopped across the country. He had lived on friends' couches and worked odd jobs before finally alighting in a studio apartment in Brooklyn. Though he said he didn't plan to stay long, he had remained for several years, and it was ultimately the last place he'd lived.

The previous summer, Jordan and her brother and sisters had spent a week in New York to be with Aiden. The photograph before her was the last of all the siblings together, taken at Coney Island one sultry afternoon. Like always, whenever she and Aiden were together, she had wondered how they could ever stand to be apart—both joking and laughing and perfectly understanding each other.

Eight months later, Aiden was dead. Overdosed on prescription pain medication. Pills that no one knew he was taking. Some questioned whether he had taken his own life, Jordan included, until she felt sick from her attempts to rationalize his death. Aiden had debts, but he never seemed to give them a second thought, and he quickly recovered from any bouts of melancholy. He always shrugged off despondency like an ill-fitting jacket.

Jordan sighed as worn feelings of doubt and regret began to pool around her. She had already waded through such waters countless times over recent months, so much so that her emotions felt too muddied to ever settle and clear. She thought moving to Japan would place enough distance between her and the memory of Aiden, as though the hurt would dull with each mile.

His beaming face in the photograph began to blur, and Jordan wiped away a tear with the cuff of her blouse. She closed the album and sank into the couch, listening to the frogs and crickets mutter outside the open window.

TWO

JORDAN CURSED AS SHE WHIPPED AROUND THE CORNER TOO tightly, skidding on a spray of loose dirt and shooting her heel to the pavement to avoid tipping the bicycle. She breathed hard as she righted the overlarge mountain bike—left for her use by her predecessor—and pedaled quickly past the grocery store, only to wait at the stoplight along the highway.

She was late. She instantly regretted her choice to stick to the roadway proper instead of navigating through the underpass. If she hurried, she could arrive at the high school with enough time to make the start of second period. She tapped her hand impatiently against the handlebars, stretching over the too-high seat to keep the bike upright. As soon as the light changed, she was off, pedaling past the fire station and to the school's parking lot, not bothering to lock the bike before rushing through the front doors.

Once inside, Jordan walked as softly as possible to her shoe cupboard and then up the stairs. The teachers' room was almost empty, since most of the instructors had gone to class. She slid open the door quietly, hoping that her untimely arrival would go unnoticed. But as she entered, her hope shriveled when she came face to face with Vice Principal Nakamura.

"Excuse me," Jordan said meekly and bowed to Ms. Nakamura, whose eyes narrowed and lips pursed like the top of a drawstring bag. Jordan scurried to her seat, more flustered than before. She opted, then, to wait for second hour instead of interrupting the first class at its conclusion, which would only worsen her embarrassment.

Across from her sat Mr. Mori. He had not acknowledged Jordan when she arrived and continued to disregard her presence, engrossed in reading a stack of assignments and striking at them with a pen that left red slashes across the pages.

Jordan left him undisturbed and unbuttoned the collar of her blouse in an attempt to cool off. She wished she had been on time, if for no other reason than to be served iced green tea with the morning meeting.

"Did your bike have a flat tire?" a raspy voice said near Jordan's ear, and she jumped in her seat with surprise. Jordan turned to see Ms. Nakamura standing close to her chair, hands clasped together at the waist.

"Excuse me?" Jordan said, breathless.

"You were late," Ms. Nakamura said, and crispness edged her words. "I assume there is a reason for your tardiness."

"Yes, I know. I'm very sorry for—"

"You will apologize to Principal Kikuchi for missing the morning meeting."

"Yes, of course. I intend to," Jordan said around the tightness in her throat, feeling choked. "I accidentally slept in, but I do apologize."

Ms. Nakamura remained silent for a moment, her face inscrutable, before finally opening her puckered lips. "I taught at elementary and junior high schools for decades before becoming Vice Principal here," she said and paused. Jordan nodded, but Ms. Nakamura was looking past her and didn't seem to be waiting for a response. "If any children were late to my class, they were made to stand in the hall with buckets on their heads."

Jordan had seen this exact punishment depicted in Japanese children's books but considered it an exaggeration, like the idea of an unruly student being rapped across the knuckles by a ruler-wielding nun. She almost grinned at the image of students donning bucket-hats, but every muscle within her withered under the vice principal's frosty stare.

"I guess I'm lucky to be a teacher instead of one of your students," Jordan said with a self-deprecating smile, desperate to salvage any measure of standing with the older woman. Ms. Nakamura raised a single eyebrow, almost imperceptibly, but gave no other indication that she had even heard her.

"Only the most...disappointing students let tardiness become a habit." Ms. Nakamura nodded to herself, satisfied with the effect, and turned her back to Jordan. Her heels clicked as she walked away. Jordan turned back to her desk, feeling both relieved and still surprised.

Mr. Mori had been drawn by their conversation and looked plainly at Jordan. A lopsided smirk tugged at one corner of his small mouth in obvious amusement. Jordan bristled but tried to recover herself.

"Where can I buy a new alarm clock?" she asked but got no reaction from Mr. Mori. She frowned and wondered if her Japanese was too poor to convey humor.

"Vice Principal Nakamura is like that around everyone." It wasn't clear whether Mr. Mori was trying to reassure her or was merely stating a fact. "Or so I understand. I haven't known her for very long, I just arrived in April."

"You've only been teaching since April?" Jordan said with surprise, since she guessed him to be in his early forties—much older than most new teachers.

"No, I transferred from Sagae to here. It's quite common, required actually, for the staff to rotate between schools in the prefecture," Mr. Mori said slowly and clearly for Jordan's benefit. "In fact, Ms. Nakamura transferred here to Ogawa High School when I did, along with Mr. Ota, the head teacher."

"She certainly made a reputation for herself, then, if she has only been here a few months." Jordan smiled as she spoke, thinking she had an ally, though Mr. Mori retained a placid expression.

"Not exactly. She taught at Ogawa's elementary school years ago. She's well-known in town."

"I see," Jordan said and nodded. She realized this was the longest she had ever spoken with Mr. Mori. They usually only exchanged greetings at the beginning and close of each day. He seemed nice enough, but perhaps a bit solitary.

He patted at the slicked-back hair along his temple, though it seemed perfectly in place, then adjusted his tie. A dark birthmark crept down his neck and under his collar. Just as he was about to return to work, Jordan interjected, hopeful to get to know him better. "So, how do you like Ogawa?"

"I could ask you the same question," Mr. Mori said and smiled with amusement at his remark. "It's a very charming town, don't you think?"

"Oh, yes. It's great," Jordan said sincerely.

"How is Japan for you?" This was a common question. A safe question. Everyone was endlessly bemused by a foreigner's take on their country. Almost any comment Jordan made—whether about the humidity, how she struggled with chopsticks, or how difficult *kanji* was to read—was met with knowing nods and smiles.

"I really love it so far," Jordan said. It was true, and it seemed like what people wanted to hear. "I experience something new every day— it's exciting."

"Your Japanese is good," Mr. Mori said without much expression, which made his comment seem more like an observation than a compliment. Still, Jordan smiled graciously.

"Thank you very much. I studied for years in college, but I still have a lot to learn." She considered humbly objecting to the compliment, as she had heard many Japanese people do, but felt too proud of her progress to refuse. Praise of her grasp of the language was another comment she had heard many times over, and though she knew she was fairly proficient, she couldn't help but wonder if most were just being polite. "What subject do you teach, Mori-*sensei*?"

Someone had probably already told her the answer to this question, and perhaps Mr. Mori had even mentioned it himself, but it was difficult for Jordan to keep track of the other teachers' classes. She only team-taught English, after all, and worked exclusively with Mrs. Okubo. Jordan hoped Mr. Mori wouldn't be offended that she had forgotten. It was something of a relief to see he was unaffected by the question, possibly even bored.

"Japanese history," Mr. Mori said and fell silent, apparently not seeing a need to elaborate or comment further. Before Jordan could formulate a follow-up question, a bell sounded to signify the end of first period, and students began to pour into the halls for the short break.

"Well, I had better prepare for the next class," she said.

"Yes, you wouldn't want to be late," Mr. Mori said with a pinched smile. Jordan felt there was something a bit unfriendly in his tone.

"It was nice talking to you, Mori-*sensei*," she said, even though their conversation was marred by his parting remark.

"Yes, you too, Jordan-*sensei*." He uncapped the pen and returned to his work.

———

Shrill laughter carried from the back of the classroom, cutting between Mrs. Okubo's words like buzzing midges. Jordan looked away from watching Mrs. Okubo write on the chalkboard to see a group of three girls forming a small clutch, gesturing and smiling without any pretense of paying attention to the lesson. One girl threw her hair over her shoulder and laughed again.

Though the student faced away from her, Jordan knew who it was: Emi Hirata. Of the over two hundred students at Ogawa High School, only a surprising few were disruptive in class, Emi foremost among them.

Jordan stepped away from the board and circuited through the desks as the students practiced a short exercise from the textbook. She looked over their shoulders and offered some quiet suggestions as she made her way toward Emi and her friends. The girls were talking so loudly that, at first, they did not notice Jordan approach.

"Okay, girls. Let's be quiet and pay attention now," Jordan said in a soft but firm voice and adopted a stern look. If their English grades were any indication, they did not understand her reprimand, but there was little mistaking her expression. One girl's cheeks bloomed with color, like a silk blouse soaking up spilled wine, and she ducked her eyes to her textbook. The other friend looked ashamed but didn't turn back to her desk before glancing at Emi for permission.

Emi glared at Jordan, peering at her through lowered, dark lashes that were caked in mascara. Emi wore more makeup than Jordan had seen on most Japanese women, and her hair was dyed a light brown color—an act that could draw punishment from school officials, or so Jordan understood. She was surprised that Emi had not been asked to remove her makeup, or even to pay attention, and wondered if perhaps the teachers had given up on disciplining her.

"What?" Emi said in Japanese, molding the word into a demand for Jordan to justify her presence. She glowered with such hostility that Jordan felt a twinge of nervousness.

"Where's your textbook?" she said in English, refusing to make the conversation any easier for the willful student.

"*Where's your textbook?*" Emi said in Japanese in a high falsetto. One friend laughed, and even the more timid girl who had returned to studying gave a weak chuckle.

"I will bring you my extra textbook," Jordan said, spitting out the words. "But for now, turn around and take notes." She began to walk away, feeling heat rise to her face.

"Whatever, bitch."

A derisive snort followed, and Jordan made every effort not to increase her pace, though she felt repelled by the girl's toxic presence. When Jordan rejoined Mrs. Okubo at the chalkboard, the English instructor spared her a knowing, apologetic look. Jordan clenched her teeth, annoyed that Mrs. Okubo had no intention of backing her up.

Defeated and embarrassed, Jordan faced the blackboard with forced interest and tried to block out the girls' niggling laughter.

Jordan took her seat in the teachers' break room with a sigh, feeling both frustrated and famished. The lunch hour had just started, and she was one of the first to arrive. Jordan smiled at another young teacher at the neighboring table but made no move to join her.

Before, after weeks of taking the same seat every day out of habit, Jordan had once decided to spend lunchtime at a different table—to meet different teachers—but the principal had insisted that she keep her usual place beside him the instant she had picked up her tray. The request had been made in a friendly, smiling manner, but there had been a current of disapproval pulling at his words like an undertow. Ever since, she had continued to take the same seat without question or hesitation.

At the thought of the principal, Jordan remembered that she had missed his morning meeting and began to formulate an apology. She stared at the meal placed before her as though she could divine the perfect wording from the steam swirling above her soup bowl. A minute passed and the sounds of the students rearranging their desks to form lunch groups died down, replaced by the shuffling of teachers as they migrated from the classrooms to the break room.

Soon, Jordan was joined by the head teacher, the lunch lady, Ms. Nakamura, Ms. Tatsuya, and finally, the principal. She nodded to him as he pulled up his chair beside her, but he seemed not to notice, patting at his bald head with a handkerchief and blinking rapidly behind his glasses.

Jordan looked anxiously at the tray of food before her—breaded pork *tonkatsu*, rice, lotus root soup—but waited for the customary cue to begin eating. As though summoned by the thought, the voice of the student body president crackled over the PA system, high and scratchy with static. He made a brief announcement about after-school club meetings for the day and then bade the listeners a good lunch. As his voice gave way to a dulcet cover of an American pop song, the teachers picked up their plastic chopsticks.

"*Itadakimasu*," Jordan said in flat concert with the others and pinioned a thin cut of pork between her utensils. She waited minutes for Principal Kikuchi to say something to her—maybe to ask if she ever ate lotus root in Las Vegas or to tease her for not finishing her rice—but he slurped at his soup without a word. Finally, no longer able to stand his silence, Jordan interjected when he set down his chopsticks to reach for a carton of milk.

"Kikuchi-*kouchou*, I'm very sorry for missing today's morning meeting. I'm afraid I forgot to set my alarm clock," Jordan said and scratched behind her bowed head with one hand—a gesture she had come to learn indicated embarrassment or apology.

"I see," he said and inclined his head in her direction but kept his eyes on his plate.

"It won't happen again," Jordan said with resolve. The principal merely nodded and scooped a clump of rice into his mouth, chewing loudly as he stared at his near-empty tray.

Since any further interaction was plainly unwanted, Jordan hurriedly swallowed her soup in silence, eager to be finished. Just as the last gulp of broth slid down her throat with a warm stroke, the door to the break room slid open.

"Excuse me, Takahashi-*sensei*?" Through the small gap in the door, Jordan could see Emi's friend from earlier—the girl who had, at least momentarily, listened to Jordan's reprimands. Without waiting for an answer, the student shouldered her way into the room, staggering as she pulled Emi along with her.

Emi was leaning on the other girl, one arm draped listlessly over her friend's neck and the other wrapped around her own stomach. Her face was drained of color except for the magenta of her lipstick and the smoky, almost raccoon-like circles of eye shadow. It was odd for Emi to be so uncharacteristically quiet, and Jordan almost felt sorry for her.

Mrs. Takahashi, the school nurse, rose from her seat and hurried to Emi's other side.

"Emi-*chan*, are you all right?" Mrs. Takahashi placed the back of her hand across Emi's forehead as she spoke. With a disgusted grimace, Emi shook her head and pulled away. She clenched her hand against her stomach, puckering her shirt in her grip.

"I think she fainted, Takahashi-*sensei*," the other girl said meekly and looked even more abashed when Emi glowered at her.

"Well, let's get you to my office." Mrs. Takahashi said without alarm and pressed a guiding hand against Emi's shoulder. Emi groaned as she turned away, and the three of them left the room. As soon as the girl was out of sight, many teachers exchanged glances and whispers—some sympathetic murmurs, some exasperated admonishments. Jordan gathered her dishes and cleared them away without remark.

Though the halls were bustling with students, Jordan knew she could pass the period undisturbed if she spent her time on the first floor, where only a few classrooms were housed. She still felt prickly after her encounters with the principal, Ms. Nakamura, and Emi, and she was overcome with a flush of annoyance that rekindled every time she dwelled on the events of the day. She blew out an angry puff of breath and stalked toward the stairs.

As she rounded a flight, Jordan darted to avoid a long cord winding across the steps and the large, bucket-shaped vacuum it was attached to. She nodded at the boy manning the vacuum's hose, knowing any greeting would not be heard over the machine's raspy whirrs ricocheting through the stairwell. When she arrived at the first floor, many more students were caught up in cleaning: dusting and watering plants, washing the windows, and running along the floor with stooped backs, cleaning cloths in hand. Every single school day devoted a short time in the afternoon to cleaning the school, involving every student.

Jordan could hear chairs and desks scraping and knew that the classrooms were getting similar treatment. As she passed an open door-way, she heard a boy coughing as he dusted the chalkboard erasers, his friends laughing and calling him an idiot. For the first two weeks, Jordan had asked what she could do to help, but she was told not to trouble herself and was often ushered to her desk, though she saw other teachers directing students and cleaning.

Instead of sitting in the teachers' room, she had taken to strolling through the halls, striking up conversations with students. Sometimes a student would be convinced to hand her a broom or allow her to arrange desks.

A few first-graders passed by without greeting, still timid around her. It was unlikely that any would approach Jordan or engage her in conversation due to shyness. Perhaps that was for the best, she decided, considering her sullen mood. Jordan ambled away from the stairs and gave quick hellos to students, who replied mostly in Japanese before returning to their assigned tasks.

Before long, she turned a corner and found herself in a recessed room she had never seen before. Unlike the rest of the school, which was always bright and sun-gilded by its windows, the alcove was dark and narrowed into a low hallway that led away from the classrooms. It wasn't until Jordan's eyes adjusted to the dim light that she noticed she was not alone. A boy leaned against a large heap of stacked chairs, facing away from her.

"Hello," Jordan said. Her voice rang loudly in the small room. The boy jumped and scrambled for the broom at his side as he whipped around to face her.

"Oh! Jordan-*sensei*. Hello." He was still startled but seemed relieved to have not been caught by another teacher—one who actually wielded authority.

"Sorry to scare you. And don't worry; I won't make you clean." Jordan smiled and touched her finger to the side of her nose.

"I wasn't scared...but thanks." Instead of smiling back, he frowned petulantly and let his eyes trail away along with the strength of his voice. His gaze landed on a tiny object at his feet. Making a small noise, he quickly stooped to pick it up. He seemed to forget Jordan for a second and fiddled with the item he had snatched. Jordan moved closer and saw a flash of red between the boy's fingers. He didn't seem too interested in engaging her, but she gave conversation one more try.

"What's that?"

"It was my brother's," he said and opened his hand toward Jordan. In his palm, like a single maple leaf on the surface of a lake, was a crimson origami crane no larger than a penny.

"Your brother made that? It's amazing."

"Yeah. He was really good."

Jordan wondered a moment at the use of past tense, unsure of whether she had misheard. She glanced over his palm to his white name tag. *First Grade: Shun Watanabe.* Her breath caught.

"Are you Yuki's brother?"

Shun nodded and kept his head down. He set the broom against the stack of chairs and then ran his fingers gently over the paper figure as though he were petting a real bird.

"I'm very sorry, Shun," Jordan said and wondered whether she should pat his shoulder or offer some other condolence, feeling a twinge in her chest at his miserable expression. "I would have liked to have met him."

"Yuki didn't kill himself." He spoke so softly that Jordan could barely decipher his mumbled words. An instant later, he snapped up from his slouch with a defiant, almost angry look. Shun's plump cheeks were blotchy and flushed, his small teeth bared in a grimace. "He didn't kill himself! I know he didn't! He promised to teach me origami and he never goes back on a promise. He never—" Shun sobbed and sprinted past Jordan toward the opening to the hallway. He almost barreled into another boy who turned the corner, but Shun pivoted at the last moment and fled without another word.

"Shun!" the other boy called after him, but Shun was already gone. The boy shook his head and turned away, eyes widening when he noticed Jordan.

"Jordan-*sensei*! Hello," he said in English.

"Hello." She couldn't quite place the spindly, thin boy—a second-grader by his name tag. Obviously he was in one of her classes, but he looked familiar for some other reason. "I'm sorry. I didn't mean to upset Shun."

"It's not your fault," the boy said, reverting to Japanese. "Shun usually comes down here when he's sad. Yuki and I would always hang out here." Jordan recognized him then. He was the boy who had been speaking with Ms. Tatsuya in the teachers' room on Jordan's first day. Ms. Tatsuya had described him as Yuki's sole friend.

"Are you Akira?"

"Yes."

"And you were Yuki's friend?"

"Best friend." Akira said and straightened with pride. "Yuki was pretty happy when he found this place. Did you see the science room?"

"Science room?" Jordan repeated the words phonetically, not knowing what he meant.

"Yeah, over here." Akira moved past the stacked chairs to a closed door flush against the wall that Jordan hadn't noticed. He motioned her over and then cupped his hands against the sides of his face to peer inside. "Check it out."

He stood aside and pointed to the window. Jordan looked in as Akira had, but she had to strain to see its contents in the low light. Inside were small stacks of books with yellowing pages covered in a patina of dust. Lining the walls were shelves and display cases with curious specimens—objects suspended in bile-like liquids, moths pinned to boards, a taxidermy pheasant with brittle feathers, and other bottled and preserved oddities. A cabinet held empty beakers, test tubes, and glass vials containing various liquids.

Except for a burnished lock on the old cabinet, every inch of the room was dull, dust covered, and yellowing, like a tableau frozen in a sepia photograph. The window on the door was at least clean enough to let her see what the light would allow. As she pulled away from the door, a shiny padlock against its handle rattled.

"Kinda creepy," Jordan said but knew Akira was happy to share his discovery, so she amended her comment quickly. "But interesting! Doesn't anyone use that room? The science teacher?"

"There's a new science lab upstairs with microscopes and burners and all that." Akira shrugged. "Guess the teachers didn't want to use these old supplies. Yuki always thought they were pretty cool. Always wanted to check them out..." His expression changed, and he abruptly fell silent.

"I read that Yuki wanted to study to be a chemist," Jordan said to fill the sudden quiet.

"More like a mad scientist." Akira grinned. "But, yeah, he was crazy-smart. Couldn't shut him up about attending Yamagata University." He looked thoughtful and a little sad despite the smile.

"Sounds like Yuki had big plans." Jordan paused, unsure whether to continue, but ultimately pushed ahead. "Maybe that's why Shun can't believe he killed himself."

"Shun said that, huh?" Akira shook his head with a knowing look. "He was the one who found Yuki, suffocated in his bedroom by a kerosene heater. The doors and windows were blocked up with rags and stuff, so Yuki must've... Anyway, they were really close. It's no surprise Shun can't believe it. Poor kid."

"I know how Shun must feel," Jordan said. Akira nodded in understanding though he had no notion of the weight pulling at her words.

They stood there for a moment, saying nothing. Akira looked at his feet, and Jordan listened to the scrape and shuffle of activity from the floor above. The class bell wedged through the relative silence and pushed Akira out of his contemplation.

"I have to go now, Jordan-*sensei*." His smile was ready, but it didn't quite reach his eyes. "Come back and visit me and Shun down here sometime, okay?"

"Sure, Akira. Thanks."

Akira waved and left quickly, leaving Jordan alone for a moment before she collected Shun's broom and left.

Jordan could feel the pimpled warning strip indicating the edge of the platform, like smooth river rocks beneath her shoes' thin soles. As she waited for the train to Yamagata City, she rocked on her heels, massaging away the soreness of standing up for hours on end.

It was just before five o'clock and the air was still thick and warm. She hadn't bothered to change from her work clothes, opting to bike straight for the station, and could feel her dress shirt clinging to her back. The cool bottle of green tea pressed against her forehead dripped with condensation, offering at least a touch of relief.

Ogawa Station, like every other feature of the town, was small. The station house itself was a short, squat building with seats for barely twenty people, an automated ticket machine, and a small office with a windowed counter that was more often unmanned than not. There were two platforms for boarding and exiting trains—northbound or southbound—bridged by a pedestrian walkway that made a cornered arch from one side to the other.

Jordan had left the school earlier than usual, slipping out before she had to make apologies to Kenji and Ryusuke about missing the team practice, which she attended almost every day. From arriving late to school that morning to her conversation with Shun, Jordan felt worn out and more than a touch disheartened.

She had decided to dawdle in Yamagata City for the evening, where she could enjoy some freshly brewed coffee, Italian pasta, and maybe a little window shopping before the last train back. Plus, Yamagata City had an odd way of making her feel less out of place. Sometimes just a glimpse of an American fast food chain would offer enough comforting familiarity to cheer her up.

Ogawa station was surprisingly empty, considering it would be in the thick of rush hour back home in the United States. But if Jordan's coworkers were any indication, then most working men and women wouldn't begin the commute home until at least seven.

Mingling with the hums and screeches of the cicadas came the low whine of metal against the tracks. Jordan spied the train's headlamps,

low between the rails on the horizon. She stepped away from the edge
of the platform and waited as the train slowed its approach.

The train's doors slid open with a squeal, and she boarded, noticing
with surprise that the car was as empty as the station. The few front-
facing seats were occupied by older women and one gentleman who
had fallen asleep. Jordan moved to one of the long bench seats that ran
along either side of the car and sat at its far end, relaxing against the
wall at her side.

As the doors began to close, a young woman darted inside, looking
flustered. She stumbled as the train lurched forward and practically fell
onto the seat opposite Jordan. Though the girl was no longer clothed in
a telltale high school uniform, Jordan recognized her as one of her
students. She was Emi's friend—the one who had returned to her work
once chided and had helped Emi to the school nurse earlier that day.

The girl pinned her long hair behind one ear as she fumbled in her
shoulder bag. Eventually, she drew out an apron but almost dropped it
with surprise when she noticed Jordan. The girl's cheeks went red and
she looked away nervously. Several seconds passed before she returned
her gaze and spoke.

"Hello, Jordan-*sensei*," she said, near to a whisper.

"Good evening." Jordan couldn't remember the girl's name and felt
a little embarrassed herself.

"I'm...I'm sorry about class today." The girl blurted out the last few
words, wringing her apron in her hands.

"Apology accepted. But please pay attention tomorrow, okay?"
Jordan smiled to put the girl at ease. After all, it was mostly Emi who
was to blame. At the thought of Emi, she decided it would be rude not
to ask whether her friend was feeling better. "How's Emi doing? She
looked pretty sick earlier."

"Oh, she's f-fine, I think." The girl's eyes dropped to the floor and
she began to tap her foot, nervous and distracted. She lowered her voice
again and looked around as though afraid of being overheard. "I understand if you're still mad at me, because of what happened in class, but
please don't tell anyone about this. Please!"

"About what?"

"My part-time job." She looked in her lap. Jordan's eyes followed to the apron being anxiously twisted between the girl's fingers. The corner of the apron had an embroidered logo of a local chain of gas stations. Jordan also noticed the girl's nametag pinned to the apron's front: Nanami.

"What's wrong with working at a gas station?"

"You don't know?" Jordan shook her head, and Nanami continued. "The high school doesn't allow students to have part-time jobs. We're supposed to spend every single minute studying, I guess." Her grimace expressed her thoughts on that subject. "Anyway, I could get in big trouble if the head teacher—or anyone—found out."

"I won't say anything," Jordan said and couldn't help but grin as a look of immense relief washed over Nanami's face.

"Thank you! I promise I'll pay attention in class and study every night. I promise!" Still seated, Nanami gave a series of short, bobbing bows from the waist. When she righted herself, she looked around surreptitiously once more, nodded shyly at Jordan, and then moved her attention to her cell phone.

As recently as a week before, this might have seemed rude to Jordan—dropping a conversation without any given explanation or farewell—but it was uncommon to speak on the train, and Nanami probably felt they were being disruptive. Though Jordan felt a little sorry for the nervous girl and had forgiven her for the day's misbehavior, she preferred to have the rest of the trip to herself instead of being locked into small talk anyway.

The train stopped at and then continued past another station identical to Ogawa's, only picking up a handful of passengers. Jordan looked over Nanami's shoulder to watch the scenery pass by. The sun had begun to drop but was at the perfect level to stun Jordan's vision each time it reappeared from between tall poles and trees sprinkled alongside the tracks. Expanses of square rice paddies shone in the golden light. Streaks of water beneath their lush blades sliced through the fields like rivulets of molten metal.

Between these perfectly spaced paddies stood groups of white- and blue-painted homes, bunched together as though pushed up from between the seams of the fields. Near many of these homes were lozenge-shaped greenhouses about the size of panel vans. The lamps inside made the translucent structures glow with eerie light, like phosphorescent bugs, and their arched roofs formed spindly ribs.

As the train approached another town, the homes began to overtake the paddies, joined by businesses' colorful canopies, billboards, and flashing signs. They arrived at the first of the larger stations on the way to Yamagata City, with multiple platforms and pedestrian walkways. As the train slowed to a stop, Nanami stood and waited beside the door. She paused a moment even after it opened and tossed a look over her shoulder.

"Bye, Jordan-*sensei*. And thank you!" She hopped to the platform and scurried away without waiting for a reply.

THREE

JORDAN'S PEN DRIFTED ACROSS THE PAGE, FORMING A BRIGHT "Good Effort!" in the top margin. She couldn't bring herself to write anything else, even though the student had nearly failed the vocabulary test. He seemed to be trying, at least a little bit. Jordan was trying, too. Impossible though it seemed, she still wanted everyone to like her. Even the sulking, petulant students, like Emi, who hated English. Even Ms. Nakamura. The vice principal's frostiness seemed utterly unmeltable, but Jordan couldn't help but wonder whether she was truly frozen to the core.

Jordan swept her eyes sideways to take in the vice principal sitting at her desk. The older woman didn't move save for the shuttling of her dark eyes, which raked across the papers before her with a sharp, critical look. Jordan sighed but quickly brightened when she saw a student approaching over Ms. Nakamura's shoulder.

Akira pushed open the door and made a quick series of jerking bows, bobbing his way to Jordan like a windup toy.

"Jordan-*sensei*, good afternoon," Akira said with a bright smile.

"Hello, Akira-*kun*. Shouldn't you be with your club?" Jordan tuned her voice so that it was clear she was asking out of curiosity, not accusation. Most of the students had already filtered away from the halls to participate in their after-school clubs and activities. "Ping pong, wasn't it?"

"Yes, that's right. W-would you like to join me?" He rubbed at the back of his head and neck with one hand self-consciously.

"Sure! Though I'm not very good," she said and began to stand up to leave. The remaining vocabulary tests wouldn't take more than a few minutes to complete anyway.

"That's all right. I'll teach you."

Jordan had just pushed in her chair when Ms. Tatsuya returned from the single computer shared among the teachers, which she had been squinting at since the end of the final class. She still seemed preoccupied and visibly startled when she noticed Jordan and Akira standing before her. With a small, almost sad smile, she addressed Akira.

"Akira-*kun*, how are you doing? Better?" Ms. Tatsuya said in a cooing voice. "I'll be happy to speak with you in a moment. I just have to print off an assignment first."

"I'm doing fine, Tatsuya-*sensei*, thank you," Akira said. "Actually, I'm here to see Jordan-*sensei*, and we were just about to leave..." His expression was apologetic but he also took a tentative step toward the door, obviously anxious to go.

"Oh, I see." Ms. Tatsuya's smile wilted. She busied herself by removing her thick glasses and swiping at them with a handkerchief, eyes down. "Don't let me interrupt."

"I'll see you again before I leave for the day, Tatsuya-*sensei*," Jordan offered, but the other teacher only nodded and wouldn't meet her eyes. Jordan and Akira shared a glance, and both made for the hallway, neither speaking until they hooked around the corner. Akira broke the silence first.

"Tatsuya-*sensei* is nice—really nice! And she did help me a lot with Yuki," Akira said, thrusting his hand behind his head once more. "It's just that...she always wants to talk about him, even if I don't want to. And she can talk for a long time!" He ended with a laugh.

"I understand," Jordan said, meaning it. After Aiden died, his presence had lingered like a silent shadow over every conversation. When friends greeted her, their eyes would soften and they would ask how she was in a delicate, distant way that suggested they already knew. Even if they didn't know at all, or didn't really want to know. They joked less but smirked indulgently when Jordan might laugh, like they were only rewarding her effort. Jordan wouldn't be that for Akira. She'd try to float along with his current instead of swimming against it.

As they continued walking, Jordan realized Akira was leading her away from the gym, toward the third floor of the school.

"Isn't the ping pong club in the gym?" Jordan said breathlessly, trying to keep up with the boy's long-legged strides as they rounded the top of the stairs.

"Oh, actually, I wanted to show you someplace else." Akira threw a glance over his shoulder, mouth split wide by a wolfish grin. "Since you liked the old science room so much."

Jordan was glad when the boy's back was once again turned so he couldn't see her look of surprise and confusion. At best, the room had been a curiosity to her; at worst, it was downright creepy. Still, she was happy to at least have conveyed her interest in Akira's activities, as one of her students. She couldn't help but chuckle at his eagerness to share more with her, but she also made a mental note to be wary of—and quash—any hints of a schoolboy crush developing.

They soon arrived at a utilitarian door with a small window through which she could see yet more stairs. Akira shot a quick, wary glance down both ends of the corridor, and Jordan felt her stomach drop a few ribs lower. Akira reached for the door handle and she quickly interjected.

"Akira, are we allowed in there? I don't want you to get in trouble." *She* didn't want to get in trouble. She was supposed to be the responsible adult, after all. Jordan shivered as she imagined Ms. Nakamura's bleak eyes glaring at her in reprimand.

"Well, it's only the roof. Lots of us go up here to eat lunch." He shrugged. "It's kind of off-limits after school, but no one really cares. Yuki and I hung out here loads of times."

Jordan pursed her lips, unconvinced.

"It's no big deal. I promise!" In direct contradiction of his own words, he raked another cagey look around them and then pushed through the door. Jordan winced at the loud creak and hesitated for a beat before following him into the narrow stairwell beyond.

When they emerged on the flat rooftop, Jordan squinted and had to shield her eyes against the rays of kindled sunlight that sliced across the horizon. In the moments it took her to blink away the temporary blindness, she didn't realize they were not alone on the roof. Startled, she heard Akira cry out.

"Shun-*kun*!"

"Shun...?" Jordan used both hands now to block the sun and search for the boy who had caught Akira's attention. Once she saw Shun—his small figure smudging the sunlight around him—a blade of fear plunged into her chest and she struggled to even pull in breath.

Shun had climbed over the tall chain-link fence that encircled the roof. He had even scaled the shelf of fencing that folded toward the center of the building, designed—no doubt—to deter students from doing exactly what Shun had accomplished. There, the boy clung to the outside of the angled fence, curled like a cicada shell on a tree. He was near enough to the edge that he could push himself free of the fence, or even slip and fall.

"What are you doing up there?" Akira's question was punctuated by a nervous laugh. Shun said nothing but cringed against the fence and pressed his cheek between the chain links. The boy's silence only furthered Akira's confusion, and his eyes darted between Shun, the fence, and the ground below, searching for some sort of explanation to the boy's behavior.

"Akira," Jordan said as calmly as she could, keeping her voice steady. "Go to the teachers' room and get help from Ms. Nakamura."

Akira nodded once, slowly, but Jordan couldn't be sure whether he had really heard her. He was reluctant to look away, and an expression of growing worry crinkled his features. When he made no move to leave, Jordan raised her voice.

"Akira. Go to Ms. Nakamura, *now*." She tried to sound authoritative, but anxiety and impatience fissured her words. The change in tone was enough to startle Akira into attention, and he whipped his head toward her. Noiselessly, mouth open and eyes wide, he nodded and sprinted toward the door. She could hear the rattling echo of Akira bounding down the steps as the door eased shut behind him.

Jordan took a deep breath and let it out in a slow stream.

"Shun?" The boy didn't respond or even look in her direction. Carefully, she inched closer toward the fence. "I want you to slowly make your way back here to the roof. Can you do that?"

"No," Shun snapped. His small fingers tightened around the fence, shaking. "I don't want to."

"Why don't you want to come down?" Jordan hoped her question came across as conversational, friendly even, not as terrified for the boy's safety as she felt. She took another step forward and could finally see Shun clearly, his huddled form blocking the sun behind him. The boy looked at Jordan, but then his gaze strayed to the ground far below and he shied back against the fence, face drawn tight.

"I want to be with my brother again. I miss him," Shun said in a small voice, and Jordan could hear the wet sniffle of held-back tears. Once again, he buried his face against the fence.

"I know you do, Shun. Believe me. I know exactly how you feel." Aiden's smiling face floated to the surface of her thoughts. Then, Aiden's studio apartment—a jar of peanut butter on the counter, left open like he would be coming right back to make a sandwich. Jordan swallowed. "My brother died, too. Less than a year ago."

"Really?" Shun raised his head to look at Jordan, his eyes puffy and wet. The zig-zag pattern of the chain link had indented his pillowy cheek like a brand. His gaze was expectant and curious, and he waited for Jordan to say more.

"Yes. And I miss him every day, and it hurts to remember him—to be away from him. But I know he wouldn't want me to..."

She stopped short of saying the words, as though speaking of suicide would be an incantation that could bring her words to fruition. Besides, she wasn't sure if Shun even fully grasped what he was doing, and if he hadn't truly committed to taking his own life, she didn't want to be the one to utter the thought. She drew a shaky breath and tried again. "I know he would want me to be happy again. I know Yuki wants the same for you too."

"What's his name? Your brother?"

"Aiden," Jordan said and allowed herself a smile. "Maybe we could share some stories. If you'd only come down so we could talk. Please."

Shun worried his bottom lip between his teeth, raking one final, lingering look across the ground below before nodding.

"Okay," he said and reached upward to grab at the fence above him. The linked fence sagged and groaned as he climbed toward the inner edge of the shelf, bulging as though it were an animal taking in deep breaths. As Shun moved his foot to find a new hold, his sneaker slipped and he fell flat against the fence with a sharp clang. Jordan gasped.

"Are you all right?" She jumped forward, arms outstretched despite the fact that it would be impossible to catch him from her position.

"I'm fine," Shun said with anemic bravado and doggedly continued up the fence, more slowly than before.

"Be careful. Take your time." Her eyes never left him, hoping that—somehow—the force of her will would be enough to tether him to the roof, like tying a ribbon to a balloon before it could float away. Before it slipped forever beyond reach.

Just as Shun pulled himself to the top of the fence and hooked one leg across the lip, Jordan heard footsteps resounding on the stairs. A moment later, the door flew open, and Ms. Nakamura, the head teacher, and the principal burst onto the roof.

Shun paused, shocked, both legs now dangling over the inside of the roof and his stomach folded across the jutting fence. Jordan positioned herself to guide the boy down, but her fingertips had barely grazed his shoes before she was shouldered out of the way.

"I've got you," Principal Kikuchi said. His voice was gruff with admonishment, but Jordan could see the worry in his eyes—blown wide behind his smudged glasses. The principal's hands clamped around Shun's calves and the head teacher moved to hook the boy under the armpits as he was lowered. With a sigh of breaths and shuffling limbs, Shun finally set both feet on the roof.

No time was allowed for celebration or relief before Shun was hurried away. The head teacher guided Shun toward the door, his hand squeezing the nape of the boy's neck in a reassuring gesture. Ms. Nakamura's face was lowered to Shun's and she spoke urgently, but her voice was too quiet for Jordan to hear whether she was reprimanding or consoling him. Shun nodded and kept his eyes to the ground, not once looking back toward Jordan before he disappeared into the stairwell.

The principal had hung behind. Unmoving, he stared across the horizon. His gaze was fixed on some point far into the hills, which were glazed with the honeyed light of the lowering sun. He rubbed his head, pushing furrows into his bald scalp, and looked straight ahead without blinking. Finally, he seemed to awaken from his stupor and walked to the door in a few long strides. There, he paused, turned toward Jordan, and nodded once as he exited.

Jordan supposed it was the only recognition she would receive, if what little she had done was even deserving of gratitude. Not that she had spared a single thought for herself at the time—her entire world had narrowed to a pinpoint that only had room for Shun. She wondered, though, whether she could feel true relief.

No doubt another new lock would appear on the door leading to the roof—a twin to the one that clung to the old science room.

Jordan let out a long, unsteady breath and rested her hands against the honeycombed fence, feeling rough flakes of rust catch her against her skin. She didn't move until the edge of the sky dipped into darkness and a growing chill pushed her away.

FOUR

"Spring came. Freddie, za leaf, was born on a small branch of a tall tree," Akira said, reciting haltingly in English as he stood beside Jordan's desk in the teachers' room. She nodded with encouragement when he paused to consult his textbook with a frustrated shake of his head. "Hundreds of leaves were born on za tree. They were all friends."

She had given Akira her full attention for the last hour—and for many hours after school during the previous week—but it was getting late and she let her mind wander. Akira had been practicing his recitation diligently to prepare for an upcoming English competition between nearby high schools. Jordan offered to be his coach, to help him improve his pronunciation and general skill. Though he was enthusiastic and hardworking, he struggled. Happily for Jordan, he had improved his efforts in English class. He often chatted with her during breaks and became one of her most vocal, if not most proficient, students.

Jordan looked past Akira, through the large windows facing the rolls of low mountains that traced the eastern side of town. The hillside trees had turned to rust with the arrival of autumn, coppery colors winding through the veins of each leaf. A few fat evergreens dotted the banks of trees, forming dark, green patches among the vibrant orange and red. The sky churned with ash-colored clouds that crested and crept down the mountainside like slow waves over rocks. A few drops of rain dotted the window and Jordan saw Kenji, Ryusuke, and the rest of the baseball team leave the field. It was late for the students to still be at school, and Jordan decided to send Akira home as soon as he finished.

"He did not know this, but in za tree and za ground, there were already plans for new leaves in spring."

"Nice job, Akira. You've really been practicing—I can tell. But remember, it's 'the' not 'za.' Practice putting your tongue under your teeth." She mimed with her own tongue, exaggerating for effect, and Akira laughed.

"Freddie *the* leaf," he said before adopting a serious look and returning to Japanese. "I'll never memorize the whole thing."

"Don't worry about that now. We're working on pronunciation, right? There are still two more weeks until the competition. You have plenty of time to memorize."

"Okay." Akira nodded but didn't look convinced.

"Ask one of your friends to help you practice. It'll be fun." The words had barely crossed her lips before she remembered that Yuki's passing had left a social void in Akira's life. "Umm, maybe Shun?"

"Yeah maybe."

"How's Shun doing?" Jordan hadn't spoken to the boy after the incident on the roof. She learned that he had spent the following few days at home and was seeing a counselor who visited the school once a week. In class, he was quiet and withdrawn, but this behavior was no different from how he had acted before. Still, she was concerned.

"He's doing better, I think. He said he won't try anything like that again," Akira said and attempted a reassuring smile that fell short of its mark.

"I'm glad to hear that."

"Well, I'd better head home," Akira said stiffly. He ran a hand through his bowl-cut hair, which looked too boyish for a young man halfway through high school, and then began to collect his books. "Thanks, Jordan-*sensei*. I'll see you tomorrow."

"Yep, see you tomorrow," she said and watched him leave. Akira was clearly still struggling with the loss of his friend, perhaps as much as Shun. Though she was happy to tutor Akira, and help fill the time he might have otherwise spent with Yuki, Jordan missed afternoons with the baseball team.

If she left soon, she thought she might be able to catch a few of the players near the cubbies or the bicycle lot. Jordan pulled on her jacket, gathered her purse, and made her way to the door. There, she turned to face the many teachers still crouched over paperwork and gave her studied farewell.

"*Osaki ni shitsure shimasu.*" The phrase literally translated to "please excuse my rudeness for leaving before you." Almost everyone parroted this expression upon departing, but Jordan felt it only applied to her, almost always the first to leave. But she had no assignments to grade, no lessons to plan, and could only keep up the appearance of working at her desk for so long before her eyelids started to droop and her head nodded forward.

"Thanks for your hard work," a few teachers said back. The customary response. But many were smiling, and Jordan knew she had something of a free pass being a foreigner. Though, she caught a glimpse of Vice Principal Nakamura looking at her sourly as she slid the door shut.

There were few lights on, and the hallways were dark due to the woolly clouds stitched in the sky. Jordan shivered, mostly at the sudden chill of the open halls, but partly because of the eerie stillness that seemed so at odds with the bright, peopled room she had just left. She could hear the shuffle of feet and low voices every now and again, carried from a far corner through the empty corridors.

Just as Jordan was about to head to the exit, she noticed a large smudge of ink across her hand and decided to take a moment to wash it off. She pivoted toward a sink basin with several faucets that was wedged in an alcove set off from the main hallway. Jordan turned on the tap, which ran shockingly cold, and reached for the bar of gold-yellow soap hanging in a net from the faucet. Above the rush of water, she heard movement over her shoulder. Startled, she whipped around to see two shadowy figures in the far corner of the alcove.

"Jordan-*sensei*," a voice said from the darkness. She recognized it as Kenji's. The young man stepped forward, looking as surprised as Jordan felt. His boyishly handsome face was flushed, and he seemed at a loss for what to say.

"You scared me!" Jordan said with a small laugh of relief.

"What? You're the one who scared us, Jordan-*sensei*." This came from Ryusuke, who stood a little apart from Kenji and smiled his usual sheepish grin. Kenji shot him a look that Jordan was unable to read, and Ryusuke dropped his gaze to his feet, straightening his jacket with a sort of fumbling nervousness. Kenji cleared his throat but said nothing.

"Well, I'm terribly sorry for startling *you*," Jordan teased. "How was practice today?"

"It was great," Kenji said almost happily, but his smile was forced. "We've got a big game coming up this weekend."

"Yeah? Well, good luck! Sorry I haven't been watching the team's practices lately."

"That's all right, *sensei*. You have your own competition to win. Or Akira does, I guess," Ryusuke said.

"Excuse us, Jordan-*sensei*, but we should really go home now," Kenji said abruptly and slipped by her, motioning for his friend to follow.

"Bye, *sensei*." Ryusuke hurried past and the two boys rushed toward the exit.

"See you later."

Their heads had already dropped out of sight down the stairs, the low light making them appear to sink into the floor. Even over the running tap, Jordan could make out Ryusuke saying,

"—wasn't my fault!"

This was followed by the chuff of the large entry door sliding shut. She shook her head and washed her hands in the bitingly cold water, wondering why they had been acting so strangely. Jordan shrugged to herself, dried her hands on her slacks, and made for the exit downstairs.

Once outside, she immediately wished she had left sooner. The intermittent rain had grown into a steady drizzle that obscured everything in a sheaf of gauzy grey. Even if she had remembered an umbrella, it would do little good during her bike ride home, and her light jacket would soak up the rain like paper.

Jordan trotted to the covered bike lot, only to find her bicycle leaning against the rack at a crooked angle. She saw that both tires were completely flat, the caps gone from their valve stems. Her curse mingled with a high laugh over her shoulder. Jordan turned to see Emi and her friend Nanami—the girl Jordan had spoken to on the train weeks before, and many times since. The girls were perched on an empty bike rack under the neighboring veranda, waiting out the rain. Emi merrily splashed her toes in the growing puddles and swung her long legs, pale and bare up to the thigh despite the cold weather. She grinned and her teeth flashed in stark contrast against her bright lipstick.

"What's wrong—bike troubles?" Emi asked in a sing-song voice and stuck out her lip with an exaggerated pout. Nanami gave Jordan a helpless, apologetic look. Though it was completely unsurprising that Emi was behind the flattened tires, the predictability of her vileness did not temper it. Simmering fury welled up inside Jordan, as white-hot as when Emi had first put mud in Jordan's shoe cubby, or when she had "accidentally" spilled food coloring on Jordan as they had passed in the hall, to name just a few occasions.

With considerable effort, Jordan silently turned away and stepped out from beneath the shelter of the bike lot, hoping the effect was that she couldn't deign to be bothered by Emi. She walked without hurrying her pace, though her hair and clothes became drenched within moments. Through the staticky shushing of the rain, shrill laughter burrowed into Jordan's ears.

She wished the storm would swallow up Emi.

FIVE

Emi Hirata was dead.

Jordan's mouth fell open in shock as Mrs. Okubo relayed the news. Before Jordan could formulate even a word of response, the short English teacher turned to leave the teachers' room and spoke to Jordan over her shoulder.

"I have to collect my homeroom students for the assembly. Please go to the gym with the other teachers, Jordan-*sensei*."

Mrs. Okubo left in a hurry, but the school seemed deceptively calm. There were no students milling in the halls and the teachers' room was empty, quiet. Jordan could see the movement of pacing feet under Principal Kikuchi's closed door, but she was otherwise alone. Though Mrs. Okubo had told her to go to the gym, Jordan was hesitant, still disoriented by her initial surprise.

She grabbed her coat from her chair and shrugged it on as she entered the hallway. Jordan stayed on the upper floor, walked past the school library, and approached the enclosed walkway between the main building and the gym. Instantly, she felt the cold as she set foot in the walkway. There was a lacquer of frost on the shadowed trees below, their leaves unmoved by the still morning air. The gym was only a bit warmer, despite its loud furnace, which chugged and thrummed more impressively than it worked.

Jordan descended the stairs to the main floor of the gym and joined the head teacher, Vice Principal Nakamura, the lunch lady, and a handful of other staff members at their posts along the sidelines of the basketball court. They gave perfunctory greetings, then resumed their silence. The gym also served as an auditorium and had an inset wooden stage along one side; a podium and microphone stood in its center.

After a minute, the principal arrived and the students began to file in by grade level and class. Jordan watched Nanami and Emi's other close friends as they entered, their eyes wet and red with tears. The girls' classmates offered quiet condolences as they passed.

When their students were situated, the teachers joined Jordan and the others at the sidelines one by one. Mr. Mori came to stand by Jordan, nodded down at her in greeting, and turned his attention to the students still trickling in.

"Hello, Mori-*sensei*," Jordan said, raising her voice to be heard over the swelling murmur of the students. She stood close enough to Mr. Mori that she had to crane her neck to see his face.

"Jordan-*sensei*." He spared her the slightest glance.

"Do you know what's going on?" Jordan wasn't sure what made her ask Mr. Mori, with whom she seldom exchanged more than a few short words, despite being neighbors in the teachers' room. Still, she was anxious and felt a disquieting curiosity boil up and spill over, with no one else nearby to direct it toward.

"You don't know?" He gave Jordan his full attention then, looking interested and disbelieving at the same time, eyes narrowing behind his square glasses.

"Well, yes. I mean, I know that Emi has...died." Jordan thought she had spoken just loud enough for only Mr. Mori to hear, but Ms. Tatsuya's head swiveled in their direction. The woman blinked owlishly and craned her neck to listen as Jordan continued. "But how did she die?"

"Another suicide," Mr. Mori said plainly. His eyes flitted to hers. "Suffocation, or so I understand."

"Just like Yuki," Jordan said to herself, but Mr. Mori replied.

"That's right." He still wore an attentive expression and seemed on the verge of saying more, but a loud pop of static radiated from the stage and swept away all conversation. Principal Kikuchi stood at the podium, his face waxy and solemn. He leaned so close to the microphone that his drawn lips brushed its fine mesh. Then he cleared his throat, sparking a cascade of shrill feedback.

"*Kiritsu.*" The students smartly straightened their ranks per the command; each held out their arms straight in front of their chests and shifted so that not a single fingertip brushed the student ahead in line. Nearly in unison, they dropped their arms to their sides, as uniform as soldiers.

"Good morning, everyone." Under the yellow stage lights, Principal Kikuchi's bald head glistened sickly as he bowed forward.

"Good morning, Kikuchi-*kouchou*," the students and teachers replied, bowing, their words ringing hollow.

"I'm sorry that my address to you today is brought on by such a tragic, sorrowful event." He paused and his gaze shifted from face to face. "As your homeroom teachers have informed you, Emi Hirata passed on yesterday evening. As her friends, teachers, and classmates, we are all grieved by this sad news, and our condolences go to her family."

The principal stopped to pull a folded paper from his suit jacket pocket. Carefully, he laid the sheet against the podium and pressed out its creases. A student sniffled.

"*Life is a lamp-flame before a wind,*" he said stiffly as he read from the paper. "Only two months ago, we also parted ways with Yuki Watanabe. Ogawa has suffered great losses—Ogawa High School especially. In light of yesterday's events, all classes are dismissed. Please return home and spend today with your families."

Principal Kikuchi bowed and turned from the podium so abruptly that his paper fluttered to the stage, but he seemed neither to notice nor care as he hurried down the hollow steps. His face was tight—pinched with the strain of suppressing some emotion—and he made his way toward the exit instead of waiting for the students to file out, as was usual.

The students were bewildered, both because of the principal's uncustomary behavior and the shock of losing a fellow classmate, and they whispered among themselves. One of the teachers approached a group of students nearest the back and led them out the door.

"Homeroom won't be the same without her," Mr. Mori said, to no one in particular.

"Oh, I forgot she was one of yours, Mori-*sensei*. I'm so sorry!" Ms. Tatsuya said and straightened up a bit. Her breath wheezed wetly through her reddened nose. "Your students must be so upset."

"Yes. Emi was quite singular." Mr. Mori's lips drew into a subdued smile. Jordan was unsure whether he was expressing genuine fondness or attempting to be polite, considering Emi had been the proverbial thorn in every teacher's side. "I believe your class is waiting, Tatsuya-*sensei*."

A crowd of second-graders looked expectantly toward their math teacher. Ms. Tatsuya gave a small yelp and scurried to her students. A minute later, Mr. Mori stepped away to collect his own homeroom class without a word to Jordan. Steadily, the students emptied from the gymnasium. When only the lunch lady and the head teacher remained, Jordan left, collected her belongings from the teachers' room, and biked home against the still-crisp morning air.

SIX

Jordan stepped out of Mrs. Okubo's car after it eased to a stop in front of Emi Hirata's home. There were several vehicles wedged in the driveway and even more along the street. As Jordan waited for Mrs. Okubo, yet another car pulled up and deposited three women at the doorstep, all wearing somber black dresses.

Jordan pulled at her own dress, which was tight across the thighs and fell shorter than she would have liked. It was borrowed, since she obviously hadn't thought to bring mourning clothes with her overseas. She yanked down at the hem in one last fruitless attempt.

"You look fine," Mrs. Okubo said. Jordan couldn't tell whether she was admonishing her for fidgeting or trying to put her at ease. She looked Jordan up and down once more and nodded. "It's lucky you're about the same size as my niece."

"Please thank her for me, for the dress."

"Oh, it's no trouble. You should meet her sometime," Mrs. Okubo said as they walked toward the Hirata household, feet crunching on the gravel driveway that led to a manicured home surrounded by groomed trees. "Do you use Mixi? The social network? My niece is on it all the time. I could give you her username and...What's wrong?"

Jordan had stopped at the open door, too uncertain to step inside.

"Are you sure it's all right for me to be here?" she asked, though she suspected it was too late to turn back now. "Do all the teachers come? I didn't know Emi very well."

"Many people will come to pay their respects, especially for a child." Mrs. Okubo smiled in a motherly, reassuring way Jordan had never seen before. Not even with the students. "Don't worry."

Jordan smiled for a moment too, despite her nervousness, and they let themselves in.

At least a dozen pairs of dress shoes were already lined up in the entryway, black and shiny like beetles. Jordan and Mrs. Okubo slipped into flimsy indoor slippers and padded down a hallway decorated by watercolor paintings with fine script as tiny as ants.

Just outside the threshold to the living room was a young man with an open ledger. Mrs. Okubo bowed as she handed him an envelope; then, she began to write her name in the book. Jordan let her gaze wander to the adjoining room, but she only caught glimpses of strangers sitting silently in rows of chairs.

Jordan felt a nudge at her elbow, and Mrs. Okubo motioned to the ledger. Jordan wrote her name in blocky *katakana* letters under Mrs. Okubo's cramped *kanji* and handed her own envelope to the young man, who took it without comment.

The man made a note and placed Jordan's offering in a box filled with identical envelopes, all tied with thread-thin black and white ribbons. They contained condolence money for Emi's family.

Hesitantly, Jordan followed Mrs. Okubo into the living room, just managing to swallow a gasp as she entered.

Beneath the window stood a long altar bearing an open coffin. Emi Hirata was inside. Devoid of makeup and clothed in a snowy kimono suffused by sunlight, Emi looked oddly, strikingly beautiful. It seemed impossible that Emi had taken her own life just hours after Jordan had seen her in the rain, as bright-eyed and sharp-tongued as ever.

Jordan's throat tightened with guilt and she tamped down a

sudden, intense urge to leave. Somehow, she forced herself to walk up behind Mrs. Okubo, who was in a line leading toward the altar.

About a dozen mourners flanked Jordan, sitting stiffly in folding chairs, their gazes fixed toward the altar. At the head of the room sat a middle-aged woman with serene, even features that mirrored Emi's. The woman, no doubt the mother, wiped at her eyes with a handkerchief but made no noise. Her husband squeezed her shoulders with one arm.

Jordan was startled out of her quiet observations by a bell tinning through the room. The noise had come from the man in line before Mrs. Okubo. He placed the bell on a low table he knelt before. The man got to his feet, bowed toward the altar, and took a seat among the rows of chairs. Mrs. Okubo turned back and motioned for Jordan to join her.

"Just do as I do," she said in a low voice. Mrs. Okubo knelt in front of the black-lacquered table that squatted low to the ground, leaving enough room for Jordan to sit alongside her. Jordan's dress pulled uncomfortably as she folded her legs beneath her thighs, and she could feel her feet begin to tingle under the weight of her body.

Like a child, she mimicked Mrs. Okubo's every movement, bowing and pressing her palms together. After ringing the altar bell, Mrs. Okubo pinched a dab of incense from a dish, brought it close to her forehead, and then placed it in a smoking urn. Jordan did likewise. Her nostrils flooded with the incense's musky, perfumed fragrance as she brought it toward her face.

Repositioning her hands, Mrs. Okubo began to recite what sounded like a prayer, so quietly that Jordan could only make out every other word. She soon gave up on any notion of repeating the sutra and simply knelt in silence with her eyes closed. A minute later, Mrs. Okubo stopped her recitation. She got to her feet and nodded to Jordan, who gratefully followed her to sit among the others.

She wasn't sure how long they would stay to pay their respects but noticed that only a couple of people had left since their arrival. Already feeling uneasy and impatient to leave, Jordan balled her hands together to keep from fidgeting and surveyed the room. The air was thick with the smell of incense. Lazy wafts of its pungent smoke clouded the columns of sunlight from the windows.

In the gauzy shafts of light and undulating smoke, Emi looked ethereal, as though it were her spirit at the altar and not her body. Despite their brief and antagonistic relationship, Jordan felt a swell of sorrow press against her chest and she had to look away.

Jordan's memory of helping her mother choose a suit for Aiden to be buried in crept through her thoughts. She clamped her eyes shut to block it out, like shuttering a window against a storm.

At the sound of voices, Jordan opened her eyes again and saw a woman she recognized as Ogawa High School's nurse, Mrs. Takahashi, talking to the mother and father. The nurse clasped the other woman against her in a brief embrace—Emi's mother only pressed one hand against Mrs. Takahashi's back in the barest of hugs—before bowing and making her way out of the room. The school nurse pulled a tissue from her handbag to dab at a stray tear. She gave no sign of noticing Jordan.

As Jordan watched her go, another mourner across the aisle caught her eye. The man was young, no more than thirty or so. His delicately handsome features were schooled into a calm but alert expression. He adjusted his glasses as he wrote in a small notebook cradled between his long fingers.

Even though his suit was similar to the other men's, Jordan could tell it was expensive, tailored to accent his tall, lean frame with its crisp material. His dark hair was worn just long enough to look casually tousled. This seemed to be the popular style among young, fashionable men she had seen in Yamagata City.

"Jordan-*sensei*? Let's go now."

Jordan jumped at Mrs. Okubo's voice so close to her ear and felt her face flush. She chided herself for gawking at a man while attending a wake, but she was relieved to see that no one seemed to have noticed. Jordan nodded to the other woman, still feeling embarrassed, and followed her out of the room.

As they left, Jordan spared a glance over her shoulder. She saw the well-dressed man turn away, as though he had been looking in her direction, and scribble in his notebook.

SEVEN

Jordan ached for a cup of coffee. Between the train fare to Yamagata City, the cab ride to a French cafe at its outskirts, and the return trip, it would probably be the most inconvenient, expensive coffee she would ever drink. But the autumn winds were chilling, her apartment had no central heating, and the instant coffee crystals from the local grocery store tasted more like dirt than coffee beans.

Jordan envisioned a cup of coffee made caramel-tan by cream, sweetened with a lump of unrefined sugar. She smiled in anticipation as she boarded the train at Ogawa Station and filled the black space behind her closed eyes with images of the warm cafe.

Soon after Jordan took a seat, Nanami—Emi's friend—entered behind her. As was customary now that they had grown to know each other, the young woman sat beside her and they exchanged greetings.

"I haven't seen you since Emi..." Jordan trailed off and softened her voice. "Nanami, I am so sorry for your loss. I know how much your friend meant to you."

"Thank you, Jordan-*sensei*." Nanami dropped her gaze to her lap, her shoulder-length hair obscuring her expression. A long moment passed in silence.

"Are you doing all right? Do you want to talk about anything?" As she spoke, Jordan couldn't help but be reminded of Akira and his own grief. She hoped she could find the right approach to reach Nanami, too. Though, she regretted the need to have to console so many students in the first place. Nanami remained silent.

Jordan swallowed thickly and wondered if she was going about it all wrong, but finally, Nanami mumbled something in response. So quietly that Jordan couldn't hear, even though their shoulders were brushing. "I'm sorry. What did you say?"

"Emi didn't kill herself." Her words were low but urgent. Nanami turned toward Jordan and her hair whipped like a dark sail in a turbulent wind. The girl's eyes stuttered back and forth, intently searching Jordan's face. She wore an odd expression of defiance tinged with hopefulness. Jordan felt a pang of sympathy and recalled Shun's similar denial of his brother's passing. She doubted either student had experienced the loss of a loved one before, both desperate to explain away what they couldn't comprehend.

"Nanami, I understand that you're upset, but some people are able to hide parts of themselves, even from their closest friends."

"You sound like my mom." Nanami sounded disappointed and looked away. "You don't understand."

"Why are you so sure Emi didn't kill herself?" Jordan said, trying a different tack to re-engage the girl. Nanami shook her head and fell silent, but Jordan could see her hands wringing in her lap, skin white across her knuckles. "Nanami?" The girl looked around the car nervously before leaning in and cupping her hand to Jordan's ear.

"Emi was pregnant."

Jordan shivered as Nanami's breath brushed against her throat. "What? You're sure?"

"Yes." Nanami nodded vehemently. "She told me a few weeks ago."

"Did anyone else know? Her parents maybe."

"No way she told her parents!" She looked aghast at even the thought. "Mrs. Takahashi though..."

"Mrs. Takahashi—the school nurse? She knows?"

"Maybe. Well, no, I don't think so..." Nanami shrugged and continued. "Emi was feeling really dizzy one day at school and started bleeding—she thought she was having a miscarriage. Remember the day I brought her to the teachers' lunchroom? Well, Emi went to the nurse's office, but when she came back, she said she hadn't told Mrs. Takahashi anything." She paused for a moment and worried her lip as she thought. "I think she was telling the truth. Mrs. Takahashi and Emi's mom are good friends. They probably don't keep any secrets from each other, so I doubt Emi would tell her."

"Emi would have been in serious trouble if she was found out," Jordan said, realizing it was quite the understatement. The highschoolers were discouraged from harmless dating—even from holding hands. Emi probably would have been expelled at best, possibly even thrown out by her parents for such a transgression. "Maybe her pregnancy was why she—"

"No," Nanami said with firm certainty. "She was excited. Happy, even. She was sure the baby would convince her boyfriend to marry her." She smiled ruefully and shook her head.

"So even the father didn't know yet."

"I don't think so."

"Do you know who he is?"

"No. Emi said she was seeing a boy from Sagae High School. She never told me his name or even showed me a picture." Nanami frowned. "She always loved having a secret."

Nanami fell silent when the train stopped and a trickle of passengers walked by on their way to the door; she eyed them warily. Jordan had to admit that Nanami's reasoning for why Emi wouldn't take her own life was plausible. But the girl was still young and seemed naive about her friend's motivations, and Emi had clearly been impetuous and volatile. Though Nanami couldn't fathom her friend committing suicide, Jordan could see few other alternative explanations.

They both tipped sideways in their seats as the train once again continued its path down the dark tracks. Jordan spoke up after a few minutes.

"You think Emi's death was an accident?"

"I'm not sure..." Nanami bit her bottom lip and looked on the verge of saying more when the train once again rolled to a stop. "I have to get off here, Jordan-*sensei*. I'll see you tomorrow."

Jordan itched to hear more and wanted to urge Nanami to stay and talk, but she decided it wouldn't be fair to pressure the girl.

"Okay," she said reluctantly. "Bye, Nanami."

The girl already had one foot on the platform before she turned around and scurried back to Jordan.

"Don't tell anyone, okay?" She didn't wait for agreement before rushing away into the blue-blackness of early evening and merging with the crowd of figures departing into the streets.

EIGHT

On the surface, school life had returned to normal. Classes ran on schedule, there were no more solemn assemblies, and the students, for the most part, seemed happy. Akira had politely declined a few of their practice sessions for the English competition, and Jordan suspected Emi's death had stirred his not-yet-dormant remorse over Yuki's passing. Akira still spoke to her in class and sometimes sought her out during breaks, but his subdued smiles rarely eclipsed the distracted look in his eyes.

So it was with a mix of regret and pleasure that Jordan once again watched from the bleachers as the baseball team practiced. Their season had ended not long before—after losing their final game by a large, disheartening margin—but Kenji insisted they would benefit by practicing throughout the year. Jordan suspected they might benefit more from a break but didn't have the heart to tell him.

The afternoon was bright but cold. The players' hands and cheeks looked red, abraded by the dry, biting air. Jordan settled gratefully into her knee-length wool coat, her cheeks and ears hidden in a winding scarf wrapped about her head, as she watched the balls' lazy arcs through the air.

With a crack like a branch splitting, a ball sprang almost vertically into the ash-blue sky. Jordan shielded her eyes against the cold sun and watched the ball turn into a small fleck at its pinnacle. It seemed to hover for a fateful moment before racing toward the ground—straight into an unsuspecting passerby.

Jordan's surprised gasp mixed with too-late shouts of warning from the players. The man grunted with pain as the ball thudded meatily into his shoulder. His briefcase struck the pavement and documents burst forth like confetti from a New Year's party favor. Jordan was already on her feet, rushing to his side, and was joined by Ryusuke and two infielders. Everyone else on the field stopped to watch with curiosity.

"Are you all right, mister?"

"Hey, are you okay?" The boys nervously ran over each other's words.

"Oh, yes, I'm fine. Thank you," the man said pleasantly, but his smile slipped into a grimace when he rolled his shoulder. Massaging the base of his neck, the man knelt and began to collect his papers. Jordan crouched as well, already feeling the chill seep from the concrete through to her knees. She plucked up a few scattered pages of thick, cream-colored paper with gold and bronze letterhead. Curious, she looked at the bold emblem at the top of the documents: a three-pointed crest embraced by leaves, surrounded by thick *kanji* lettering and the English words "Yamagata Prefectural Police." Her concern for collecting his documents vaporized instantly, and her head shot up to look at the stranger.

The man's head was bent over his briefcase, but Jordan suddenly recognized his distinct features, from his carefully styled hair to his pressed suit and fog-grey dress shirt. Jordan's pulse quickened when he raised his sharp eyes to meet hers, smiled, and extended his hand for the papers.

"Sorry about that," Jordan said with an unsure smile as they both got to their feet. "Ogawa's usually far more welcoming to guests, I promise."

"Yeah, we're really sorry, sir." Ryusuke piped up and sheepishly ran his fingers through the hair at the back of his head.

"I have to say, I'm the one who's embarrassed—I played shortstop in high school." The man's lips turned up in a small grin and the students laughed, looking relieved. "Go on. Get back to practice."

Ryusuke and the others jogged away, tossing more hasty apologies and goodbyes over their shoulders as they left.

"You're sure you're all right?" Jordan said once the boys had gone.

"Yes, thank you for your concern. You must be the assistant language instructor," he said in flawless English.

"That's me," she said, happy to be able to speak easily, and held out her hand to shake his. "I'm Jordan Howard."

"Toshihiko Sakurai." He nodded and returned the handshake. "Pleased to meet you."

"Officer Sakurai, is it?"

"Inspector, actually." His eyebrows quirked at her comment but he didn't seem surprised by the question.

"From the Yamagata Prefectural Police Station?"

"Yes."

"Ogawa's small, I know, but it can't be *that* small. Surely the town has its own police force."

"Indeed it does—and he's a very fine officer. But Ogawa is not equipped to handle investigations," Inspector Sakurai said plainly. The following pause stretched until it was clear he did not intend to offer more.

"You're conducting an investigation...at Ogawa High School?"

"Yes." He adjusted his tie. Jordan wasn't sure whether she was amused or annoyed by his terseness.

"Does this have something to do with Emi and Yuki's deaths?" An unreadable look flashed across the inspector's features and he stood a bit straighter. For a moment, he searched her face and Jordan wondered whether he would say anything at all. Jordan spoke up again instead. "I saw you at Emi's wake."

"I remember." He paused for a long moment before seeming to

come to a decision. "There have been a number of recent deaths of high school students near Yamagata City. We're investigating the possibility of a suicide club."

"Suicide club!" Jordan wasn't sure what answer she had been expecting, but his reply caught her off-guard. She had heard of so-called suicide clubs but had dismissed the notion as a singular incidence the media had inflated into a pandemic, like America's pregnancy pacts. "But Emi and Yuki barely knew each other."

"Well, that's what I'm here to find out," Inspector Sakurai said with an assuring air.

"Yuki...died before I arrived in Ogawa, but I'd be willing to talk about Emi if it would help your investigation," Jordan said.

"Thank you, Ms. Howard. I'll be here throughout the week to conduct interviews, and I'll let you know if I have any questions."

For a moment, neither spoke. Inspector Sakurai didn't appear inclined to leave right away, taking in the campus, the field, and Jordan with sweeping looks. She was intrigued, both by the newcomer himself and by his purpose at the high school. Though the prolonged silence seemed to slide right off the police inspector, Jordan began to feel uncomfortable.

"Your English is excellent," she said, unsure of what else to say—and it was true.

"Thank you." He smiled. "I studied at Doshisha University before I attended the National Police Academy." Jordan nodded, though she knew nothing of either institution.

"You should do some guest teaching while you're here," she said wryly. "Show these students that English isn't as impossible or as dumb as they make it out to be."

He chuckled and his glasses slipped down his nose a bit.

"You're American, aren't you?"

"Is it that obvious?"

"Americans have a...certain way about them," he said with a smile, not quite mocking nor teasing.

"I'll take that as a compliment." Before either could say more, a distant speaker wrung out an innocuous ditty of tinny notes that echoed off the school and surrounding buildings. A network of speakers broadcast this chime across Ogawa every day, four times each day, signaling the times to wake up, eat lunch, return home from work, and go to bed. No one seemed to pay these notices much heed, or even comment on them, but the tune prompted Inspector Sakurai to look at his watch.

"I need to return to Yamagata City soon." He reached into his breast pocket and retrieved a business card, bowing as he extended it to Jordan with both hands. "It was very nice to meet you, Ms. Howard."

"You too, Inspector." She bowed as she accepted the card and looked it over with careful interest, as was polite, though she could not decipher many of the *kanji* characters that represented his name and title. After a moment, Jordan returned her attention to his sharp, arresting face. "I'll see you here tomorrow?"

"Yes. Have a good evening." The inspector picked up his briefcase from the pavement and bowed once more before making his way to a nondescript white sedan.

"Goodbye," Jordan called after him and watched his car drive away between the buildings on the darkening road. She turned the business card in her palm, feeling its sharp points press into the pads of her fingers, and slipped it into her pocket.

NINE

"JORDAN-*SENSEI*."

Jordan flinched at the sound of Vice Principal Nakamura's voice. The words caressed her spine like an ice cube sliding down the back of her shirt.

"Yes, Ms. Nakamura?" She turned in her seat to see the rigid woman standing at the door to the break room, wearing her usual expression of disinterest bordering on annoyance.

"The inspector wishes to speak with you." The vice principal had spent the last twenty minutes or so being interviewed. She had been preceded by the principal, head teacher, Mr. Mori, and a handful of other faculty members who had flowed in and out of the break room throughout the morning. Ms. Nakamura had left the door ajar, but Jordan knocked against its glass pane before entering.

"Come in, please," a man's voice said from the other side of the door.

Jordan entered to see Inspector Sakurai seated at the end of a long lunch table, surrounded by a horseshoe of stacked papers, photographs, and file folders. He leaned over a thin notebook and continued to write in quick, small letters before placing his pen aside and giving her his full attention.

"Ms. Howard, nice to see you again." He smiled, speaking in Japanese now, and stood to bow.

"Nice to see you, too. Hopefully we won't be interrupted by any rogue baseballs this time."

"Indeed," he said politely, more reserved than the day before. He motioned to a chair with his open hand. "Please have a seat."

"So, you have questions about Emi?" Jordan sat close to the inspector, glancing at the paper nearest to her but not gleaning much.

"Yes. If you could please let me know generally about your relationship with and impression of Emi. Almost any information about her or her life outside of school may be helpful." He laced his slender fingers over his notebook and looked at Jordan calmly but intently.

"Have you heard the phrase, 'Speak no ill of the dead'?" she said. At this, the corners of his mouth twitched.

"Ms. Howard, I have interviewed nearly a dozen people about Emi. At this point, I have a...distinct impression of her personality." Inspector Sakurai stifled a wry look and continued. "Please do not hesitate to include any details. This is a police investigation, after all."

"I didn't speak to her much, if at all, outside of class, during which she was disruptive at best." Jordan continued to describe Emi as she only knew her to be: obstinate, defiant, and sometimes cruel. As she spoke, Inspector Sakurai took careful notes, only glancing at Jordan occasionally. A digital recorder stood in the center of the table like a miniature obelisk. She soon came to the end of her limited firsthand knowledge of Emi but remembered her recent conversation with Nanami. "Have you interviewed her friends yet?"

"Not all of them. Why do you ask?"

"Her close friend, Nanami, told me that Emi was pregnant," she said after a moment of hesitation, recalling Nanami's insistence on secrecy. If the inspector was surprised by this information, he didn't show it. Without so much as raising his eyes from his pen, he continued his diligent note-taking. "You already knew?"

"I really can't divulge anything, Ms. Howard," he said, not impolitely. "Did Nanami say anything else—how Emi felt?"

"She said Emi was happy—excited, even. Apparently Emi thought she'd marry the father."

"Who was the father?"

"I don't know. Nanami didn't seem to know either. Only that Emi often spoke about a boy at Sagae High School."

"I'll be sure to ask Nanami." He again laced his fingers and adopted a more conversational tone. "Thank you for your cooperation, and I apologize for interrupting your schedule. I believe I have no more questions for you at this time, unless there's anything else you'd like to add..."

"Yes, actually. Nanami's convinced that Emi didn't commit suicide." Inspector Sakurai nodded and his eyes narrowed with interest as she continued. "Yuki's younger brother was adamant that he didn't kill himself either."

"You asked them what they thought about their loved ones' deaths?"

"No, not exactly. I spoke with them about...what had happened, and they volunteered their thoughts. I am their teacher, after all." Jordan's pulse rose and she felt defensive. "Seeing as you're investigating a suicide club, I thought you'd like to know."

"Of course, and I thank you," he said sincerely and stood. "If you remember anything further, please don't hesitate to contact me. Do you still have my business card?"

"Yes. Will you be in Ogawa much longer, Inspector Sakurai?"

"At least a few more days."

"I'll let you know if I learn anything else from the students," Jordan said as she rose from her seat and pushed in her chair.

"I would appreciate that," he said but a look of curiosity and vague suspicion crossed his features as she turned to leave. "That is to say, if they happen to mention anything. Please leave the questioning to me, Ms. Howard."

"Of course. But you never know what students will share with their teachers." She smiled as she began to slide the door shut behind her. "Goodbye, Inspector."

Jordan breathed into her cupped hands to warm her fingers before returning them to the laptop's keys. Though in her apartment's living room, she felt little relief from the autumn chill. She sat on a cushion atop the wooden floorboards and folded her long legs under the *kotatsu* —a low table with electric coils and a quilt hanging off its edges to capture the heat. She let as little air as possible escape from under the quilt and sighed as her thighs began to warm.

On the *kotatsu*'s tabletop sat a Styrofoam tray and bowl, empty save for a few grains of rice and drops of broth left over from her dinner of store-bought sushi and miso soup. Despite being from the supermarket, it was better than most sushi she had back home in Nevada, thanks to the region owing its livelihood to fishing.

She finished the last gulp of green tea and clicked "Send" on an email to her eldest sister with a tap of cold-stiff fingers against the track-pad. With a stretch and a sigh, Jordan leaned against the couch and glanced at the television. She had left it tuned to *IQ Sapuri*—a quiz show based on logic puzzles and riddles—though many of the Japanese plays on words were beyond her. A spiky ball landed on a contestant's head as punishment for a wrong answer, and Jordan grinned.

She usually paid more attention to the show but found herself easily distracted that evening, flitting between checking bookmarked webpages, uploading some photos to her seldom-updated blog, and replaying her conversations with Inspector Sakurai. Though she had little reason to question his purpose for being at Ogawa High School, she felt his presence was odd—seemingly unnecessary for two isolated deaths in a remote town.

Jordan then remembered that he had mentioned other recent suicides near Yamagata City. She opened the laptop's internet browser. After some wrangling of its translation settings, she searched for "high school suicide Yamagata prefecture" and limited the results to within the last year.

The browser's translations were ungrammatical at best and nonsensical at worst, but it allowed Jordan to skim articles that would have otherwise taken her hours to translate herself. Most results spoke of national suicide statistics or were unrelated. After fifteen minutes and as many more searches, a blurb caught her eye: "Mother Warns Against Bullying, Suicide Clubs."

When she saw the headline was no more than a week old, Jordan clicked it hurriedly. The article, which was fairly comprehensible, detailed one mother's campaign to raise awareness about school bullying following the death of her son, Junichi Sato. The boy had taken his own life on the day following Emi's death, Jordan noted with increased interest. His mother's statements became mangled in the translation program but generally spoke of how, despite being seemingly well-liked, her son was believed to have committed suicide due to pressures from peers at Sagae High School, where he attended as a senior.

The article went on to widen its scope to the national level and mentioned a letter from an anonymous student sent to the Minister of Education. The letter had received widespread media coverage the month before, speaking of troubles with bullying and the author's intention to end his or her own life.

The local article's accompanying photograph showed a petite woman with a severe expression and her hair pulled back so tightly that her skin looked painfully stretched. In her hands, the woman held a framed photograph of a young man, a black ribbon drawn across its upper corner like a shadow. The boy looked somber but handsome, with dark, defined brows and stark cheekbones. The caption read, "Mari Sato and photograph of son, Junichi."

Jordan's fingers shook as she clicked the "Print" button—from cold or anxiousness, she couldn't be sure. The article wasn't much to go by, she knew, but there were too many coincidences to let it pass unnoticed. The printer whirred to life and spit out the paper in short, noisy bursts until the boy's dark eyes stared at her from the lip of the machine. With a few quick keystrokes, Jordan bookmarked the page, pausing for only a moment before entitling the webpage, "Emi's boyfriend?"

A half-hour more of searching for unusual deaths or suicides revealed little else. As she moved to close her laptop, she thought once again of Inspector Sakurai and instead opened a new search window. To her surprise, Jordan was presented with a long list of links related to "Inspector Toshihiko Sakurai," almost all of which were also ornamented with the word "Yakuza."

Curious, she leaned forward and clicked on the first link to an article from the *Japan Times*: "Investigators Arrest Yakuza Lieutenant." The inspector gazed back at her through the monitor—an official-looking headshot that had probably been supplied by the police department. She didn't think it possible for him to appear more reserved, but the photograph somehow accomplished exactly that.

His hair was shorter, for one, cut close to the head in severe planes. His mouth was drawn taut in a sober, solemn line that didn't seem capable of softening around a smile. The article was dated from two years before, but he didn't look any younger. If anything, he seemed world-wearier, like an invisible weight had settled over him. Though, it didn't diminish his handsomeness, Jordan thought with a private smile.

She looked from Inspector Sakurai's small photo, halfway through the article, to the main picture that perched atop the page. A middle-aged man with small eyes and a face like granite was being escorted by a throng of uniformed officers to a waiting police cruiser. He stared straight at the camera—a dark looked imbued with so much anger that it reached through time and across the miles to grip the base of Jordan's spine. The photo's caption identified the man as a lieutenant of the Inagawa-kai Yakuza, arrested in Tokyo under suspicion of a laundry list of charges.

Much of the article detailed a then-recent spike in organized crime attributed to actions of Yakuza groups in the region, accompanied by only a smattering of information about the lieutenant and the charges against him—details still unfolding at that time. The remaining paragraphs lauded the young Inspector Sakurai as being instrumental in the arrest, having painstakingly built a case against the Yakuza leader for well over a year. His quotes were dry and formal. He rejected the praise and thanked his team for their hard work, of course.

Nearly an hour and a dozen news articles later, Jordan knew a few things for certain about the inspector. He had been the youngest in the Tokyo Metropolitan Police Department. He was credited as spearheading the investigation against the Inagawa-kai Yakuza. He was clever, talented, and something of a prodigy. An overnight celebrity. And then, nothing. Any news about him had simply dropped off—petered away in the few months following the high-profile arrest he had orchestrated. Not surprising, Jordan decided, seeing as the news cycle thrived on fresh blood and the lieutenant had yet to be found guilty on any charges, his lawyer expertly tying up any legal proceedings.

Still, Jordan wondered what had brought Inspector Sakurai to the Yamagata Prefectural Police and Ogawa. It hardly seemed like the ideal career trajectory for a young man who had just proved the worth of his salt in Japan's largest police department. Not to mention that investigating a couple of small-town suicides was a strange use of his skills and experience. Unless something more was at work—some silently spinning machination that Jordan couldn't see.

She considered searching more, perhaps for some falling out between him and the Tokyo police, but the tiredness tugging down her eyelids convinced her otherwise. Besides, maybe she could use the topic as an entry to conversation with the inspector—a way to dip in her toes without causing splashes that would scare him off. His stoic, unsmiling face followed her thoughts as she brushed her teeth and went to bed.

TEN

"Nanami!" Jordan said excitedly and waved the young woman over. Jordan had hurriedly finished lunch and was chatting with students in the hall, lingering with the hope of spotting the girl. Nanami hesitated before trudging over with her head down. Jordan stepped back until they were in a small recess, away from the flow of students.

"You told him about Emi's secret," Nanami said and glowered. She could only mean Inspector Sakurai; Jordan had seen her enter the inspector's makeshift office in the break room earlier that morning. "You promised you wouldn't say anything."

"I'm sorry, Nanami, but he *is* a police officer. Besides, anything we can do to help Inspector Sakurai find Emi's—" Jordan stopped short when she realized she was about to say Emi's killer.

Her breath caught and she paused for a moment, feeling strangely disoriented. Certainly she thought Emi's and Yuki's deaths were odd, but she hadn't seriously considered murder. Not really. Nanami was still angry, but a look of confusion seeped into her expression when Jordan continued her silence. Another moment passed and Jordan forced herself to set aside her thoughts, at least for the moment.

"That's actually what I wanted to ask you about—Emi and her boyfriend."

"Oh, yeah?" Nanami's mopey attitude shifted to interest.

"Yes. Do you know this boy?" Jordan pulled the printed article from her pocket, which was folded so only the photo of the young man showed.

"Actually, yeah, he does look familiar somehow." Nanami brushed her long hair from her face and leaned closer, squinting. "I feel like I know him."

"Do you know anyone named Junichi?"

"Yes! That's who he is—Junichi Sato!" Nanami clapped her hands once in excitement and kept them clasped against her chest. "I was classmates with Ju-*kun,* but he moved away from Ogawa when we were first-graders in junior high school. I haven't heard from him in years."

"I think he may have been Emi's boyfriend—the father of her child —do you think that's possible?"

"Oh, definitely!" Nanami said without hesitation and Jordan felt a small thrill of excitement. "Emi had a huge crush on Junichi ever since she met him in elementary school. Later, right before he left for Sagae, she said she kissed him on the cheek, and he gave her a button from his school jacket. That's totally romantic, don't you think? She kept that button on her dresser until she...Well, anyway, Emi would sometimes say he had been her true love." Nanami's cheeks colored and she ducked her head.

"But she didn't say they were together recently? Or even that she had seen him again? That seems odd." Jordan frowned.

"You didn't know Emi," Nanami said wistfully, almost proudly. "We were best friends, but she was secretive, too. She probably didn't want to jinx anything by telling me. She would say that a lot: 'Don't talk about how you think you did on the test, Nanami. You'll jinx it!' You know?" She smiled.

"I see. Well, did Emi have a blog or anything? Facebook? Some-place where she might have talked about it, maybe shared a picture of the two of them?" Jordan had actually already checked Facebook, and

Instagram, but couldn't find the Emi she was looking for. She supposed there were probably Japanese social media sites she was unfamiliar with and hoped Nanami could shed some light. Her spirits sank when Nanami shook her head.

"Emi used Snow a lot, but I never saw pics of her with boys. I would've remembered that." Nanami shrugged apologetically. "She kept a diary, I think."

Inspector Sakurai had likely taken any diary as evidence, or at least read it. Jordan nodded to herself as she thought. Before she could ask Nanami more, one of her classmates spotted the girl and walked over to chat. Jordan paused for a moment as the girls spoke, contemplating whether she should inform Nanami of Junichi's death. She didn't know if the girl could take the blow of losing another friend, and Jordan conceded selfishly that she didn't want to be the one to break the news.

She excused herself with a fumbling apology and hurried back to the teachers' room, hoping to catch the inspector before the next class hour. Most of the instructors were at their desks, and she heard no movement or voices behind the frosted glass door to the break room. She knocked.

"Yes?"

"Inspector Sakurai, do you have a moment?"

"Ms. Howard. Please come in." He smiled briefly as she entered, and then resumed collecting the neat stacks of documents from around the table. "What can I do for you?"

"Inspector, I think I may know who Emi's boyfriend was," she said, deciding it was best to just jump in. Inspector Sakurai's hand halted midway to his briefcase; the documents he held were left suspended midair.

"Oh?" His attention on her was rapt and he remained unmoving.

"Yes. A senior at Sagae High School named Junichi Sato." Jordan swallowed hard. "They knew each other from elementary through junior high school, and Nanami said Emi still carried a torch for him." Slowly, the inspector laid the documents in his briefcase, running his gaze and his palm smooth over the paper. He seemed lost in thought but eventually refocused his attention on Jordan, as though he had made up his mind about something.

"What makes you so certain they were seeing each other?"

"Junichi died the day after Emi."

"Suicide?" he asked. Jordan suspected he already had the answer and was only asking to gauge how much she knew.

"Yes, presumably," she said. He raised an eyebrow at that but she continued. "Inspector, you said you were investigating serial suicides around Yamagata City, but besides Junichi, Emi, and Yuki, I haven't found nor heard word of any others." After discovering the article about Junichi the night before, she had run yet more searches that morning and plumbed the recent obituaries for Sagae, Nagai, Higashine, Yamanobe, Kahoku, and a few more major surrounding cities, but no additional information about teen suicides had bubbled to the top.

"I really can't discuss the particulars of any ongoing investigations at this point, Ms. Howard. I'm sorry."

"Are you really here to investigate a suicide club, Inspector?"

"Pardon me?" He smiled enough to show teeth, whether in amusement or to disguise a grimace, Jordan couldn't tell.

"It's odd that Yamagata Prefectural Police would send one of their best inspectors to the sticks of the *inaka* over two kids' suicides." She considered revealing what she had found in her online searches, about his successful arrest of the Yakuza lieutenant and all the articles lauding him as an unparalleled inspector. His assignment to the Ogawa case did begin to make sense if murder was involved. She pressed forward, now feeling some substance to her empty musings. "I find it even more suspicious that Junichi died right after Emi."

"You don't think that points even more strongly to a suicide club? If, as you say, they were lovers, then it's not a far leap to assume they were in the club together, or that a distraught young man would take his life after his lover died. What *do* you believe is going on, Ms. Howard?" Surprisingly, his interest seemed genuine, but Jordan felt too self-conscious to answer right away, especially since he was asking her to share her admittedly drastic conclusions.

"I think they were targeted...by someone else," Jordan said finally. He nodded and the corner of his mouth quirked.

"I like you, Ms. Howard." He placed the remaining files in his briefcase and snapped its latches shut, the sound expanding to fill the space of the open room. "But once again, I cannot divulge details of the investigation."

"Are you leaving?"

"Yes. I've learned all I can here for the time being." He removed the suit jacket from the back of his chair and shrugged it on, preparing to depart. "I'll be back to ask any follow-up questions, and to let the community know about the results of my investigation."

"Where are you going? Or can't you divulge that either?" Jordan said, realizing she'd be sorry to see him leave and feeling somehow a little abandoned.

"Sagae High School." He adjusted his glasses before reaching for the door handle. "Goodbye, Ms. Howard."

ELEVEN

THE STUFFED PHEASANT'S BEADY EYES SHONE IN THE LOW LIGHT as Jordan peeked through the door to the science supply room. Though they hadn't agreed to meet, Jordan had waited for Akira in the dusky hall near the science room in hopes of asking about the English competition the week before. Though, she already knew that he hadn't placed and felt partially responsible, guilty even, having spent the last few days leading up to the contest with the baseball team instead of Akira.

After a few minutes of waiting for him, her attention had wandered and she remembered the bizarre menagerie of taxidermy specimens sitting in the forgotten room. She pulled against the lock on the door experimentally, but it held tight. A squeaky voice behind her suddenly piped up.

"Oh! Jordan-*sensei*!"

Jordan jumped with surprise and spun to see the small figure of Ms. Tatsuya perched a few feet away.

"Tatsuya-*sensei*, hello," Jordan said.

"My goodness, whatever are you doing in this gloomy place?" Such tucked-away corners of the school certainly were uninviting that day, the overcast sky letting no more than a hint of grey light inside.

"I was hoping to speak with Akira, actually."

"He still comes down here?" Ms. Tatsuya asked, and Jordan nodded. With a sigh, the small woman shook her head and flipped through a large set of keys in her hand. "I'm not terribly surprised, since this was his and Yuki's favorite spot, even after they were reprimanded."

"Reprimanded? What happened?" Jordan said and followed Ms. Tatsuya into the room once she had fumbled the lock open. When the light flickered to life, it cast a yellow pallor over the already fading and discolored equipment. As Jordan took in the room, she realized Ms. Tatsuya's presence there was just as odd as her own. "I didn't know you taught science as well, *sensei*."

"Oh, I don't! I need vinegar for today's Home Ec. club, but the school's all out—there's not even a single bottle in the main science lab. Goodness, even if there is some here, I don't think I want to use it." She grimaced as she wiped a finger across a desk and came away with a pat of chalky dust. She continued to poke through large plastic bottles on a shelf, not showing any intention of answering Jordan's initial question. Jordan wondered whether the other teacher's silence was indeed her answer but pushed ahead regardless.

"Tatsuya-*sensei*, what did Yuki and Akira get in trouble for?"

"Oh, that...Yuki used the room without permission and stole some chemicals. That's why everything's locked up now." She clucked her tongue, sounding sad. "Apparently, Akira tried to stop him, that dear boy. He eventually told the staff about it."

"What happened then?"

"There was talk of expelling Yuki, even after he'd apologized. Vice Principal Nakamura especially wanted him gone, saying there was no room for thieves in Ogawa High School," Ms. Tatsuya said and continued rummaging. "Principal Kikuchi saw that Yuki was bright and promising, and he only suspended him for a time. Yuki had only been back for a week or so before he..." Ms. Tatsuya straightened and set down the plastic jug she had been inspecting. Her mouth twisted into a frown and her eyes drifted as though trying to follow the tail of a stray thought bounding away. Then, the short woman snapped her head toward Jordan. "Why do you want to know?"

She sounded so accusatory that Jordan was taken aback and had to think for a moment. "I'm just sorry that I never got to know Yuki—not even meet him—I'm curious to know what he was like." Ms. Tatsuya's eyes darted from left to right, as though reading sentences lined on Jordan's face, until finally her attention returned to the jug left on the counter.

"There's not much left. I can't use this."

"I'd be happy to go to Ai-Yu for you," Jordan said, eager to change the subject. The grocery store was only a few minutes' walk away, and she had no more classes for the day anyway. "It's not far."

Ms. Tatsuya agreed after a few minutes of weak, almost perfunctory protestations that Jordan not go out of her way. Jordan had insisted, hoping for an excuse to be away from her desk for the remainder of the afternoon.

Once outside, however, she regretted it, greeted by a bitter wind and a few feeble smatterings of snow. She took one look at the muddy paths and decided to walk instead of taking her bike, not being an experienced cyclist. She hadn't taken more than a few steps when she heard a voice behind her.

"Jordan-*sensei!*" A tall student loped from the school's doors, one of his hands raised as though to be called upon in class. It was Ryusuke. In two more long strides, he was at her side. His sun-dark face was flushed by the cold and breath streamed from his lips like steam from a bowl of soup. "Hi."

"Ryusuke! Playing hooky?" Jordan said with a smile.

"Nah, the school nurse sent me home. I'm not feeling so good."

"I'm sorry to hear that." Jordan took another look at the tall boy as they walked together, noticing the redness of his nose and cheeks and a puffiness around his eyes.

"Oh, shit, almost forgot." Ryusuke pulled a paper face mask out of his pocket—commonly worn by those who were ill or wished to avoid being so—and hooked its elastic loops over his ears.

"Can't one of your parents pick you up?"

"My older brother works at the pharmacy by Ai-Yu. I'll hang out there. Looks like you're the one skipping school, *sensei*," Ryusuke said teasingly. Even though Jordan couldn't see his smile behind the mask, his eyes scrunched up with amusement. They stopped chatting after a few more steps, hunkering into their scarves, giving Jordan a moment to think.

Inspector Sakurai had been gone for several days, but even without anyone to report her findings to, Jordan had continued to ask questions of Nanami, Akira, and anyone who knew the deceased. As far as she knew, Ryusuke wasn't particularly familiar with either of them, but she decided it couldn't hurt to ask.

"Ryusuke, did you know Yuki and Emi well?"

"No, not really. Emi and I were in the same class, but, well... She was popular and always hung out with the *cool kids*, you know?" Jordan was getting to know the students' dynamics and cliques but was surprised to hear that Ryusuke didn't consider himself popular. No one would argue that he wasn't a bit awkward, but he was always friendly and smiling, well-liked, and one of the baseball team's star players. Jordan looked back at him. The mask obscured much of his expression, but his brows were drawn down and he looked almost sad. "I didn't have a clue that Yuki existed at all, until he got in trouble a few months ago. Maybe I should get to know the underclassmen better."

"Did the inspector speak with you?"

"About the suicide club? No, I don't know anything about that. I just don't get it." He shook his head and they waited in silence near the traffic light, which glowed like a Christmas ornament against the snowy sky. Jordan could see Ai-Yu's bright red and white sign across the street —peppered with spots of ashy snow—and decided she couldn't leave Ryusuke in an uncharacteristically melancholy mood before they parted.

"I almost didn't recognize you without Kenji. I thought you two were inseparable. You're like Downtown—that comedy duo on TV!"

Ryusuke laughed and had to catch his breath before he replied.

"No! No, *sensei*! That's so uncool." Ryusuke's cheeks raised and she could tell he was smiling under the mask. He slowly recovered himself. "Actually, *sensei*, I was hoping to ask you a question. You're always so nice to us, hanging out after school, and I thought you might answer something."

"Yes?"

"Well, what if you like someone, and you think they like you back, but you're not sure?" He lowered his head and then muttered something incomprehensible that sounded like he was admonishing himself.

Jordan thought a moment and felt a sudden flush rise to her face that had nothing to do with the cold. Was Ryusuke asking about her? She sometimes wondered if any of her students were stoking schoolboy crushes, remembering her own daydreams about her high school math instructor. She bit her lip to keep from smiling and adopted a tone of flat seriousness.

"Ryusuke, you're an excellent student and I consider you my friend, but—" she stopped as Ryusuke let loose a bark of laughter and stumbled to keep walking.

"No, no! It's okay, *sensei*. Forget I said anything." He raised both gloved hands in front of him as though to stop an oncoming car. Jordan took a breath to ask what he meant and caught a waft of chicken *yaki-tori* on the swift breeze, realizing they were at their destination. Ryusuke jumped in before she could continue. "Well, thanks for walking with me. I'll see you next week," Ryusuke said.

"Bye, Ryusuke. I hope you feel better." She waved as he jogged toward the small pharmacy and bowed to her before stepping inside. Smiling to herself, Jordan brushed through the grocery store's sliding doors in search of a bottle of vinegar.

TWELVE

"INSPECTOR," JORDAN SAID, SURPRISED TO SEE HIM AT THE entrance of Ogawa's train station. She hadn't noticed him at the school that day but doubted he had any other reason to be in town besides gathering information for the investigation. As always, he was dressed in a smart suit, briefcase in hand, this time with the addition of a scarf and warm-looking overcoat. His glasses fogged as he stepped inside the station. The inspector carefully removed the frames as he took a seat across from Jordan, and she was once again struck by his attractive, almost feline, features.

"Hello, Ms. Howard," he said and smiled, removing a cloth from his briefcase to wipe at his glasses. "I trust you've been well?"

"I've been cold." She grinned and moved a little closer to the barrel-sized kerosene heater planted between the rows of benches in the tiny station house.

"Japan must be very different from Las Vegas," the inspector said.

"Did I mention I was from Las Vegas?" Jordan asked, knowing full well she had not, and felt somehow pleased that the inspector had been asking about her.

"You will forgive me? I am an inspector after all."

"Were you at the high school today? Do you have some news about the investigation?" Jordan said and leaned forward, though there was no one to overhear their conversation besides the man behind the ticket counter.

"Yes. Unfortunately, I had to tell the principal and the children's families that the results of my investigation are so far inconclusive." He looked and sounded displeased yet retained an ever-present air of professionalism.

"So you don't know whether there's a suicide club or not?" Jordan said, trying not to sound accusatory despite her disappointment.

"Correct."

"You didn't turn up anything about Emi and Junichi in Sagae?" She was fishing. The inspector had never said that he was going to Sagae to investigate Junichi, after all. His answers were always carefully crafted, but perhaps he would reveal more if only she kept asking.

"Inconclusive," he said and grinned ever so slightly at her latest attempt to wrest away information.

"Will you come back to Ogawa?"

"My superiors have assigned me to another case. Unless new information arises, I don't expect to," he said and paused. "Not for work, at least. But Ogawa has other charms."

"I see," Jordan said and ducked her head to hide an involuntary smile. Certainly she was attracted to him, but she hadn't held out hope that he felt the same. She felt her stomach flip with nervous excitement, though she wasn't confident that she was reading him correctly, between her imperfect Japanese and his previous attempts to distance himself.

Jordan also hadn't entertained the thought of pursuing anyone during her time in Japan, but neither had the opportunity presented itself before. Inspector Sakurai was clearly intelligent and undeniably handsome. In a more casual setting, she imagined he could be rather personable. She smiled wider, mind made up. "Inspector, would you like to get coffee sometime?"

"I would like that very much, Ms. Howard," he said, looking pleased and slightly surprised.

"Please call me Jordan," she said. "And I certainly can't keep calling you 'Inspector.'"

"It's Toshihiko."

"I look forward to it, Toshihiko."

THIRTEEN

COFFEE ONE FRIDAY EVENING HAD BEEN FOLLOWED BY DINNER the next week, and another, and Jordan once again found herself sitting across from Toshihiko, sharing a meal and conversation. They sat in the corner of a *shabu-shabu* restaurant, crowded near a window that sweated with condensation from the boiling broth at the center of their table. Outside the window, fat drops of freezing rain slid and spattered against the glass.

"I guess I should head back to Ogawa soon—wouldn't want to get caught up in this storm. It'll be bad enough as it is," she said and turned her attention from the window to Toshihiko. Picking up her chopsticks, she pinched a leaf of cabbage from the roiling, golden broth and brought it close to her lips to blow on it. "Or you could show me your apartment." Toshihiko coughed, and she smiled widely.

"Yes, well, the station's not far. I'll see you to your train if you like," Toshihiko said after taking a sip of the dregs of his beer.

"Sure," Jordan said with a sigh, unsurprised by Toshihiko's answer but still disappointed. It wasn't the first advance he had deflected. Toshihiko was a tough enough nut to crack already, and approaching him from a romantic angle didn't do much to pierce his shell.

Jordan knew Toshihiko's hesitation wasn't from lack of attraction to her, or at least, she saw no evidence of that. He was always the one to propose their next date—which she always gladly accepted—and she would sometimes catch him admiring her. There was no coldness when he would press his hand or lips to hers—quite the opposite. Infrequent though they might be, each touch was brief and searing, like an electric spark.

She also knew there must be some men who simply wanted to take things slowly, but none whom she had ever met. Though, she had only been in a handful of short-lived relationships before, so she didn't have much to compare Toshihiko to.

Also, unlike Jordan's other romantic interests, Toshihiko made her feel...fuller. She couldn't think of another word for it. When Toshihiko was with her, his presence filled in the small hollows of her life in Japan —little pits she seldom realized were there, until Toshihiko left and they were emptied. Neither feeling—the gain nor the loss—was over-powerful, but Jordan had to admit she enjoyed Toshihiko's company, enjoyed the realization that he was one of the few she cared for among a sea of strangers.

She didn't love him, though. And she wondered whether her isolation from friends and family was honing her feelings for Toshihiko—whether the weight of her loneliness lifted up her fondness for him, like opposite ends of a scale.

Jordan liked him, and admittedly, she liked to watch him squirm from time to time. At the moment, however, his rebuff irked more than amused her.

She eyed the last piece of Kobe beef somersaulting through the broth. She knew Toshihiko would not take the final piece, as it was polite to refuse it, and decided to eat it herself without offering. As Jordan scooped the dripping meat into her rice bowl, she saw Toshihiko smirk and nod once to himself, though he didn't say anything for some time. Finally, he met her eyes and spoke.

"I've been wondering—why did you come here?"

"A handsome friend of mine said it was the best *shabu-shabu* restaurant in Yamagata City, and that we should give it a try." She grinned around a mouthful of rice.

"To Japan, I mean," Toshihiko said, either not picking up on her joke, or more likely, choosing to ignore it. "Do you want to be a teacher when you return?"

"Not really." Jordan shook her head and thought for a moment. "I thought it would be exciting—like an adventure. Strike off on my own in an entirely new place."

"Is it as foreign and exotic as you hoped for?" Toshihiko pushed up his glasses as he said this, obscuring his expression with his hand. Jordan wasn't sure of his tone but felt edges of sarcasm poke at her.

"Yes," she said and took a long swallow of water, not wanting to comment more. Either she had read Toshihiko incorrectly, or he was easily defused, as he smiled and calmly set aside his chopsticks instead of prodding further. Jordan kept her eyes on her water glass as she set it down. "Actually, there's another reason why I came here."

"Oh?" Toshihiko clasped his hands on the table.

"My brother Aiden...died. In March. He overdosed, and no one knows whether it was an accident or not. Everything back home reminds me of him. I thought if only I left, if only—" She heard her voice quaver and felt the familiar sting of tears at the back of her eyes. Toshihiko could see the change in her demeanor and his expression softened. In different circumstances, Jordan would have milked Toshihiko's unexpected show of tenderness, but not when it came to Aiden.

She couldn't fall to pieces every single time she thought of her brother—it was too frequent an occurrence—and Toshihiko's warm look bolstered Jordan's resolve to pull herself together. She took a deep breath, slumped back against the booth's stiff cushion, and sighed. "I thought if I left home, maybe I could get away from it all. But now, after Yuki and Emi..."

"I'm very sorry, Jordan. You have my deepest sympathy." Toshihiko placed his hand atop hers and gave it a brief squeeze. He didn't let the touch linger, yet Jordan was grateful for the gesture, small as it was. He wore a sincere look but was also entirely calm, leading Jordan to wonder just how many grieving families he had consoled in his line of work.

"Why did *you* come here?" Jordan said after a pause, hoping to redirect the conversation. "From Tokyo to Yamagata City."

"Ah. So you know about all that?" Toshihiko settled back in his seat. He looked intrigued, and maybe even a shade embarrassed.

"Who doesn't Google their dates these days?" She shrugged. "Seriously, though, that Yakuza arrest was quite the accomplishment. And so early in your career. I'm surprised you left the Tokyo police."

Toshihiko said nothing, his energies diverted to his thoughts. Though his neutral expression didn't change, Jordan could tell he was weighing what to say next, if anything at all. After a moment more of silence, Jordan tried again.

"I mean, didn't you have more opportunities in Tokyo?"

"I left because a Yakuza *shatei* attacked me in retaliation. Four stab wounds. I spent weeks in the hospital recovering," Toshihiko said with controlled calm. He continued over Jordan's choked noise of surprise, his steady gaze holding hers. "Even then, I wished to stay in Tokyo, to see more members of the Inagawa-kai brought to justice. But once they learned that I had survived, they made threats against my family."

"Toshihiko..."

"I convinced my parents and sister to move to Akita. When another —unsuccessful—attempt was made on my life, I transferred to Yamagata City."

"I don't know what to say." She ached to reach for his hand then, to return the same small reassurance he had given her, but his chilly expression was as much a deterrent as the distance. "You must—"

"You don't have to say anything," Toshihiko said firmly, though not unkindly. Jordan took his meaning clearly: he didn't want to speak more about it. A beat of silence followed before he permitted a wan smile. "At least now I can concentrate on solving cases. I wouldn't have been able to perform my duties well in Tokyo, not with the distraction of the Inagawa-kai."

"Distraction? That's an understatement." Jordan was too over-whelmed by Toshihiko's story to check her incredulity.

"I suppose it's better this way. People in Yamagata need help, too, after all." Toshihiko's smile broadened a touch, but Jordan could see little warmth behind it, or his words, despite his effort to build up a serene exterior. He sounded like he was trying to convince himself. "I don't regret coming here."

Even saying as much seemed to make the case for him feeling the opposite. Still, Jordan grinned back.

"Because you met such charming people?"

"Of course." A short laugh escaped him despite himself.

They finished their dinner, and he paid the check without much more conversation beyond casual comments on how delicious the meal was. Once outside, most of their attention was focused on staying dry, angling their umbrellas just so in order to deflect the plump raindrops without allowing the wind to catch underneath. Through the clear wings of her umbrella, Jordan could see the lit sign of Yamagata City's train station, and they were through its main doors within minutes.

"I can find my train from here, thank you," Jordan said and stamped her shoes and umbrella against the already sodden floor mat. She looked up and smiled brightly. "And thank you for the lovely dinner."

"Of course," Toshihiko said pleasantly as he removed his glasses to wipe at their fogged lenses. "Have a safe trip home."

They parted with a few more friendly words and suggestions to meet again soon, before Jordan purchased her ticket and rounded a staircase leading to the lower level. Though it was already late into the evening, most of the station's shops and restaurants remained open, and Jordan had to squeeze past crowds of customers on her way to the platform.

She passed stalls selling souvenir cookies, candies, cheeses, and meats from the region, boutiques and makeup counters, and cafes fragrant with coffee and hot chocolate. Many stores were also ornamented with Christmas decorations, and some notes of holiday music danced on the air. Jordan paused by a bright bakery window housing rows of Christmas cakes, each frosted with smooth white icing and topped with a circle of strawberries that stood like red trees on a snowy hilltop. She smiled to herself at the warm scene as she pushed onto the platform and was met with the night's cold, wet air.

FOURTEEN

Only Jordan's hands were warm: one squeezing a disposable warming packet in her pocket and the other wrapped in Toshihiko's gloved grasp. He held her hand lightly, easily. They had spent every weekend of the past month together and seen each other even more often since the school's winter break had begun the week before.

Without work to distract her, Jordan eagerly sought out Toshihiko to occupy her time, and her thoughts. It would be her first Christmas away from home. She had considered flying back to Las Vegas for a few days, but she was on a tight budget and trying to pay off college debts, maybe even build up her savings...for what she wasn't sure. Graduate school, possibly, or her own home. Her parents had insisted that she not go out of her way, not to worry about them, but the undertow of sadness was unmistakable.

It was also their first Christmas without Aiden. Jordan couldn't imagine trying to celebrate a holiday without him there—what it would be like to see so many familiar faces together except for the one. Those faces wearing the same hollow pain she felt. Even thinking about it was too much for her to bear. And now, because of her staying in Japan, there would be two people missing. Perhaps it would be better, for everyone, if they simply held onto the memories instead of trying to live out some weak mockery of times before. Or maybe it was just easier for her not to face it.

Jordan was yet again overcome with guilt over her own selfishness and cowardice. Shaking her head, Jordan wrapped her fingers tightly around Toshihiko's and leaned her shoulder into his.

"It's beautiful," she said, hoping he didn't hear the catch in her voice. Her sniffling she could blame on the cold.

They walked together slowly along the mountain path. It was packed with snow and groups of visitors bundled in thick jackets, snow pants, and scarves. Laughter and plumes of breath floated from the passersby's plump shapes as they shuffled alongside Jordan and Toshihiko. Snow crunched below their feet when their boots broke through untrodden patches of crust.

Just beyond the path, they were joined by more figures. Rows upon rows of hunched forms loomed tens of feet tall—trees bent under the weight of rime wrapping them like batting. The Snow Monsters of Zao. The countless trees wore hoary shells pocked and lined by the wind, huddled against the elements, utterly frozen.

In the dark of the evening, the shapes did look truly monstrous—an endless phantom army of defeated warriors plodding forward in an inexorable march. They continued so far up the mountainside that they disappeared beyond sight, swallowed by the night as though sinking into deep, dark waters. A stiff burst of wind shunted through the rime-covered trees, making their covered branches moan and shudder.

Jordan was awestruck by the distorted creatures. She felt a shiver crawl across her neck at their ghostly sounds and almost imperceptible swaying in the dark. Some were illuminated by colored lights mounted high on scaffolding on the other side of the path, making them look incongruously cheery, awash in greens, pinks, and purples. The trees' shadows were lined by ribbons of color from the multiple lights, as though the snow had been dyed. Opposite the mountainside, the golden lights of the Zao Onsen spa glittered below.

Jordan sighed appreciatively at the sight, only to have her teeth snap back together with a shiver of cold. They had been outside for a half-hour, and the biting wind was beginning to overpower her enjoyment of the scene. She glanced at Toshihiko, who seemed unperturbed despite the redness of his nose and cheeks. He looked at the icy trees with cool regard, his lips forming a very small, private smile. Jordan squeezed his hand.

"How about some hot coffee at the lodge? I'm freezing."

"Of course."

They walked to the queue for the suspended cable car that would transport them down to the lodge at the mountain's base. After a few minutes, Jordan and Toshihiko arrived at the front of the line and waited as a car floated down the cableway. They scurried inside and sidled into a seat together to make way for the handful of other visitors who boarded. The car bobbed and rocked like a cork as the passengers settled before drifting down the mountainside.

The windows were already foggy and teary with breath, and Jordan had to swipe her hand across the glass to see outside. Now far below, the snow monsters seemed less magnificent, trudging away in their snowy, bunched coats. Jordan pressed a gloved finger against the window and closed one eye, obscuring a lavender-washed rime creature, and imagined just how luxurious a simple mug of coffee would taste. She turned back to see Toshihiko quickly direct his gaze at his feet, as though embarrassed to have been caught watching her. He recovered himself in a heartbeat.

"Did you enjoy the *Juhyo*?"

"I hardly ever see a single flake of snow back home! This was... amazing." Jordan smiled. Toshihiko returned a pleased look but said no more, instead directing his attention out the window.

Even after a month of getting to know Toshihiko, Jordan was still learning how to navigate a conversation with him. He was always polite —almost professional—and tended to toe around the edges of topics, slowly circling his way to the core point. Jordan had thought she would get to see the man behind the collected inspector but began to wonder if his badge was grafted to his bones. Not that he spoke about his job often—far from it—but rather she wouldn't be surprised if he pulled out his digital recorder mid-conversation and took notes with his usual calm demeanor. At the thought of Toshihiko and his casework, an idea settled in Jordan's mind.

"I'll be in Yamagata City tomorrow. Your office isn't far from the train station, is it?"

"My department's not exactly open to the public," he said and looked coolly out the window.

"But you can get me clearance. Come on; you promised to show me one day—I'd like to see where you work."

"Some other time. I hoped to enjoy this weekend without thinking about my investigations." Toshihiko looked at her then and smiled. Jordan decided not to press any further, though he had deflected her request more than once before. Because they had met due to her students' deaths, and because Jordan's curiosity still lingered after the investigation's non-resolution, she couldn't help but probe the inspector for details. Often. Once, Toshihiko had let slip that Emi and Junichi had indeed been involved with each other, as she suspected, but he had schooled himself more carefully since.

They spent the rest of the ride to the base of the mountain in comfortable silence and Toshihiko politely took Jordan's arm to help her from the car as it skirted along the loading platform. Many other cold-weary visitors shared the same longing for a warm drink, and Jordan and Toshihiko followed a trickle of people into the wooden lodge nearby. Upon entering, the warmth from the twisting fire in the hearth and the crush of people swallowed Jordan. She unwound her scarf and pointed to two armchairs edging one of the large windows.

"I'll get the seats. You get the coffee."

Toshihiko nodded in agreement and Jordan slipped away to the chairs. So near the window, she could feel the cold curling its fingers through the glass, but she sighed at the pleasant ambient warmth, feeling her cheeks tingle as her blood pumped with new vigor. She sank into the cushioned chair as she removed her gloves and watched the stream of people outside. The lodge's bright interior made it difficult to see much beyond what was illuminated by its bubble of light cast onto the snow, but Jordan was happy to watch the pink, smiling faces that passed rather than the snowy grotesques beyond them.

The rime-encased trees reminded her of lost spirits roaming the mountainside, and she felt a familiar ache at the thought of Aiden, and her students. Even Emi. She let her shoulders slump and realized she was scowling when Toshihiko returned with two steaming mugs.

"Are you all right?"

"I'm fine, thank you." She took the mug gratefully, taking a moment to enjoy the nutty, woody aroma of the coffee and the warmth that seeped from the ceramic cup to her fingers. She paused before taking a sip. "Did you know that Yuki was reprimanded for breaking into the school's science room a few weeks before his death?" Toshihiko smoothly navigated his own coffee to his lips, but Jordan thought she saw a muscle in his jaw twitch.

"Yes." He eyed her over the top of his glasses. "You believe this is relevant?"

"I assumed anything out of the ordinary relating to Yuki or Emi was relevant. I guess neither were model students."

"And perhaps they both felt deeply ashamed of their actions," Toshihiko said and continued firmly over Jordan as she began to speak. "Jordan, I don't know how else to say I shouldn't be discussing a case, especially with someone so closely involved, even if the investigation has been tabled. I'm sorry, but you may never find the answers you're looking for."

"I understand," she said and sighed before sitting up a little straighter so that she could place her hand over Toshihiko's. She felt his fingers relax under her touch. "I'll stop raining on our outing."

"So we *can* talk about something else for a change?" he asked teasingly.

"You were going to tell me about that man who was born in the castle we visited the other week—Yonezawa Castle. You know, the guy who wears the eye patch and the banana hat in all his statues."

Toshihiko laughed. "Date Masamune. You know very well that it's a crescent-moon helmet and not a banana. He's the founder of Sendai, actually. Back in 1584..."

Jordan smiled to herself as she listened and watched the lights of the town below disappear and blink back to life as person after person drifted by.

FIFTEEN

School had only resumed that day, the students still lethargic and resistant to acclimating to their lessons. Jordan felt much the same way and made little effort to stifle a yawn, drowsy and unenergetic so soon after lunch. The days were still bitterly cold, but a large kerosene heater thrumming a few feet away from her desk suffused the teachers' room with warmth, if also a cloying smell of gas. Jordan finished marking the last vocabulary test in the stack and lifted her gaze from her work.

Mr. Mori was the only other teacher at their group of desks. As usual, he didn't appear receptive to chatting, leaning over his papers with his glasses perched on the edge of his nose.

Over Mr. Mori's shoulder, Jordan could see part of the soccer field —brown with cold—the low-crouched hills, and another section of the school, which was something like a mirror image. By looking straight out the window in front of her, Jordan could see inside another room at the opposite end of the U-shaped building.

The other room had collapsible walls, few pieces of furniture, and no blackboard—seldom used except for the occasional student council meeting or other impromptu activities. Jordan grinned as she remembered her surprise when, one day, she had looked up from her papers only to be faced with the junior boys stripping down to their under-shorts, their locker room out of service.

Now, Jordan was intrigued to see a large group assembled in that room. Such gatherings weren't unusual during break times, but the students were keenly interested in something, all forming a haphazard circle to face the middle of the room. One student shifted his weight and Jordan glimpsed a flurry of activity at the center—white shirt-sleeves and flailing limbs flashed between the onlookers like paper caught in a gust of wind. Over the hum of the heater, she heard muffled shouts and cheers.

"I...think there's a fight," Jordan said hesitantly to Mr. Mori and pointed out the window.

"What's that?" Mr. Mori sounded disinterested, but once he followed Jordan's gaze to the scene, he jumped to his feet. At that same moment, a first-grade girl threw open the door to the teachers' room without so much as a greeting and scurried to the head desk.

"Vice Principal Nakamura, come quick! Kenji-*senpai* and Tadao-*senpai* are fighting."

Jordan's ears perked at mention of Kenji, and she quickly followed the student, Ms. Nakamura, and Mr. Mori out of the teachers' room and down the hall. The commotion of excited voices and wordless shouts from the observers and combatants rushed into Jordan as they approached the huddled group.

Without a word, Ms. Nakamura grasped the shoulders of one boy and began to move him aside. The boy whipped his head around with a look of annoyance aimed at whomever was disrupting the show, but his expression melted into one of cowed fear when he saw the vice princi-pal. He slunk back, pulling worriedly at his friend's sleeve as he retreated. Everyone nearby soon followed suit, peeling away to create a small opening for the adults to pass through.

Either Kenji and the other boy did not notice the interruption or they were too embroiled to care. Kenji threw a wild punch at the taller boy, who dodged easily, mostly because another student was hanging on Kenji's side, pulling and urging him to stop. Both boys were utterly disheveled—shirts pulled out of waistbands, hair mussed—and Kenji wiped at a trickle of blood from his nose. Tadao balled his hand into a fist and made a move to strike but stopped upon noticing the change in the room. He looked at the silent students with confusion until his eyes fell on the vice principal. Instantly, he dropped his hands to his sides and bowed in her direction.

Kenji paused, seemingly tempted to lash out while his opponent's defenses were down, but instead turned to see Ms. Nakamura's stormy visage. A look of worry and panic crossed his face before he, too, offered an apologetic bow. He bent so deeply that his hair almost brushed the floor.

"Vice Principal Nakamura, please—"

"Be silent," she said and glared. Kenji swallowed. "Everyone else, leave." The students who had not already crept to the door hurried away, more than happy to increase the distance between them and the older woman. Kenji sniffled wetly as a fresh ribbon of blood trailed down his face; he swiped at it with an already reddened shirtsleeve. Ms. Nakamura barked out her next command. "Mori-*sensei*, take Tadao-*kun* to Principal Kikuchi. Jordan-*sensei*, you may return to the teachers' room."

Jordan hesitated for a moment, wishing to discover just what had happened. But Ms. Nakamura was unkind on even her best days and was clearly not in a mood to be contested, so Jordan reluctantly obeyed. Tadao shuffled to Mr. Mori, who peered at the student disapprovingly over his glasses. Jordan followed them to the door.

As she turned to slide the door shut, Kenji caught her eye, looking both contrite and pleading, as though she could somehow help. Jordan mouthed, "I'm sorry," with an apologetic look, leaving him alone with the vice principal.

Mr. Mori and the other boy were already turning the corner down the hall. Instead of returning to her desk, however, Jordan scanned the dispersing students for anyone she could ask about the incident. She was confident she could eventually get the story out of Kenji, but curiosity gnawed at her, making her both tense and excited. Just down the hall, she spotted Akira's gangly figure shuffling away and hurried to meet him, calling out to get his attention.

"Akira!" She continued forward quickly, and he smiled to see her. "Did you see the fight just now?"

"Yeah! Pretty intense," he said and ran a hand through his straight hair. His eyes drifted off to the side as though he could still see the tussle, looking almost awestruck. "I didn't know Kenji-*senpai* had it in him."

"Do you know what they were fighting about?"

"I'm not sure...They were already going at it by the time I heard shouting," he said, and as he thought of it, he became more animated and excited. Jordan doubted Ogawa High School saw many fights. "Actually, Tadao-*senpai* did say something."

"Yes?" She leaned forward. Akira hesitated and looked at his feet. "It's all right, Akira. I'd like to know what he said."

"Well, after he landed that wicked punch on Kenji-*senpai*, Tadao-*senpai* said, 'You really are a homo.'" Akira spoke in a whisper and looked about nervously as though he were in trouble. "Kenji-*senpai* got really mad, but Tadao's always saying things like that, just because he's bigger than everyone."

"He's a regular bully then?"

"Yeah, you could say that. Everyone knows he's a real jerk, and Kenji-*senpai* is usually so cool... Must've gotten under his skin today."

Jordan nodded thoughtfully. "Thanks, Akira. You'd better head to class now—lunch break will be over soon."

"Okay, Jordan-*sensei*. See you later." He waved and loped away through the empty hallway. Jordan hadn't taken more than two steps toward the teachers' room when she heard the echoing footfalls of someone running up behind her.

"*Sensei!*" It was Ryusuke, barreling clumsily toward Jordan like a retriever after a tennis ball. "*Sensei*, what happened? Where's Kenji?" Jordan relayed what little she knew, including what Akira had told her. Ryusuke's eyes went wide with concern when he heard that Kenji had been left to the vice principal. He stared intently at the door, as though he could divine what was occurring behind its wood panels.

"Tadao, that asshole," he said suddenly and with more venom than she thought Ryusuke capable of mustering. "Dammit, I should've been there."

"Ryusuke, then you would have only gotten in trouble too." She smiled gently. "Come on. It's not your fault."

"No, *sensei*, you don't understand." His voice came shuddering through his clenched teeth, and Jordan thought she saw a glint of wetness in his eyes before he ducked his head. Ryusuke took a few slouching steps away before returning and repeating the circuit. He paced and ran a hand through his spiky hair, eyes to the floor, seeming to forget he was not alone. Jordan frowned, feeling sorry for his obvious distress but also confused by what seemed to her to be an overreaction.

"Ryusuke, this will all blow over," she said in what she hoped was a tone of reason. "Why don't you head back to class and wait for Kenji?"

He slowly looked up, still lost in thought, before offering the barest shadow of a smile.

"You're right, *sensei*." He didn't seem convinced but he nodded and turned to leave. "Make sure Nakamura-*kyoutou* doesn't eat him alive, okay?"

"I'll try." She chuckled, and Ryusuke's smile widened for the briefest of moments before he raised his hand in a parting wave, let it fall to his side, and walked away.

SIXTEEN

Jordan dipped her head to her chest, bracing against the cold wind and snow until only her eyes were visible between her scarf and ear-flapped hat. Her booted foot quailed at a patch of ice, shooting to the side, but she managed to right herself before falling into the snow. Jordan let out a sigh of relief, breath unfurling in smoky curls, when she saw the school just a few yards away. It bobbed in her vision, grey and spliced with static-like snow.

A few students trickled inside, but one boy shot through the open doors, hurrying outside.

Kenji.

He clumsily tried to juggle his book bag and coat, one arm halfway through each, before making a noise of frustration and increasing his pace. He threw his items to the ground, uncaring of the slushy snow his coat sank into, and began to fumble at his bike lock. Jordan approached cautiously, uncertain of whether he would welcome any interaction, even with her.

"Kenji?" When she spoke, he spared her a brief look over his shoulder before returning to the lock. "Is everything all right?"

"No," he said simply and choked back a noise in his throat.

"You haven't been expelled, have you?" After the fight a couple of days before, she had heard nothing about how Kenji and Tadao were to be disciplined. She had watched the door to the principal's office for what had seemed like hours, as the silhouettes of the boys, the principal, and the vice principal played across the window's frosted glass. Eventually, she had gone home without an answer, and she now felt a pinch of worry in her chest.

"No, Jordan-*sensei*." Kenji shoved his dripping belongings into the bike's rear basket and wrangled it onto the sidewalk. His bare hands held the handlebars in a strangling, shaking grip and his handsome features contorted with a look of intense sorrow. "Ryusuke's dead."

Without another word, he swung onto the seat and pedaled away through the snow, flakes as big as leaves falling.

Jordan's breath thickened in her throat and she simply stared, watching the furrows of the bike tracks collect snow. She thought she heard someone call her name, but the sound was muffled by the wind whistling through the wool against her ears and the pulsing of her heart through every muscle. Disbelief and grief overtook her, seeped into her inch by inch, as if she were lowering into a gelid lake toe-first, slowly, until her head sank far below the surface.

Unable to move, much less think, she felt for the cell phone in her pocket. The slim device rested in her gloved palm, feeling heavy as she methodically brought up Toshihiko's number. She watched her fingers tap out a message seemingly of their own accord, like a planchette sliding across a spirit board. She read over the short text—*Ryusuke is dead. What's happening? Where are you?*—pressed Send, and waited. Minutes passed without a response. The bell signaling the start of class rang, and still she stood as the winds began to pile snow at her feet.

SEVENTEEN

JORDAN FELT STRANGELY NERVOUS AS SHE WAITED FOR TOSHIHIKO at the izakaya outside Yamagata City Station. Not the sort of girlish nervousness that had bubbled up before their first few dates, but leaden, murky worry.

Toshihiko's reply to Jordan's text message about Ryusuke had been kind and consolatory, but brief. This was followed by nearly a day of silence, and then Toshihiko's suggestion that they meet in person. Something was amiss about his messages, though Jordan couldn't put her finger on what. Toshihiko was always to the point, but now his few words hinted at hesitation, or obfuscation.

Or maybe she was overthinking it, she conceded. Thoughts of Ryusuke's death were ever present, and Jordan's moods were constantly ping-ponging between utter grief, numbness, anger, and disbelief. Probably anything Toshihiko could have said would have strummed an overtight nerve. Even the weather seemed willfully dreary—outside the izakaya's windows, the snow cast a cold pallor as it hustled to the ground, grey and wet.

Jordan had arrived early, but as minute after minute passed with no sign of Toshihiko, her nerves bunched impossibly tighter. When he finally emerged through the curtained door—perfectly on time—it was with a flash of dumb relief that Jordan rose and walked to him.

"Toshihiko," she said as she encircled him with her arms. She had meant for it to be a quick embrace, but Toshihiko's comforting sturdiness made her tighten her hold and press her cheek to his chest. Through the chilly specks of snow on his overcoat, she could feel the warmth of his body, and she sighed gratefully.

The press of Toshihiko's hands hugging her back was firm but short-lived, and he soon pulled away. This wasn't unusual—nor was the lack of a kiss—but worry crept back to Jordan.

"Hello, Jordan." Toshihiko gave a small smile. "How are you holding up?"

"Not well, to be honest. But I'm better now that you're here."

"You give me too much credit," he said, and his eyes skirted away to latch onto a nearby booth. He gestured toward it. "Shall we?"

They settled in and placed their orders, Jordan eyeing Toshihiko when he requested only hot tea. Not even a beer, as was his usual.

"Aren't you hungry?" she said, trying to sound nonchalant.

"I can't stay long, I'm afraid." As Toshihiko spoke, he removed his glasses and began to wipe off a smudge of melted snow, not meeting Jordan's eyes.

Jordan waited while Toshihiko deliberately cleaned and returned his glasses, but no further explanation came as to why he had to leave so soon. *Overthinking it*, she reminded herself, and forced her voice into a pleasant timbre.

"Well, I'm glad you were able to spare some time to see me. I need the pick-me-up."

"I *am* sorry about Ryusuke," Toshihiko said. His words were soft and held genuine warmth, but this gesture of kindness lanced Jordan with incongruous anger.

If you're so sorry, why aren't you doing anything about it? Why couldn't you stop this? Jordan came dangerously close to blurting out her thoughts but was interrupted when the waiter served their drinks and her meal. Jordan stared at the chicken drooped over the plate, her appetite supplanted by aimless fury. She took a swallow of sake, more to allow her temper to cool than for the enjoyment of it.

"So why can't you stay? Because of an investigation?" Jordan said. Though it was a Saturday, Toshihiko working through the weekend was not unheard-of, and she allowed herself to hope that he was working on *the* investigation. If he wasn't forthcoming with an answer, she resolved to keep pressing. After so long, she was done tip-toeing around his notions of propriety.

As though he had heard her thoughts, Toshihiko pinned Jordan with a firm look over his glasses before he continued.

"Yes, I'm working on an investigation. Actually, that's why I asked to see you today."

"You've taken up Ryusuke's case?" Jordan felt a burst of something close to happiness, despite the circumstances, when Toshihiko nodded in reply. Yet this was quickly tempered by a dark look that shadowed his eyes.

"Jordan. We can't see each other anymore," he said simply.

"Wh-Why not?" Jordan huffed, too incredulous to muster more words. Not that she could have voiced them through her choked throat.

"Ryusuke's death has reopened Ogawa's other case files. As you know, we began our relationship only after investigation of the suicide club was tabled and I was reassigned. This was quite purposeful on my part—to avoid any conflict of interests, you see."

As Toshihiko spoke, Jordan could only look on, searching his face for...what, she wasn't sure. His tone and demeanor had shifted ever so slightly, and Jordan realized she was no longer facing Toshihiko as she had grown to know him, but rather Toshihiko the cop. *Investigator* Toshihiko Sakurai.

With each word that passed Toshihiko's lips, Jordan felt the last few weeks with him fall away and disappear, one by one. When he had finished, it was though they had walked backward through time and she was looking into the eyes of the stranger who had just been hit by a fly ball and dropped his briefcase.

Jordan fumbled through her thoughts and fought against the prickling sensation that threatened to coax tears to her eyes, so she said nothing for a long moment. Silence didn't typically faze Toshihiko. If anything, he would gladly wait out the other person and let them fill in the space, but now he shifted and cleared his throat.

"I'm sorry, Jordan. Perhaps I made a mistake by pursuing you in the first place."

"Oh?" Jordan said hotly, any trace of tears evaporating. "So sorry to disappoint."

"No, that's not—Please allow me to explain," Toshihiko said and ran one hand through his already mussed hair—a telltale sign that he was flustered. "I always believed it was likely that the investigation into your students' deaths would continue. And now that it *has* resumed, I have to maintain a professional distance—from you."

Jordan's ears pricked at that: Toshihiko's belief that the investigation had never been truly over. Had he suspected that more students were at risk, or simply that new evidence would come to light? Despite the numbness piling atop her, a spout of curiosity broke through too quickly to quell.

"You thought more students were going to die?"

"Jordan." It was equal parts a sharp reprimand and warning to tread lightly. He even looked a bit shocked that she had asked.

Both of them refused to break the taut silence that followed, but Jordan finally gave in, reluctantly returning to the subject at hand.

"Don't I get any say in this? Relationships are usually a two-way street, you know." She hated the note of defeat in her voice but didn't know how to overcome it. Toshihiko's pronouncement had already settled heavily on her shoulders, too oppressive to shrug off.

"You're too close to the case, Jordan. I can't let partiality sway my inquiries, or my judgment," he said as though it were the obvious, and only, solution.

"*Partiality*. That's a funny way of putting it," Jordan said dryly as she poured another glass of sake and drank it in a single gulp. "You might want to brush up on your sweet nothings before wooing other women."

Toshihiko was taken aback, and he said nothing for a long while. For the first time that night, Jordan saw unchecked emotion color his face. He looked pained, and then disconsolate. It was such an alien expression on Toshihiko that Jordan felt her chest constrict with reflexive sympathy.

With stubborn resolve, she tamped down the feeling and watched Toshihiko's turmoil play out through his lowered eyebrows, his tense shoulders, his bobbing throat. Finally, he forced words past his drawn lips.

"Don't you understand?" His voice was reined, despite everything. "I'm interested in *you*, not other women. That's the problem."

"Oh, I'm the *problem* now?" Jordan was on her feet in an instant, grabbing at her purse and jacket as she scuttled away from the table.

"Jordan, you know I didn't mean that—"

"You won't have to worry about me troubling you anymore," she said loudly and stabbed her arms through the jacket's sleeves, already halfway to the exit. When she reached the door, she paused and turned to spare a last look at Toshihiko. He was on his feet, his expression distraught, but he made no move toward her.

"Jordan..."

The threat of tears again lanced at her eyes and she ducked her head as she pushed out the door of the izakaya and onto the street. Jordan took several lunging, sliding steps along the snow-strangled road before stopping at the sound of a voice calling out. But when she looked over her shoulder, there was no one behind her.

She waited for the izakaya's door to fly open, for Toshihiko to push through the pall of snow to her side. She waited, and then walked away.

EIGHTEEN

Jordan didn't go to Ryusuke's funeral, or the wake. Simply imagining Ryusuke lying too-still in a black suit, his skin pale and smiling mouth drawn, caused tears to sting her eyes.

"I'm sorry, Ryusuke," she said to the black marble pillar standing before her, nearly as tall as the boy had been. The stone surface was glassy, lined with morning sunlight along its tiered corners. Jordan could recognize the thick, brushstroke-like symbols of Ryusuke's name only upon close inspection, but his grave marker stood out among the thicket of carved stones that dripped down the hillside.

Bundles of flowers coated the low mantle as though they were growing from the grave itself. A single crimson flower rested between the others' snowy petals like a pinprick of blood. Jordan wasn't sure what the red flower symbolized but felt its uniqueness spoke of deep affection. Below the flowers, small offerings were placed—a bowl of the crisp, golden pears that Ogawa was famous for, a *mikan* orange, and a shallow dish of clear liquid.

Even at such an early hour, she had not been the first visitor. Beside the pears, a thin line of blue-white smoke twisted from a stick of musky incense. Perhaps the grave had been visited by his mother and father, who remained with their son even then, in a way. Their engraved names joined Ryusuke's on the coal-dark marble, painted in red until their ashes, too, were to be interred in the family altar.

With the back of her gloved hand, Jordan wiped at her nose, raw from the cold and crying. Uncertain of what else to say to the lifeless, somber stone—so unlike Ryusuke—Jordan let her eyes stray.

The path to the cemetery branched from the road between Jordan's apartment and the high school, climbing in a tight zigzag up the narrow, tall hillside. Below, Jordan could see the road to Ogawa High School where it bisected columns of rice paddies—fallow and brown but gilt with a layer of early-morning frost. The school building was also visible in the distance. She could even see tiny figures filing through the doors and realized she would have to leave soon to be on time for class.

Jordan took a deep breath of frosty air and faced her shadowed, distorted reflection in the stone. She recalled that Japanese people were bestowed new names upon death so that when families and friends spoke of those who had passed, their spirits would not be summoned back. She wondered, then, if they believed the deceased could hear their old names upon their loved ones' lips, spoken in sighs and empty rooms.

"Goodbye, Ryusuke." She turned and left quietly.

"Kenji hasn't come back."

Jordan barely heard Ms. Tatsuya's meek voice over the mingled sounds of the teachers eating their lunches. Ms. Tatsuya had directed her comment at her plate, but the principal answered.

"I just received a phone call from Kenji's mother this morning." Many teachers set down their plastic chopsticks on their lunch trays as they paused to listen. "As you may know, the Ito family has lived in Tsuruoka for years now. But Kenji commuted here with his father every morning, to learn alongside his old friends and classmates. Because of...what happened, he has elected to finish his schooling closer to home. Ms. Nakamura, let's talk about his transfer paperwork later." Principal Kikuchi finished speaking quickly and returned to his soup.

"And he will simply get away with fighting and disorderly conduct, I see." Vice Principal Nakamura added with a terse sniff.

"Kenji has been through enough. With his best friend gone, why should he come back here?" Ms. Tatsuya said with enough heat to contend with the vice principal's icy shell. But Ms. Nakamura merely raised a single eyebrow and pursed her lips at the edge of her teacup.

"Well, Tadao has been temporarily suspended and will serve detention when he returns. As well he should," Mr. Mori said, nodding toward the vice principal, almost hopeful for her approval. "For what it's worth, Tadao was sincerely apologetic, and he insisted he was merely defending himself. Maybe Ogawa High School is better off without Kenji, after all."

A few teachers murmured—some in agreement, most decidedly not. Ms. Nakamura gave no comment, looking as though she had just sipped lemon juice instead of tea. They resumed eating and all conversation gave way to the slurping of broth and the click of chopsticks against plastic bowls. Then came a firm knock at the door, followed by a soft *whish* as it opened to admit someone. The visitor smoothly announced his arrival.

"Please excuse me. I decided to let myself in."

Jordan nearly dropped her bowl at the sound of the voice, splashing soup on her fingers as she spun to face the door. Inspector Toshihiko Sakurai stepped inside and bowed.

"I'm sorry for disturbing your meal." He took in the room as he spoke. "Unfortunately, in light of Ryusuke Suzuki's death, I must resume my investigation from last year. Kikuchi-*kouchou*, I trust you received my message."

"Yes, of course, Inspector."

Principal Kikuchi stood up to greet him, and the teachers resumed eating their lunches only after the curiosity of the inspector's arrival had died down. As the inspector and principal exchanged pleasantries,

Toshihiko didn't look at Jordan once. She realized this with irritation, watching him like a hawk as she finished her plate.

Even when she loudly dropped her tray and utensils in a nearby washtub, he didn't so much as blink. For a few minutes, Jordan hovered at the opposite end of the room and waited as the other teachers filed out.

Since her conversation with Toshihiko at the izakaya, and his decree that they could no longer be together romantically, Jordan had heard nothing from the inspector. She had likewise refrained from contacting him, despite the occasional urge fueled alternatively by anger or regret.

She wasn't proud of how she left things with Toshihiko. Storming out like a petulant child didn't leave the best impression, and Jordan's gut churned at the thought that that would be the ultimate moment of their relationship. She had never plainly expressed the fondness she had felt for him, even at the best of times. But she hoped she would have the grace to do so now, even if it were in goodbye.

As the inspector began to remove files from his briefcase and set up a makeshift workstation, Jordan finally strode over.

"Toshihiko."

"Good afternoon, Ms. Howard," he said, giving her a placid, level look, free from any whiff of emotion. The address caught Jordan off guard and she came up short of words. The ensuing silence felt brittle and Toshihiko's eyes silently entreated her to leave.

"Do you have a moment?" Jordan finally managed.

"I'll be conducting interviews with all the teachers, as before. Perhaps later today." He looked away, piling files onto a squared-away stack.

"Very well, Inspector." Jordan turned on her heel and closed the door hard enough for the glass to shudder in its frame.

"Ms. Howard."

Jordan didn't look up from her papers when the inspector called to her. She tucked a rebellious lock of hair behind her ear and took a leisurely sip of tea.

"Ms. Howard?" Louder this time.

With a sigh, Jordan stood up from her desk and made her way toward the break room, where Toshihiko waited at the entrance. He flipped through his notebook as though her presence were of no consequence as he motioned her toward a seat and closed the door.

For a moment, neither one spoke. The whispering of the inspector's notebook pages was the only sound. Finally, Toshihiko looked up.

"Jordan, was there something you wanted to say before we proceed?"

"Oh, so we're back to 'Jordan' now?" She made an effort not to cross her arms.

"Yes, well..." He didn't finish the thought.

All the apologies and proclamations Jordan had been mentally rehearsing dropped away. She opened and shut her mouth twice before words finally surfaced.

"I understand why you said we can't see each other anymore, and I agree." She spoke softly. "I won't try to change your mind."

"Thank you, Jordan," Toshihiko said with visible gratitude. He gave a fleeting smile that held some of their old familiarity and a calm quiet followed.

When Toshihiko at last broke the silence, the cool veneer had returned to his voice.

"I'll be recording our conversation and taking notes," he said, and Jordan nodded to show she understood. She felt marginally grateful that his professional demeanor had returned—at least it was predictable. Her simmering emotions settled further as she watched Toshihiko methodically switch on the digital recorder, organize his notes, and uncap a pen. "As you already know, the investigation has reopened. In light of compelling new information."

"What new information?" Jordan felt a thrill in her chest. Toshihiko hesitated for just a moment.

"This is now a homicide investigation," he said and continued over Jordan's open-mouthed fumble for words. "Emi and Ryusuke both died of cyanide poisoning, not carbon monoxide asphyxiation as originally thought. I believe Yuki and Junichi did as well. However, their bodies were not autopsied before cremation, so I do not have the forensic evidence."

"I don't understand." Jordan finally managed to speak past the choking feeling that grabbed her throat. "Cyanide?"

"Yes. Extremely fatal even in small quantities. With the amount the victims ingested, they likely suffered cardiovascular collapse within minutes."

"Why weren't Yuki and Junichi autopsied?" She felt a twinge as she asked.

"Actually, it's quite common for no autopsies to be performed. Cause of death appeared clear in Yuki's case. His body was found in a closed room, windows sealed shut with tape, door partially blocked, kerosene heater on: apparent suicide. Also, a small town like Ogawa doesn't have the resources to perform thorough testing. Emi's parents, however, are quite wealthy and personally know the Superintendent Supervisor General of the Yamagata Prefectural Police. They demanded an autopsy for their daughter, insisting it wasn't suicide."

"And they were right."

"As it turns out, yes," the inspector said with increasing animation, caught up in the details of the case. "By the time I made the connection between Emi and Junichi, his body had already been cremated. But the circumstances of Ryusuke's death were nearly identical to theirs. The results of the autopsy produced striking similarities to Emi's."

"So you were definitely able to rule out suicide." Jordan suspected Toshihiko had already explored every facet of the case, and she wasn't hoping to find holes, but she felt compelled to press for more details. If only to reassure herself with his answers.

"Of course someone could take their own life with cyanide," Toshi-hiko said and nodded thoughtfully. "In fact, that's why my superiors lowered the priority of the case. They concluded from the available evidence that it was a suicide. Except when you consider other details."

"Like, if they purposefully killed themselves with cyanide, why would they go to the trouble of setting up a kerosene heater and making it look like they had asphyxiated? Why cover it up?"

"Exactly right," Toshihiko said empathically. "Also, cyanide is not widely available—especially not to teenagers—due to its extreme toxicity. It's unlikely that a few high school students from a small town would have the resources to acquire it. And, perhaps more compelling, there was no vehicle for the poison found near the bodies."

"Vehicle? I don't quite understand..." Jordan leaned forward, intent.

"If the victim injected the poison, for instance, we could reasonably expect to find a syringe at the scene, not to mention puncture marks on the body. Such a large dose of cyanide is so fast-acting that they wouldn't have had time to clean up. Plus, it would have been...challenging for the victims to take the poison elsewhere before entering their bedrooms—where we found the bodies. The bedroom doors were securely shut and partially blocked by blankets, and their kerosene heaters were lit. The effects of the cyanide would have been too debilitating for them to prepare their rooms. Impossible, really."

"So *how* were they poisoned?"

"That's exactly the detail that leads me to believe murder has been committed." His voice grew low and he paused. If Jordan didn't know him better, she would have thought he was being dramatic, like a teller of a ghost story. "The autopsies revealed that both Emi and Ryusuke drank the same tea shortly before death. A red hibiscus tea."

"So the tea was poisoned. But there were no teacups near their bodies?"

"No. Also, neither family had such a tea in their household."

"Meaning there must have been another person—the murderer—to remove his traces, secure the rooms, and light the kerosene heaters." Jordan ticked off the points on her fingers.

"Precisely." Toshihiko seemed to be on the verge of smiling, impressed.

"If Emi and Ryusuke—and the other boys—sat down to tea with their killer, they must have known him."

"Premeditated homicides are seldom carried out upon strangers. It's not unheard-of, of course, but it's not incredibly common, either," Toshihiko said and thumbed a file, reverting to a calm and professional tone. "Which is why I'm back in Ogawa."

"Is that the only reason?" Jordan said smoothly, unable to help herself. The inspector shot a glance over his glasses but said nothing. "I don't get it, Inspector. When this was a case of a mysterious suicide club, it was like pulling teeth to get one word out of you about the investigation."

"Yes, well..." He squinted and then frowned, which for him amounted to being flustered. Instead of finishing his thought, he tapped a paper against the table rhythmically. Jordan flattered herself to think that perhaps he had accidentally let his guard down in her company. Finally, the inspector continued. "Even back then, I suspected there was more than met the eye. But I couldn't let my speculations influence your, or anyone else's, testimony. Now that my office is officially pursuing a homicide case, some details must come out."

"And you trust me."

"Ms. Howard." Toshihiko's words grew an edge that cleaved between him and Jordan. "You will not be in my confidence and we will not see each other outside of a professional capacity while this investigation is ongoing, not even as friends. After all, no one can be outside the realm of suspects."

"Oh, really?" She snorted. "I wasn't even *in* Japan when Yuki died. Or did you forget that little detail?"

"Be that as it may—"

"You *do* trust me, though. If you thought I was at all involved, you never would have told me about the poison, or the tea." Jordan's voice quickened. "I could go back to my apartment right now, flush my stash

of hibiscus tea and cyanide, and get the first flight back to America. You
didn't tell the principal any of this, did you? Or Ms. Nakamura?"

"Owning tea is hardly conclusive evidence. But you're right. I
shouldn't have..." He dropped his head and took in the blank notebook
page before him. "At any rate, I do have some questions to ask."

"Where was I on the night of the fifth?"

"Something like that." He pushed the digital recorder closer to her
in one precise motion, like moving a chess piece across a board. "You
seemed to spend a great deal of time with the victim Ryusuke Suzuki,
more so than your other students. How would you describe your relationship?"

Jordan's first encounter with Ryusuke swam up to the surface of
her memory—his large hand swallowing hers, his lopsided smile—as she
answered the inspector's questions. The interview didn't last long,
despite her tendency to wander into anecdote before he steered her
focus back to the question at hand. True, she had known Ryusuke
better than she had her other students, but she knew nothing of his
home life, his interests outside of baseball, or even what his favorite
band or food was. What she did know was that any portrait of Ryusuke
would be half-developed without Kenji.

"You should really speak with his best friend, Kenji Ito. They were
inseparable," Jordan said as she stood to leave. "He lives in Tsuruoka,
with his parents."

"Thank you, Ms. Howard. I will." He smiled politely but made no
note, likely well aware of Kenji, if he hadn't spoken to him already.

"I'll let you know if I have any more information."

"Please do," he said hesitantly, and his eyes narrowed, as though to
show his disapproval at the hint that she would involve herself in the
investigation. Jordan let the look slide off her as she opened the door.

"Goodbye, Inspector."

NINETEEN

WHAT AM I DOING? JORDAN ASKED HERSELF FOR THE THIRD TIME as she picked up the teacup that had just been placed before her. She brought the cup to her mouth but paused as the tea's delicate fragrance touched her nose and lips. Jordan hastily set the teacup back down without taking a sip, and a few limpid drops splashed onto the worn table.

She looked away, embarrassed, and let her eyes roam across the unfamiliar living room before coming to rest on the woman sitting across from her.

"I have to admit that I've never met an American before. Much less an American reporter," the woman said modestly. "Thank you for taking an interest in my son's story."

"Well, I'm more of a blogger than a reporter, really. I do appreciate you taking the time to speak with me, Mrs. Sato." Jordan felt the words grow bitter in her mouth, and she grimaced at her own deception as she looked into the earnest face of Junichi's mother. It had been months since Jordan first saw the woman's image in the online news article, but her face was still lined with grief and shadowed by the muted sunlight that soaked through the drapes.

Jordan hadn't gone to Sagae with the intention of tracking down Junichi's mother. In fact, it was not in her mind at all as she entered the gym near Sagae's train station for her workout, Ogawa not having one of its own. But with each thud of her sneakers against the whirring treadmill, thoughts of her students had pulsed through her. Murder, poison, death—the words surged up between each heartbeat. With her hair still wet from the showers, she found herself thumbing through a local directory at the gym's front desk.

Even then, she was hesitant to go, but Junichi's family house was just a block from the station. Also, she knew she'd be unable to ask questions of Emi's and Ryusuke's parents in the same way, being known to just about everyone in Ogawa.

Junichi's mother had been surprised by the unexpected visit but had welcomed Jordan and was pleased to hear of her interest.

The woman now stared at Jordan expectantly but said nothing. Her daughter, Junichi's younger sister, sat in the corner at a small desk. At first, the sister appeared to be poring over her notebooks, but her pencil was still, and her head was turned just enough for the cup of her ear to collect their conversation. Jordan rapped her pen against her own notebook and continued.

"Could you tell me a little more about Junichi, please?"

The mother began to speak warmly of her son, saying he was gregarious and studious, and Jordan jotted down notes. She doubted her impressions would be very useful later but had to keep up the appearance of being an amateur journalist. Soon the older woman came to the subject of her son's death and her strong belief that bullies were to blame for pushing him to suicide, much as she had said in the previous interview Jordan had found online.

So Toshihiko must not have informed the mother of the homicide investigation yet. Even though there was no autopsy evidence in Junichi's case, the inspector was sure to follow up with Mrs. Sato. Regardless, Jordan had no intention of being the one to tell her that her son had likely been murdered, or that his death was tied to those in Ogawa. She thought a moment before formulating her next question.

"Were there any other student suicides in Sagae recently? Any of Junichi's classmates?" Jordan asked, wondering whether the murderer's sinister touch had reached even farther outside of Ogawa than she already suspected.

"Recently? No. There were three high-schoolers who took their lives four, maybe five years ago. Junichi didn't know them. He wasn't part of a suicide club if that's what you're thinking." She made an exasperated noise and grimaced. Her daughter sighed from the corner.

"I wasn't suggesting as much. I apologize," Jordan said quickly. "Do you happen to remember any of these students' names?"

"Haruka Hidaka I remember. I used to work with his mother." Jordan added the boy's name to her notes.

"Did Junichi have any friends in Ogawa, or does your family?"

Mrs. Sato nodded. "We used to live in Ogawa, and Junichi kept in touch with some of his old classmates. Why?"

"Some students at Ogawa High School died within a few weeks of your son," Jordan said, and Mrs. Sato's eyes narrowed. "My article will be about suicides in the region, so I'm trying to create a complete picture of Yamagata Prefecture's teenagers—there might be a social connection."

"I see." She nodded, the answer seeming to satisfy her.

"Did Junichi make any new friends or acquaintances recently? Maybe you saw him with someone unfamiliar in the days before his death?"

"I don't believe so." As Mrs. Sato answered, her daughter's gaze twitched toward them, her head turning fast enough to flick her hair over one shoulder. She didn't look at them directly, but it was impossible for Jordan to miss the girl's sudden interest.

Jordan continued chatting with the mother, asking questions she felt were appropriate of a reporter but doubting their usefulness for her real purpose. The longer she spoke with Mrs. Sato, the more she wished she could talk to Junichi's sister. The girl kept silent, but several more furtive looks betrayed her interest.

After almost an hour, Jordan excused herself to leave. As she stood from the couch, she placed her pen on the coffee table and made for the door.

"Will you let me know when your article is published, Ms. Johnson?"

"Yes, of course." Jordan lowered her head into a bow. She was grateful for the chance to hide her face, feeling both guilty and embarrassed about using a false name and pretense. "Thank you for your time, Mrs. Sato."

Soon she was descending the apartment building's stairs, going slowly to avoid tripping in the dim light. A single, rattling light bulb did little to illuminate the stairwell, despite its noisy efforts.

As soon as she exited the stairwell, she heard light footsteps padding toward her. Jordan turned to see Junichi's sister, short and bird-thin, scramble around the corner. The girl stopped abruptly to avoid running headlong into Jordan.

"Oh, Ms. Johnson! I'm glad I caught you—you forgot your pen." The girl thrust the pen into Jordan's hand then retracted her own instantly, as though it had been bitten. She was clearly anxious, wringing the hem of her shirt in tight fists.

Jordan was so pleased that her "forgotten" pen had worked as hoped that she had to rein in a satisfied smile.

"Thank you—" Jordan started but was cut off.

"That question you asked, about whether Junichi had any new friends..."

"Yes?" Jordan felt her heartbeat quicken.

"Well, on the night that Junichi...died, I left the house to study at my friend's place. Like I always do on Wednesdays." She paused and looked around the stairwell nervously. Already soft-spoken, she lowered her voice even more. "As I was coming down the stairs, I bumped into someone. It was my fault—I was using my cell phone and didn't see him, so I apologized. He passed me and didn't say anything at all. It was kind of creepy, so I just left. Anyway, I got downstairs and was unlocking my bike when I saw the same person at our door, but then Junichi let him in right away. I didn't think much of it until now."

"And you didn't recognize this person at all? Was he your brother's age? Older?"

"A-actually, I don't know. I never saw the person's face. I guess I don't even know whether it was a man." The girl's nervousness ratcheted up at Jordan's questions, her eyes growing wide. "I-I thought maybe it was because he was kind of tall. It was raining, so he was wearing a big coat with a hood. Hard to tell what he looked like…"

"Or she?"

"I guess so." She bit her lip and concentrated. "It might have been one of Junichi's friends. They never talk to me anyway. Or an NHK fee collector."

"Do you remember anything else?" Jordan tried not to sound too eager.

"There was a car I didn't recognize in the parking lot. A little yellow car."

Jordan nodded. Many people in Ogawa—and probably Sagae—didn't have cars, so it was easy to remember who drove what. Jordan knew instantly which of her own neighbors were home by identifying their cars in the small dirt lot in front of the apartment building. Still, the vehicle Junichi's sister saw could have belonged to a guest of their neighbors. All the same, Jordan felt a sort of nervous excitement and swept the crumbs of information into her memory as the girl spoke once again. "I'm sorry, Ms. Johnson, but I have to go back now."

"Thank you for speaking with me. And for returning my pen."

The girl nodded shyly and scurried up a few steps before pausing.

"Junichi didn't kill himself," she blurted out and left, leaping up the stairs two at a time.

Jordan thought of Nanami and Shun and their same declarations in the face of death. Beyond their shared words, they had all borne expressions of deep certainty woven with defiance, as though daring Jordan to think otherwise or to deny them. She wished to tell Junichi's sister she was right. Instead, she stepped out to the gravel path leading away from the apartments, cinched up her coat, and headed for the train station.

It was nearing eight o'clock and the station was swelling with bodies, mostly salarymen leaving to begin the commute home or join their coworkers at an izakaya. Even these ostensibly social after-work gatherings were more like mandated work meetings: a time for the low-ranked employees to pour beers for their superiors and to take ribbings fueled by alcohol and the knowledge that no one would speak of it again.

The Japanese workday was like an octopus, stretching its tentacles far into the night and beyond the reach of the actual office. For all the people present in the station's waiting area, there was little noise, most people tapping away at their cell phones or munching on *onigiri* from the corner store.

Jordan passed a vocal group of men in jacketed suits to wait at the platform. Unsurprisingly, they assumed she couldn't understand Japanese—with her corn-silk hair and green eyes—and one made a lurid suggestion of what he and "Blondie" could do together. They laughed. Jordan ignored them and dropped some yen into a vending machine near the tracks.

With a thunk, the machine ejected a warm canned latte, which Jordan popped open gratefully. The backlight of the vending machine shone harshly and illuminated its wares like diamonds on a light table, from milk teas to lemon vitality drinks. The glare plunged everything else into pitch darkness. Except for the muzzy eyes of the incoming train, Jordan could see little else. She walked unhurriedly to where the front few cars were slowing to a stop and waited for the passengers to depart. As she raised the latte to her lips for another sip, she caught sight of a man making for the train's exit and spluttered on her drink.

Inspector Toshihiko Sakurai adjusted his coat and began to disembark alongside the other passengers.

Jordan quickly pulled up her hood and looked away, keeping her eyes anchored to her feet. Of course, she had every right to be in Sagae, and if asked, she could say she was there to go to the gym, which was true. Still, she felt that Toshihiko would wheedle out her true purpose if she did so much as blink at the wrong moment. She kept still until she felt others brushing past her to board the train.

Head still tucked down, she hurried on board and fell into a window seat. As the train pulled away, she watched the inspector walk surely toward the Satos' apartment.

TWENTY

OGAWA BORE ALL THE BITTER TEMPERATURES OF WINTER without the thick layers of snow that had clung to the trees of Mount Zao. Still, Jordan felt frozen to the bone and didn't bother to hide her chattering teeth. Bobbing from foot to foot hadn't helped, so she merely stood there, shivering, arms and scarf tight around her like mummy wrappings, while she waited in line.

It was the day of Ogawa's own modest Oden and Dongara-jiru Festival, one of many community get-togethers organized by the town's Cultural Committee. As far as Jordan could tell, it seemed less of a long-held tradition and more of a stopgap celebration falling squarely between the Sweet Potato Imoni Festival and the Hanami Festival. Regardless, Jordan was not one to miss a sampling of local cuisine or any opportunity to meet with students and teachers outside of school. But she began to have second thoughts when the line crawled forward, bringing her only marginally closer to the covered stalls serving steaming pots of stew.

Like many community-sponsored events, the Oden Festival was held in front of the town hall, with its stalls spread out like playing cards. There was also a temporary stage for dancers and small bands to perform upon, but it stood empty for the moment.

The town hall was a few stories high—the largest building Jordan had seen in Ogawa, outside of the factories. On the opposite end of the town hall's parking lot were the community center and a town museum, all of which perched on the crown of a large hill.

Looking behind her, Jordan could make out the line where the Mogami River met the land a few miles away, grey and hazy with atmosphere. After a few more minutes of letting her gaze wander while waiting in line, Jordan gratefully received a plastic bowl sloshing with *oden*.

She took a seat at a cluster of benches and lunged at the boiled egg with her chopsticks. It bobbed away languidly in the brown *dashi* broth and rocked against floating islands of *konnyaku*, potato, radish, carrots, and tofu. For the moment, she was content to sip the steaming broth and feel its warmth suffuse her throat and stomach. As she sipped the stew, she saw someone approach over the white horizon of the bowl against her lips.

"Jordan-*sensei!*" It was Akira, also bundled up but not seeming to mind the cold. Jordan hadn't seen him much since classes had resumed after the winter break and she smiled warmly as she greeted him. Without further pleasantries, he took a seat next to her and leaned in close. "Do you think it's true that Yuki was...murdered?" Though his question was direct, Jordan wasn't surprised by the lack of preamble—everyone was talking about the investigation, if more discreetly.

"I don't know, Akira. Inspector Sakurai doesn't have the same information for Yuki as he does for Ryusuke and Emi, but it seems to follow. You said yourself that you didn't think he committed suicide," Jordan said. "Don't you feel the same way anymore?"

"I don't know what to think," Akira said, thrusting his hands into his pockets and staring at his feet stretched straight in front of him. "No, I guess I don't think he killed himself. But he was really down right before he died. He was pretty ashamed about all that stolen lab stuff. I guess that was before you got here..."

"Ms. Tatsuya told me," Jordan said and took another swallow of broth.

"Oh yeah? I still feel bad about ratting out Yuki, especially after everything that happened. But what else could I do when Vice Principal Nakamura asked me about it?"

"Ms. Nakamura came to you? I heard you confessed to the teachers yourself."

"No, she called me into her office one day and accused me of stealing chemicals from the storeroom cabinet. I knew it was Yuki—who else could it be? I guess I shouldn't have told." He shook his head. "She's a scary lady."

Jordan was more intrigued than she let on. Since asking Ms. Nakamura about the incident was out of the question, she would have to unearth more information on her own. Jordan felt a surge of curiosity and decided to return to the storeroom the following school week. The dusty collection of curiosities housed there seemed old and forgotten, but apparently not to Ms. Nakamura. The thought of revealing whatever the vice principal had hidden made Jordan's spine thrum with anticipation.

While she had Akira on the topic, Jordan asked if Yuki had made any new friends or hung out with any odd acquaintances shortly before his death. Akira answered "no" and changed the topic to the latest episode of his favorite anime before Jordan could ask more. Eventually, the boy was called away by his mother, and Jordan sat contemplating just how she could get into the storage room.

TWENTY-ONE

Ms. Tatsuya was not at her desk, nor would she be for the next thirty minutes. Jordan knew the math instructor had a key to the storage room, which could be sitting unattended in her desk drawer just inches away. Or lying in the recesses of Ms. Tatsuya's pockets, Jordan thought grimly.

Of the very few people present in the teachers' room at that moment, Ms. Nakamura was among them. Jordan felt a chill trickle down her back at the thought of being caught swiping keys from Ms. Tatsuya's desk—especially by Ms. Nakamura. Fortunately, as usual, the puckered woman didn't spare Jordan a glance, as though even the sight of her was somehow distasteful.

With a deep, bolstering breath, Jordan reached to the nearest drawer and pulled. She almost laughed with relief at her luck. Atop a jumbled nest of pens and pencils sat Ms. Tatsuya's key ring, sprouting more metal prongs than a jailer's.

There was no choice but to take the whole thing and return it as soon as possible. Eyes straight ahead, Jordan grabbed the keys—muffling them with her palm—and maneuvered them into her pants pocket. A quick glance showed no one was looking her way, so she stood up to head for the door. Jordan was no more than a foot away when a man's voice called out to her.

"Ms. Howard?"

She flinched and swallowed hard at the brassy jangle that whispered from her pocket. Jordan turned to see Inspector Sakurai and drew her lips into a polite smile.

"Yes, Inspector?"

"May I speak with you for a moment?"

"Well, actually, I was just about to—" She looked pointedly at the door.

"Please. It's urgent." There was an unfamiliar tightness in his voice, and he did seem perturbed—perhaps even worried. Jordan hesitated a moment longer before following him into the break lounge. He closed the door quickly behind her and launched in. "I wasn't aware you moonlighted as an online journalist, *Ms. Johnson.*"

Jordan's breath caught. She thought he might have seen her take the keys, but this was far worse. "I don't know what you're talking about."

"Please do me the favor of at least pretending you respect my intelligence, even when you so clearly do not respect my position."

"It's not against the law in Japan to ask people questions, is it? Besides, I didn't say a word about the homicide investigation," Jordan said stubbornly. "If you're looking for an apology, I'm afraid you won't get one."

"I don't think you fully understand the situation, Jordan. There's a murderer in Ogawa, likely in this very school." His voice softened, and he looked pained. "Of course I don't want interference in my investigation, but more than that, I can't simply watch while you put yourself in danger." The inspector took a step closer and his hand moved as though to reach out to her, but he let it fall back.

"You really think I'm at risk?" Jordan felt a sudden thrill of worry and embarrassment at not seriously considering such a possibility earlier. Despite the pulse of initial surprise, she realized she was not terribly concerned for her own safety. The idea that someone would target her seemed almost too unbelievable to consider.

"I still know very little about the perpetrator. All the more reason to be cautious." The inspector said nothing further and looked at her expectantly. Jordan suspected he wanted some sort of assurance that she would cease her personal investigation, but she was about as willing to wrench those words from her throat as she was to apologize. The silence continued and she felt the weight of the keys anchored in her pocket.

"Well, if there's nothing else—"

"Why do you insist on involving yourself?" he asked, not seeming to hear her. "I know that your brother's death left you with questions, but solving these murders won't help you."

"I get it—you think you know what's best for me. You think you know what I want better than I do. At least I can do *something* this time." She hardened her voice, and neither of them spoke for a while.

"Will you at least tell me if you uncovered anything about Junichi?" Toshihiko finally said with a sigh.

Jordan paused before answering, surprised by his request. She wondered if he was asking just to placate her. Then again, he was also focused enough on the investigation to welcome any bit of information, even if it came from her and her unendorsed sleuthing.

"Did his sister tell you about the person she saw the night Junichi died? And the car?"

"A tall person, gender uncertain but possibly male, wearing a hooded raincoat. A small yellow car of unknown make and model."

"That's all I got."

"You're not a bad inspector," he said and gave a hint of a smile.

"*And* I got there before you." Jordan smirked. "Listen, Inspector, I'm sorry but I really do have to go now." She slid past him to open the door.

"At least...be careful." He tried to sound stern but his hesitation held an air of uncertainty.

"I will," Jordan said over her shoulder, already scurrying away. She cursed Toshihiko silently for interrupting her plans and hurried toward the lower floor as noiselessly as possible. A few students raised their heads as she passed their classrooms, but she was soon in the empty stairwell and the secluded hallway beyond.

The entryway to the storeroom was dark, as usual, and she was startled by the looming form of the haphazardly stacked chairs, feeling even more on edge. Jordan reminded herself that time was short and began to systematically try each key in the lock hanging from the door. Finally, one sank into the metal and the tumblers fell into place. Jordan gave one furtive look behind her before opening the door and pushing inside.

The single light sputtered to life and threw a jaundiced glow on the room's specimen jars and taxidermy inhabitants. Faced with vials, bottles, beakers, test tubes, and every manner of unidentifiable substance, Jordan was suddenly struck with the realization that she had no idea what she was looking for.

All she knew was that Yuki had stolen something from that very room and died a mere week later. She knew these two instances could be unrelated, and any sort of connection wasn't immediately obvious. Still, she thought it odd that Ms. Nakamura had confronted Akira about the theft—the vice principal had somehow known something was missing.

"What was she down here for?" Jordan said to the row of glass beakers in front of her nose. Her words deadened as they hit the thick, musty air. Except for the plastic jugs near the door that Ms. Tatsuya had rummaged through to look for vinegar, all the other items seemed undisturbed. A thick layer of dust covered every surface, making the room look like a freeze-frame from a grainy black-and-white film. Jordan's and the math teacher's footprints from a couple of months before were still visible, and there were faint signs of foot traffic all around—she couldn't discern the scuff marks' age beyond the fact that they were not fresh.

Jordan laughed a bit, feeling like an archaeologist trying to parse clues from the ruins of an ancient civilization. What eventually caught her eye—and she realized she had seen it before—was a hefty glass-doored cabinet on the shelf, secured with a new padlock. Ms. Tatsuya had said that the lock on the outside door had been added after Yuki's theft. It seemed likely that the second lock had been installed at the same time, for the cabinet itself was very old and its hinges rusty.

Jordan angled the lock toward her. It was shiny and untarnished. Only a few scratches radiated from the keyhole, suggesting it hadn't been opened very often. Two minutes and a dozen keys later, Jordan had the cabinet open as well.

The inside shelves were lined with glass bottles hugged by yellowing labels, housing both recognizable and entirely foreign chemicals—from just a few drops to full. Huddled against these bottles were also a scale, crucibles, and a mortar and pestle that bore brown stains. Jordan yanked her cell phone from her pocket and snapped several photos of the bottles, labels, and the cabinet's miscellaneous contents.

Once finished, Jordan felt a pull of disappointment. Somehow, she had felt sure that investigation of the storeroom would reveal something to her. But as she stood staring at the rows of bottled chemicals, their labels and formulas failed to coalesce into some secret message. Of course, she wouldn't be so lucky as to find a half-empty vial of cyanide smattered with fresh fingerprints. She sighed and tapped a note to herself on her cell phone: *Nakamura went to cabinet, noticed something missing, what was she after?*

"She'd have to come down here a lot to notice something amiss," Jordan mused aloud. She wondered if she was inventing a connection to the murders simply because of her dislike for the vice principal. She grimaced, not pleased to dwell on the thought.

With time running short, Jordan rearranged the bottles as close to their original positions as possible, locked the cabinet, and exited the room, securing the door behind her.

As she turned and made for the end of the hallway, a sharp bang resounded behind her. She yelped with surprise as she spun to face the noise. One of the chairs had fallen from the precarious heap, still rocking on its side from the force of the impact. Jordan heard nothing else beyond the creak of the settling chair and her heartbeat in her ears, but worry that someone else was there clutched at her.

"H-hello?"

She swallowed. There was no answer, no movement. Just as her anxious muscles began to loosen, the bell signaling the end of class rang, and every nerve spooled tighter than before. Without a backwards glance, she sprinted back to the teachers' room.

She wondered whether she should slow down—whether her haste would draw unwanted attention—but decided she *must* replace the keys, above all else. Despite the distance she had to cover, Jordan arrived well before most of her colleagues, and she sagged with relief to see Ms. Tatsuya's vacant chair. Not even Ms. Nakamura was there to chide her for running, or for failing to excuse herself as she rushed to her desk.

Jordan slid open Ms. Tatsuya's drawer, shot one more glance over her shoulder, and placed the keys inside. Just as she was about to push the drawer shut, someone called her name.

"Jordan-*sensei*, can I help you?"

"Tatsuya-*sensei*!" Jordan squeaked and grabbed a pen from the pile under the keys. She whipped around and schooled her expression to be as calm as possible. "I was just looking for a pen." She wiggled the pen in her fingers, as though that proved anything.

"Oh." Ms. Tatsuya didn't look angry or offended by the intrusion, but her expression left Jordan uneasy. Her eyebrows were drawn down, her lips pressed closed over her teeth, like she was thinking hard on something.

"I-I'm sorry. I should have just waited for you to come back," Jordan said, feeling genuinely sorry that she had bungled everything. But her body had been between the desk and Ms. Tatsuya as she had replaced the keys. There was no way Ms. Tatsuya had seen her with the keys —was there?

"Oh no! It's quite all right, Jordan-*sensei*. No need to be sorry." Ms. Tatsuya's lips pulled back to offer a timid smile. "I was just a bit confused for a moment..."

"Thank you, Tatsuya-*sensei*," Jordan said and bowed before taking her own seat. Not wanting Ms. Tatsuya to dwell on her rummaging through the dusk, Jordan diverted her attention. "What do you have planned for Home Ec. club today?"

"Oh! We're just about to start sewing. Have you used a sewing machine before? No? Well..."

Ms. Tatsuya was her usual self as she spoke—at one moment animated and in the next abashed by her own excitement, swinging between these poles every few sentences. Sometimes her words would wander off with her thoughts. Nothing was amiss, Jordan convinced herself, and let Ms. Tatsuya's stream of chatter sweep away her worry.

TWENTY-TWO

THE WINTER SUN WAS SETTING EARLY. JORDAN NOTED THE lowering light with a melancholy that sometimes came upon her when she got wrapped up in thinking about the case. She had spent all day fixating on the storeroom and what she had found there, or *didn't* find.

This stoked a familiar sense of uselessness, one that led her thoughts back to Aiden yet again. She sighed as she shut the door to her apartment, toeing off her shoes in the sunken entryway.

With the reflexive, thoughtless movements born of routine, Jordan placed her shoes in the in-wall rack and shrugged off her jacket. As she tossed the jacket over the back of a chair, something fluttered out of its side pocket and landed on the floor softly.

Curious, Jordan bent to inspect the item. It was an envelope—one she had not placed in the jacket herself. The envelope was unaddressed and sealed. Jordan was surprised that she hadn't noticed it upon putting on the jacket and was now eager to open it, running her finger under the flap.

The envelope gaped open, and a dusting of red specks drifted out onto her hand and the floor. She plucked one from her cuff: a flower petal, dried and strawlike. With a tilt of the envelope, she saw hundreds more petals piled inside and a folded slip of paper poking out from the mound. Jordan felt a shiver of inexplicable nervousness as she removed and unfolded the paper. In its center was a single typed word: *STOP*.

A cold numbness embraced her as the message's meaning found purchase. The dried petals were hibiscus petals. Hibiscus tea.

The envelope slipped from her fingers, falling to the ground in a spray of red.

"Thank you, officers. I'll see you at the station shortly." Toshihiko spoke to the uniformed men who bowed as they exited Jordan's apartment, sealed evidence bags in hand. Toshihiko closed the door behind the policemen and gave Jordan an apologetic look.

"I called *you* to be discreet, not to have the whole police force tromping through my apartment," Jordan said and crossed her arms. She wasn't angry, not with Toshihiko at least. Just overwhelmed, and shaken. She attempted a smile to show she was joking, but she couldn't hold it.

"And I called the forensics team to be thorough. To do this right." Now that the two of them were alone in the apartment, Toshihiko's voice warmed. He was still firmly professional, but for once, Jordan found his unflappability comforting. He had dealt with this type of thing before. He would know what to do.

"Do you think they'll find anything? Any evidence that can point to the murderer?"

"As I said before, we first have to see whether any trace evidence can be recovered—fingerprints, fibers, hair, cyanide." The last word gave him pause. "Then we can evaluate whether this is connected to the homicide investigation."

"How can you say that? It's obviously connected," Jordan said with a huff, gesturing toward where the envelope had fallen on the floor, though there was no remaining sign of the scattered tea.

"It could be a prank." Toshihiko adjusted his glasses, not sounding entirely convinced himself.

"A prank? You said you hadn't told anyone else about the poisoned tea, so who would know to threaten me with it?" As much as Jordan wished for a benign explanation for the envelope, it was unthinkable that someone uninvolved with the murders could be so cruel to her. She hurried on before she could dwell on the idea. "And that's exactly what this is: a threat."

Toshihiko gave a thoughtful nod. "Few people know of the tea—true—but it's possible that someone else working this case divulged information when they shouldn't have. It's not unheard-of," he said, his disapproval clear. Jordan wondered whether he included himself in that rebuke. Wondered just how much he regretted allowing her to peek into the investigation.

"I didn't tell anyone about the tea, if that's what you're suggesting," Jordan said, feeling agitated, defensive.

"I didn't think that you had."

"So you really believe this is all just a prank? Because if you're saying so just to make me feel better, it isn't working." Now she *was* angry with Toshihiko. Jordan could understand if he wished to ease her fears, but not if it meant misleading her. She hardened her voice. "Please be honest with me."

Toshihiko was silent for a long moment, deep in thought. When he at last spoke, his voice was low and careful.

"I believe the message should be taken very seriously." He nodded grimly and then fell quiet once more. It was obvious he was weighing what to say next, painstakingly so, and Jordan's nerves knotted tighter the longer he stayed silent. Finally, he met her eyes with reluctance. "Jordan, what did you do to provoke this?"

"I investigated the case, obviously," Jordan said sharply. She wasn't sure if she was more annoyed by the gall of the question or by how justified Toshihiko was in asking.

"You'll have to be more specific," he said with an airy dryness as he pulled a notepad and pen from his jacket pocket.

"You already know—I spoke with Junichi's family, and..." Jordan was about to tell Toshihiko about her excursion to the school's storeroom, but stopped short. When he had confronted her before about speaking with Mrs. Sato, he had been livid—or as close as he could be to such an emotion, at any rate. She shuddered to think how he would react to her latest snooping.

Toshihiko sensed Jordan's hesitation and his eyebrows rose.

"Anything else?"

"Promise you won't be too angry with me?"

"I don't tend to make promises. Or get angry," Toshihiko said with a sigh.

Jordan worried her lip as she considered what to say. As little as she wanted to be reprimanded by Toshihiko, again, she couldn't withhold information that might be helpful. She took a breath and steeled herself.

"I went into the school's old storeroom yesterday, to look for clues. Ms. Nakamura knew something had gone missing from that storeroom, you see, which was how she found out Yuki had been stealing. I thought she might be using, or hiding, something in there," Jordan said, hurriedly pushing past a flash of embarrassment. It all sounded rather absurd when said aloud, and Toshihiko looked more perplexed than irritated.

"Someone saw you do this?"

"Well, no. At least, not that I know of." Jordan felt even more mortified, having exposed herself for possibly no reason at all. But then she remembered the chair that had tumbled to the floor—how she had felt watched. "Actually! I did hear a noise and thought there was someone in the hallway outside the storeroom. But I didn't see anyone."

"And did you find anything of interest in the storeroom?" Toshihiko said. Jordan couldn't tell whether he was asking with serious intent or just shining a light on her failure. He continued with his notes, head down.

"No. Did you?" Jordan fired back.

"I really can't say one way or the other," Toshihiko said, not taking the bait. He was unbelievably calm.

Not only did Toshihiko's failure to reprove Jordan surprise her, it irked her. Usually, the closer she got to the investigation, the more agitated he became. If Toshihiko was completely unfazed by Jordan visiting the storeroom, it could only mean that he thought she was on a wild goose chase. Granted, nothing had stood out to her amid the dusty vials, but that didn't mean the trail was entirely cold. She tried again to persuade him.

"It all makes perfect sense if the murderer is someone at the school," Jordan said, ignoring Toshihiko's attempt to interject. "They saw me snooping around the storeroom. They got nervous, decided to scare me off. Everyone knows which locker is mine and can easily get to it without anyone batting an eye. In fact, if the murderer *isn't* connected with the school, this threat would've been a lot harder to pull off."

She ended with a decisive nod, rather impressed with her own argument. At the very least, she didn't sound quite so foolish anymore.

"Well, it's not a bad theory," Toshihiko said, closing the notebook and raising his eyes to meet hers.

"Must not be a good one either—looks like you're ready to move on."

"I *am* taking this seriously, Jordan, trust me." He looked over his glasses as he spoke, as he sometimes did when he wanted to convey his sincerity. As though he wanted no barrier between them—not even a thin circle of glass.

"I know you are," Jordan said quietly, and she did. If no other reason than because of his dedication to his job.

Toshihiko didn't reply, but neither did he make any move to leave, and a taut silence stretched through the room.

Without the distraction of conversation, thoughts of the envelope and its message swarmed into every crevice of Jordan's mind. The same numb disbelief that had swallowed her as she had read that single, sinister word crept upon her again, this time with an undercurrent of real fear. She quelled an urge to run up to the window and shutter it—each car's headlights like eyes staring at her through the dark.

Her discomfort must have shown because Toshihiko's brow creased and he took a tentative step toward her.

"Would you like me to stay?" he asked cautiously.

"No, thank you, I'll be all right..." In truth, Jordan longed not to be alone that night, but not if it meant imposing upon Toshihiko, of all people. Jordan realized with a stab of regret that this was the first time Toshihiko had set foot in her apartment. She had imagined such a moment going much differently, and under much better circumstances.

For the first time since Toshihiko had dissolved their relationship, Jordan was gripped with a need to embrace him, to feel his arms fold her against his chest. It was a sensation she had experienced seldom, but the memory of it was so sharp she could almost feel the warmth of his palms pressing against her.

She sighed, hugging her own arms across her chest, and angled a look at Toshihiko. "Don't you have to meet those officers at the station?"

"Yes, I suppose I shouldn't keep them waiting," Toshihiko said without conviction. He looked at her a moment longer, came to a decision, and deferred with a polite nod. Soon, he had donned his shoes and jacket, and Jordan held the door for him as he exited the apartment.

"Thanks for coming, Toshihiko," she said with a flit of a smile.

"Of course. Call me anytime if you feel unsafe or... Just call me, if you like."

"Sure," Jordan said and paused. "It's all going to be okay, right?"

She looked to Toshihiko expectantly, hoping for some measure of reassurance, but his unguarded expression darkened with a whisper of concern. His hesitation encased Jordan in icy worry.

"I don't know." Toshihiko's face was set with a grim, apologetic look. "But I will do everything I can to keep you safe."

Jordan let out a nervous laugh.

"You should've just said everything would be fine."

"I thought you wanted me to be honest," Toshihiko said with a wistful smile and turned to leave. "Goodnight, Jordan."

"Goodnight." Her tongue grew so thick in her throat she could barely draw breath past it.

She watched the inspector retreat down the landing with a tense feeling of foreboding, as though something was lurking just around the corner. Waiting until she was alone.

Jordan heaved the door shut and secured the deadbolt with a loud clack.

TWENTY-THREE

"FANCY SEEING YOU HERE," JORDAN SAID AND SAT DOWN IN THE seat facing Toshihiko, feeling the train thrum as it pulled away from the station. He looked up from his notebook with surprise, and unless Jordan was flattering herself, he seemed pleased to see her.

"Going to Yamagata City?" he said.

"Your skills of deduction never fail to impress, Inspector," she said around a teasing smirk.

"You look much better than..." Toshihiko cleared his throat. "You're doing well?"

No doubt he was going to say Jordan looked better than the last time he had seen her, which was when he had responded to her plea for help upon finding the envelope. He hadn't been to the school in the two weeks that had followed, but they had communicated by phone during that time.

"I'm fine, thanks," she said. It almost sounded convincing. At least she had slept through the entire night, for once. And she could look her colleagues in the eye without obvious suspicion or distrust. Most of the time. "I'd be even better if that damn envelope had turned up anything."

"Though no foreign hairs or fingerprints were discovered, the envelope and its contents may still prove useful when securing a conviction, as I've said."

"If you arrest someone for the murders, you can compare their envelopes and tea and whatever else with the stuff planted in my jacket and..."

"And see if they match, yes," Toshihiko said with a touch of exasperation. They had already been through the same conversation before, after all, but he seemed to regret his impatience and softened his expression. "It's good to see you, Jordan. But if you'll please excuse me, I need to finish this before we arrive in the city." He gestured to his notebook.

"Sure. I'll shut up." Jordan smiled wanly, then directed her attention out the window. Toshihiko may have wanted to change the subject, but Jordan could think of nothing else. Rather than deter Jordan, the threat had brought the murders into sharp focus before her.

It wasn't always fear that kept her up at night, but careful consideration of every morsel of information about the case. She turned over each thought, again and again, until she was sure she had scrutinized it from every angle. Still, shadows remained that only other people could shine light upon—Toshihiko, in some instances.

Jordan fidgeted in her seat. She wiped her hands on her pants, imagining she could still feel the sticky black residue that had coated her fingers after the local policeman had fingerprinted her—to identify any marks left on the envelope.

A few minutes passed. Surely Toshihiko had concluded whatever it was he had hoped to get done. She piped up.

"Why do you think Emi and the others were targeted?"

Toshihiko spared her a brief, schooled glance over his glasses, his pen stilling against his papers.

"You see, I don't think they were targeted at random," Jordan continued, undeterred. She wasn't about to let the opportunity to speak with Toshihiko face-to-face slip by, after all. "Yuki was caught stealing,

Emi was pregnant, and Junichi was the illegitimate father. They were being punished."

"And Ryusuke?" Toshihiko said, hesitant to take the bait.

"I haven't figured that one out yet. If only I could talk to Kenji," Jordan said hurriedly. "But Ryusuke must have done *something*. Ms. Nakamura really has it out for unruly students—"

"Ms. Nakamura—the vice principal?" Toshihiko closed his notebook with a defeated look.

"Yes. She discovered Yuki's theft and she's the school disciplinarian. She really broaches no misbehavior. She practically jumped at the opportunity to reprimand Kenji and that boy he was fighting with."

"Yet those two boys are fine."

"For the time being," Jordan said, and Toshihiko raised his eyebrows. "Well, a little scuffle isn't quite as bad as stealing school property, is it?"

"You really suspect Ms. Nakamura?" He sounded almost amused, and Jordan felt her face heat. She hadn't expected him to agree, but she had hoped. Toshihiko continued more sedately. "All right. Let's assume they were murdered as punishment for their misdeeds. Who besides Emi and her friend even knew she was pregnant?"

"Well—" Jordan stopped short and thought for a moment. "The murderer must have found out somehow."

"Have you read any Sherlock Holmes stories?" Toshihiko said, and Jordan shook her head. "It is a capital mistake to theorize before one has data. Insensibly, one begins to twist facts to suit theories, instead of theories to suit facts," he quoted.

"I don't intend to stop looking for facts," she said but felt a little embarrassed.

"I truly wish you would." He sighed, sounding more concerned than annoyed, and leveled a serious look at her. "Now, if you don't mind..."

So he wasn't in the mood to lob theories. Jordan raised her hands in silent surrender and once again turned toward the window, to demonstrate that she would leave Toshihiko alone.

Outside, the sun was bright and warm, creating a fissure between days of frigid, bitter cold. Jordan watched some crows pick at bugs in an empty rice field, which was spotted with strawy weeds gilt by the afternoon sun. The pleasant warmth soon made Jordan drowsy, quieting and slowing her rampant thoughts. She closed her eyes as she rested her forehead against the cool glass.

It wasn't until the rolling thrum of the train stopped that she dragged herself back to alertness and saw she was in Yamagata Station, the last stop on the line. Toshihiko glanced at her with a soft smile, already rising from his seat.

"I thought I'd have to wake you," he said gently.

"Sorry, I wasn't very good company." She hid a yawn behind her hand. "Though you probably prefer my snoring over my questions."

"Not at all," he said with questionable conviction. "And I'm the one who should be apologizing—first, that paperwork, and now, I have to be at the police station." Toshihiko looked at his watch to confirm and took a step toward the door. "I'll be in touch. Until then, goodbye."

"Goodbye." She gave a small wave, which he returned before striding off the train. Jordan was sorry to see him go but also relieved that he had not asked how she planned to spend the day in the city. She would have felt guilty evading the question, since she certainly wasn't going to tell him the truth.

The station was busier than Jordan had seen it for a while, but she seldom came on weekdays. The high school had been closed due to an in-service day, and she had decided to take advantage of the opportunity to go to Yamagata City.

Many salarymen, housewives, and grandmothers flowed through the platforms and up to the station's main floor, moving in orderly channels. Jordan bobbed to the surface just outside one of the station's two main entrances and continued on foot, headed east toward one of the city's larger thoroughfares.

She crossed the street in front of a roiling mass of yellow taxis buzzing outside the station like a swarm of hornets. They systematically advanced in their separate columns, picking up and speeding away with passengers, the drivers' white gloves flashing across the steering wheels.

Despite the hectic appearance of the pedestrians rushing by, Jordan never felt jostled or rushed, as though everyone had been placed on separate, non-intersecting rails. She wished she had the leisure to shop as she walked between the rows of stores that lined the road, but first things first. A few salesmen hovered outside the entrances to their stores, shouting and waving fans that boasted sales on shoes, briefcases, housewares, bras, cell phones, snacks, and souvenirs.

The thoroughfare was noisy and choked, but it was also the best way to reach the prefectural government buildings without having to pay for the subway or a taxi. After about ten minutes of walking, Jordan reached the end of the road, where the stores petered out to reveal a small park and rising buildings. Jordan spotted the building she was seeking—the main prefectural office. It had a dark grey facade pocked with a grid of square, recessed windows, like a huge waffle iron.

She proceeded to the front desk, where a young woman no older than Jordan tapped away at her keyboard. Jordan introduced herself and explained that she was the assistant language instructor for Sagae City—a minor untruth, but at least she wasn't posing as an internet reporter.

The JET Program, which employed Jordan and all the other assistant language instructors throughout Japan, was partially funded by the Japanese government, and Jordan had been to this very building to attend meetings for JET instructors working in the prefecture. The receptionist didn't bat an eye at her presence, likely used to foreign teachers frequenting the building. Jordan took a breath and continued.

"I'd like to see the faculty assignment and rotation roster for Sagae's school district for the last five years," she said hurriedly. "My supervisor at Sagae's Board of Education requested it."

"That shouldn't be a problem," the woman chirped. "Please fill out this Open Record Request Form, and then you'll follow me."

A few minutes later, Jordan found herself in a small room with a single chair and desk. On the desktop, the receptionist plopped two large binders that looked liable to snap her thin arms had she held them for a moment longer. She gave an exaggerated sigh of relief and smiled as she spoke.

"Take your time. The information you need should be contained in these binders, but please let me know if you need any assistance. You can't leave with those, but I'm happy to make photocopies if you'd like."

Jordan thanked her and pulled a folded-up paper from her purse as soon as she was alone. On it, she had written the name of the boy Junichi's mother had mentioned. A student who had attended Sagae High School and died by apparent suicide four years earlier: Haruka Hidaka.

Further searching on the internet had produced two more names: Hajime Abe and Sadako Kudo. Hajime had also been a student of Sagae High School and had perished three weeks prior to Haruka. His death had been classified as a suicide.

Perhaps most interesting, however, was Sadako Kudo. Though Sadako fortunately did not die, she had been stricken seriously ill by what was determined to be cyanide poisoning. The community had been in a fervor about the possibility of contaminated water, though no one else had shown signs of poisoning, not even the girl's family. This incident had occurred a few months before the first death, Hajime Abe's.

The binders in front of Jordan were organized by year, further broken down by school and semester. Jordan flipped to spring of the same year and let her gaze skip over the list of Sagae High School's teachers' names, looking for Ms. Nakamura. She didn't know whether Ms. Nakamura had lived or taught in Sagae at the time, but that was precisely her purpose behind pulling these records—searching for a connection. Minutes passed and Jordan's frown deepened. Ms. Nakamura was nowhere to be seen. Not in the following term when students began to die, either.

As she flipped to the next page, the sharp corners of the *naka* character that began the vice principal's last name caught her eye. *Ms.*

Umiko Nakamura, principal of Sagae Middle School. Jordan's heart beat a little faster, seeming to climb its way up her throat.

She had suspected that Ms. Nakamura had been employed at the high school, not the middle school, but the dates began to slide together and interlock: Ms. Nakamura had first started at the middle school a term before the cyanide poisoning and had remained in the district until just a year ago, when she transferred to Ogawa. Granted, Sagae hadn't seen any student suicides in the years between Haruka's and Junichi's deaths, but Ms. Nakamura had definitely been present.

Pleased with her findings, Jordan asked the young woman at the front desk to make copies and offered to pay when the other woman hesitated over the thick section of papers Jordan indicated. But the receptionist politely acquiesced, and Jordan was soon walking back to the train station with a thumb-thick stack of photocopies tucked in her messenger bag.

She slowed as she passed restaurants in the train station's lower levels, mulling over displays that held plastic recreations of their signature dishes: synthetic noodles vibrant and shining as though suspended in broth. Another's rows of parfaits glistened with plastic droplets that could have easily passed for condensation.

Jordan checked the schedule on the wall and regretfully ascended the stairs to the waiting platform to catch the next train. In the island between two tracks was a cramped convenience store, hedged in by bins of newspapers. Suntory juices, shrimp-flavored chips, potato straws, Hi-Chew candies, and all sorts of energy elixirs in small glass bottles burst from the shop's packed shelves. Jordan bought a sour plum *onigiri* and a cold bottle of Pocari Sweat before taking a seat alongside the tracks. She felt the weight of the papers hanging off her shoulder, smiled, and waited.

"Hello? Is this the Ito residence?" Jordan said into her cell phone. She raised her voice in question, though she already knew the answer. After all, she had called Kenji's home three times within the last two weeks asking to speak with him.

"Yes, it is," a woman's voice said. Kenji's mother.

"May I speak with Kenji, please?" She anticipated the same answer she had received during her previous calls: that he was out of the house or otherwise unavailable. Without any expectation of actually being able to speak with her former student, Jordan busied herself with separating and bagging her recycling. She wedged the phone between her shoulder and ear and began twisting the caps off empty PET bottles as she listened.

"May I ask who's calling?" As before, Kenji's mother spoke in a crisp but not unfriendly manner, revealing little in her tone.

"This is Eiko Kitagawa. I'm Kenji's classmate," Jordan said without hesitating over the pseudonym, having chosen and practiced it before the call. She felt a pinch of embarrassment at posing as a student but was also reluctant to provide her true identity. Teachers didn't often make house calls, after all, much less temporary, foreign teachers. The less conspicuous and noteworthy the call, the better. Though, concealing her name before had done little to keep Toshihiko off her track.

Instead of replying right away, Kenji's mother could be heard speaking to someone in a low and urgent voice. Jordan stopped tossing the plastic bottle caps into their recycling bag and strained to listen.

The other side of the line plunged into near-silence, but a whisper of static and hushed voices revealed Mrs. Ito had not hung up. Jordan held her breath, wondering if she had stoked some smoldering suspicion in Kenji's mother. Jordan knew her Japanese was far from perfect, and though she had purposefully kept the previous conversations brief, she felt it likely that her accent had bled into her words. Finally, the other woman spoke up.

"I'm afraid he's not available right now. I do apologize. Have a good evening—"

"Do you know when he'll be back?" Jordan said quickly. "When is a good time to get a hold of him?"

"Good night." Mrs. Ito's words were oddly cheerful, pitched as though she had not heard Jordan, and a close quietness flowed into the empty space their voices had left.

Jordan pocketed her phone and allowed herself to think. She had purposefully called at different hours of the day each time—quite late that evening, when most teenagers were expected to be home. Still, Kenji had always been unavailable, according to his mother at least. She frowned, discouraged and unsure of what the whispers and silence actually said. Jordan hadn't anticipated that the call would be her last to the Ito family, but that particular thread of investigation had clearly been snipped.

Perhaps she could go directly to the Ito home to speak with Kenji, if he were indeed there. Tsuruoka—where the Itos lived—was far off the beaten path from Ogawa, however, and in the opposite direction from Yamagata City. It would be difficult for her to reach Tsuruoka without a car of her own. But she might have to consider it if there was truly no other way to reach Kenji.

She wrapped a twist tie around the plastic bag in her fist—the bottle caps rattling inside like dry beans in a pod—and wondered what to do next.

TWENTY-FOUR

Jᴏʀᴅᴀɴ ʟᴏᴏᴋᴇᴅ ᴜᴘ ꜰʀᴏᴍ ʜᴇʀ ᴇᴍᴘᴛʏ ᴄᴏꜰꜰᴇᴇ ᴄᴜᴘ ᴀꜱ ᴛʜᴇ ᴅᴏᴏʀ chimed, welcoming a pair of old women into the cafe—not whom she hoped to see. She checked her phone for the tenth time in as many minutes. Sadako Kudo was half an hour late and hadn't sent any texts since they had finalized their plans to meet. Just as Jordan placed her phone in her purse and prepared to leave, a young woman bustled into the cafe, sending the doorbell pinging into the wall.

Flustered and out of breath, she quickly scanned the patrons and perked up when her eyes alighted upon Jordan. The girl was to her table in two hopping steps.

"Excuse me, are you Howard-*san*?"

"Yes. Nice to meet you," Jordan said as she stood and offered a shallow bow. "Please call me Jordan."

"I'm Sadako Kudo. Nice to meet you, too!" She returned the bow swiftly, like pushing it out of the way. Pleasantries dealt with, Sadako directed a beaming smile at Jordan. She had a small gap between her front teeth that somehow made her grin all the more charming. "I'm sorry I'm late! Got a bit lost."

They settled themselves at the table, Jordan ordering another coffee as Sadako glanced over the menu, too occupied with analyzing Jordan to give it much attention.

"So, Jordan-*san*." Sadako folded her hands under her chin. "You're a reporter?"

"More of a blogger, really." Jordan felt guilty using the same ruse she had employed with Junichi's mother. But, well, it had worked. "I'm writing some pieces on life in rural Japan, with an environmental angle. Your story stood out to me."

"Yeah but I still don't get why you want to interview *me*. They never found that Sagae's water source was contaminated with cyanide. Or our food. Or anything!" she said and stuck out her lower lip in a perplexed pout. "So the whole environmental thing...?"

"But that's exactly the point: A teenager is stricken with cyanide poisoning and her rural town doesn't have the resources to pinpoint its source. What else could it be but an environmental factor? The fact that the cause was never determined may be the story. You see?"

Sadako nodded, humming a high, thoughtful note in the back of her throat. Jordan could tell she still wasn't convinced.

"Besides, I want to put a human face on my stories. The piece will be just as much about you as what happened to you. A profile, I guess you'd call it." Jordan smiled and hoped her deception would be justified. Sadako considered for a moment longer before straightening and smiling back.

"All right, then; I'm all yours!" she said and flitted her attention to the waitress. "Oh, and a strawberry crepe and milk tea for me please."

By Jordan's estimations, Sadako was about 21 years old—not much younger than Jordan—yet she was as vivacious and effervescent as a child. She readily answered Jordan's questions about her illness and spoke at length even without being prompted. Her clothes were stylish, and expensive. She wore a powder-blue blouse with transparent sleeves and tiny polka dots that dusted the garment. A matching blue bow pinned aside her short hair, which was dyed a warm, coppery color.

Sadako nibbled at her crepe when she wasn't busy answering Jordan's queries—the answers to which were joined with expressive gestures and illustrative voices or mannerisms.

Though it pained her to even think of this girl being poisoned, Jordan was at least pleased to see the incident hadn't robbed Sadako of an ounce of verve. Jordan also felt bolstered by Sadako's presence. The girl had nearly died, yet only a lingering trace of the trauma remained. If Sadako could escape the murderer's reach, so too could Jordan. With particular determination, Jordan pushed aside thoughts of the threat she had received.

Slowly, she turned the conversation in a direction that pointed toward her true motive for the interview.

"So, did the illness affect your school life?"

"Well, I was absent for some time and had quite a few doctors' appointments." She inspected her nude-painted nails.

"Of course. I guess what I mean to say is, were you a model student? A sports star? A class officer?"

"Oh, I don't see how that's relevant," Sadako said but grinned in a sly way that invited Jordan to ask more.

"A troublemaker, then?" Jordan smiled but felt her heart trip over a beat. If Sadako's case was like all the others, she must have been selected by the murderer for a reason. Or would-be murderer, in this instance.

"Something like that." Sadako lowered her gaze to her cup, hiding her doe eyes behind long eyelashes, but the slant to her lips belied the look of contrition. "I may have helped a friend change some grades. I didn't do much, really. Just distracted a teacher while he got to the faculty computer."

"I see," Jordan said, furiously taking down notes. "And this was before the cyanide poisoning?"

"Yes, right before. Oh, but please don't write about this in your blog! Honestly, I don't know why I said anything in the first place." Sadako's eyes widened imploringly and she grabbed Jordan's hand with both of hers. "Please. It was Hajime's idea all along and he took the blame. I really was the perfect student when I returned to school. Cross my heart! Almost dying has a way of setting a person on a straight path, doesn't it?"

"Hajime? Was that—" Jordan freed her hand and flipped back in her notebook to the list of Sagae High School students who had died soon after Sadako's poisoning. "Hajime Abe?"

"Yes. I mentioned him before, didn't I? How he committed suicide? He was my best friend..." Even when speaking at length about the cyanide poisoning, Sadako's liveliness hadn't faltered, but now, her eyes glazed with tears and her bottom lip quivered.

"It must have been a particularly difficult year for you. I'm so sorry," Jordan said gently. "I won't write anything about your, um, indiscretion. I promise."

"Thank you." Sadako sniffled daintily. Her flash of grief hadn't been an act—the emotion had shone clearly from her eyes—but she recovered herself in the time it took to bat back a few unshed tears. She smiled again, a bit embarrassed.

Jordan continued to write in her notebook, making nonsense scribbles as she considered in which direction to head next. She had exhausted every angle to the cyanide poisoning: when Sadako had fallen ill, details of her hospital stay, the town's brief upheaval and debate over the safety of the neighboring plastics factories.

She couldn't see any segues to asking about Ms. Nakamura. The vice principal simply didn't fit into Sadako's understanding of the situation, and Jordan wasn't about to tell the girl that an attempt had been made on her life. Or, at least, that she suspected as much. Jordan grimaced and decided just to push forward.

"Does the name Umiko Nakamura mean anything to you?"

"Yes," Sadako said and stiffened. Somehow her entire being appeared to harden, like a turtle retreating into its shell. "She has something to do with all this?"

"Possibly," Jordan said with purposeful vagueness.

"That's strange. I would have heard about her falling ill too..." Sadako tapped a finger to her lips and directed a thoughtful gaze upwards, as though the ceiling were tiled with memories for her to search through.

"So you knew her then?" Jordan said quickly, before Sadako could ask any sticky questions about how Ms. Nakamura was connected to the cyanide poisoning.

"Unfortunately."

"Ms. Nakamura was the principal of Sagae Middle School before she transferred to another town. Weren't you at the high school during that time?"

"Well, I only knew *of* her. Because of my younger brother," Sadako said. She looked like she had smelled something putrid in the air, her nose scrunched with displeasure.

"So you never met her?" Jordan's insides clenched with disappointment, disbelief. Based on what she had surmised from Ryusuke's and the others' murders, Ms. Nakamura had given them the poisoned tea in person. If Sadako really had been Ms. Nakamura's first victim, surely she must have met the woman. She *must* have. "She never came to your house...?"

"God no. Luckily for her." The cute, bubbly girl who had been perched before Jordan, delicately sipping her tea, had transformed into something hard and cold. Her frilly shirt and pink-kissed lips suddenly seemed very at odds with the sharp, flinty look that lanced from her dark eyes.

"What happened? You mentioned your brother."

"You don't know? It was quite the scandal," Sadako said with a wolfish smile that held no joy.

Jordan shook her head.

"Umiko Nakamura was a *tyrant* at that school. She treated the children monstrously." Sadako's voice shook as she continued. "She humiliated them. Made them stand with buckets on their heads and paraded them in front of their classmates for ridicule."

Jordan remembered Ms. Nakamura telling her the same story and how she had recalled her actions with pride. The woman obviously hadn't seen anything wrong with her treatment of the school's students and even seemed to lament that she couldn't follow the same tack with the high-schoolers.

"But I understood that this was a standard form of punishment for unruly students? Like putting a kid in timeout."

"Well, to some extent, yes. She would take it to the extreme, though, and punish kids for even the smallest things. But that's far from the worst part." Sadako moved her cup and plate aside so that she could lean forward. She lowered her voice to a whisper. "She would beat the children."

"Beat them?" Jordan's breath tripped after her words.

"Yes. She made them find a bamboo switch or a stick and then she would hit them across the backside. Ruthlessly," Sadako said around the catch in her throat. Her thin eyebrows jumped between a scowl and a pained look of sympathy, and Jordan could only imagine the skirmish of outrage, betrayal, and sadness within the girl. "Kouichi, my younger brother, would often come home from school in tears, but he would never say why. One day, I walked past his room as he was putting on his shirt and I *saw* all the bruises and welts on his back."

"How awful. I can't imagine..." Jordan felt her eyes begin to water but she pushed back the pinprick of tears.

"It was terrible," Sadako said with cold agreement. "I told our parents and they eventually convinced Kouichi to explain what happened. He said Ms. Nakamura would beat him regularly. We filed a formal complaint against Ms. Nakamura through Sagae's Board of Education, and a few more kids came forward. And, well...I'm sure you can imagine how news like that would ripple through the town."

"But what happened? Those are serious charges."

"Not serious enough, I guess." She shrugged bitterly. "For every person who wanted to pull Nakamura's deeds into the light, there were two more who wanted to push everything under a rock. You know how it is, living in the *inaka*."

Sadako reached for her cup and took a sip of tea that had gone cold long ago. Her pursed lips left a pink smudge against the porcelain. "Anyway, she didn't get canned, just transferred a few years earlier than she would have anyway."

"I'm surprised she didn't resign," Jordan said with a frown.

"Are you kidding? That horrible woman doesn't have a shred of shame, or honor, or any of those fine Japanese traits." Sadako waved a hand dismissively. "I still can't believe she wasn't fired. She must have had a friend on the school board."

"Who would befriend a woman like that?" Jordan wondered aloud.

"And why would someone who hates children become a teacher?" Sadako tsked and crumpled back into her chair.

They sat in silence for a minute or two while Jordan tried to absorb everything Sadako had told her. She felt like already sodden ground relentlessly pelted by rain. The girl certainly fit the profile of the other victims in many ways: she was guilty of a wrongdoing that the murderer saw punishable, she was poisoned by cyanide, and her partner in crime had been murdered by the same methods, presumably.

Still, Jordan was puzzled by Sadako's claim that she had never met Ms. Nakamura. Perhaps she hadn't recognized the woman, or she had been poisoned indirectly. Sadako was also the only one to have escaped. It was possible that Ms. Nakamura thought it was too risky to target the same person again—doubtful she had absolved the girl of her supposed sins. Not everything aligned, but there were enough connections to light a spark.

With a sigh, Jordan shrugged off her thoughts and pulled her attention back to the present. Sadako was still nursing her long-cold tea and made a displeased grimace every time the cup touched her lips. She saw Jordan watching her and set her drink against its saucer with a clatter, shyly offering up a forced smile.

"I'm sorry. This isn't what you came here to talk to me about."

It was though, Jordan thought guiltily. She decided it best to change the subject.

"I'm a teacher myself, actually," Jordan said.

"Really? Aren't you a blogger?" Sadako welcomed the distraction and leaned forward eagerly, the conversation from before instantly discarded.

"Blogging isn't exactly a day job—more like a hobby. What do you do?"

"Oh! Well I just got married, you see?" Sadako placed her hand before her, gingerly resting her fingertips on the tablecloth like it was hot to the touch. A large diamond shone from the ring that encircled her finger—big enough that Jordan was amazed she hadn't noticed it before. "I'm sure we'll add some little ones to the family soon enough." Sadako giggled.

"Congratulations," Jordan said with a soft smile.

As Sadako continued to talk, about her husband and where they met and how beautiful their wedding was, she grew cheerier and more animated, stepping back—word by word—to how she had been after first bursting through the door. The coldness that had gripped her began to thaw, and Jordan felt warmed in her presence. Jordan let Sadako talk uninterrupted, content to watch the girl's eyes light up and revel in the fact that at least one person had snatched back her life from the murderer's gnarled grasp.

Just as Jordan was considering another cup of coffee—Sadako didn't seem to be losing steam—they both startled at the low hum of Sadako's cell phone vibrating against the tabletop.

"Oh! Oh my, it's later than I thought," Sadako said as she scooped up the phone and silenced it. She was on her feet in the next instant. "I'm sorry to be rude, but I really must be going."

"No need to apologize. And thank you for taking the time to speak with me." Jordan collected her pen and notepad, also standing as she placed them in her purse.

"Please do text me if you have any other questions, Jordan-*chan*. Oh, and send me a link when you post the blog. Make me look good!" Sadako winked and Jordan felt her throat tighten. She could only nod feebly in return. Sadako continued. "It was so nice to meet you. Really, thank you for listening to me."

Sadako took a step forward and lifted her arms, as though she meant to hug Jordan, but then she let them drift to her side. Jordan wondered if Sadako had read the hesitation, the guilt, in her eyes.

"Goodbye, Jordan-*chan*," she said and hurried out the door with a fleeting wave and a smile, not even seeming to hear Jordan's farewell.

TWENTY-FIVE

JORDAN SQUINTED AGAINST THE WHITE LIGHT ON THE CEILING SHE laid facing, the bulbs shining as brightly as the sun through thin clouds. She reminded herself that she was feigning a crippling headache, so she draped her arm over her eyes and groaned. Jordan heard the school nurse approach.

"Jordan-*sensei*, how are you doing? I'm sure the pain relievers will start working soon," the nurse said in a quiet, calm voice.

"I'm sure I'll be all right if I rest a little more, thank you," Jordan said and peeked out from under her arm to see Mrs. Takahashi return to her desk just a few steps away. Since Jordan's last conversation with Toshihiko—when he had reminded her that few people knew of Emi's pregnancy, thereby eliminating Jordan's theory that the young woman had been targeted for such—she couldn't stop wondering just how many people *did* know and sheltered the secret.

She couldn't shake loose the idea of Ms. Nakamura appointing herself as some sort of moral vigilante—it was firmly moored to Jordan's thoughts on the murders and the motives behind them. There was also Nanami's story of Emi's dizzy spell, and how she had been worried that her friend's pregnancy would be found out by the school nurse. The simple fact that Emi hadn't been expelled seemed to suggest her secret had gone unearthed.

Jordan closed her eyes and waited for the opportunity she knew was coming. Not a minute later, a quiet knock shook the door and a female student stepped inside.

"Takahashi-*sensei*, Akira tripped on the stairs and can't walk—he thinks he sprained his ankle. Can you come please?"

"Of course. Jordan-*sensei*, please excuse me."

Jordan had to keep from smiling and silently thanked Akira for agreeing to help with her ruse, though he hadn't needed much convincing when told his faked injury could help reveal Yuki's killer.

Jordan waited for the door to swing shut, checked to ensure that she was alone, and sprang to the large filing cabinet near the nurse's desk. As she had guessed, the drawers were filled with student files, but she required a minute to orient the jutting and swishing characters denoting proper names before the filing arrangement became clear. Once the system was deciphered, she soon found a manila folder with Emi's name on the tab and hastily opened it against the desk.

Inside were photocopied papers. Large red letters reading "COPY" were stamped on the upper corners of each page, sitting on tiny, ant-like scrawl that said the originals were with the police. She tamped down a rush of annoyance at Toshihiko and continued on quickly. The topmost page was dated the week before Emi's death. Jordan struggled to hold her cell phone steady over the page with her nervously shaking hands as she read the notes and snapped pictures.

"Student complained of feeling nauseous and dizzy...administered two caplets of...Student asked whether fainting was a symptom of pregnancy."

Jordan perked up and read closer.

"Student also asked if prescribed pain relievers were 'safe.' Did not admit to being pregnant but reported last menstrual cycle occurred approximately 40 days ago. I suspect—"

Jordan suddenly heard Akira's voice, muffled but near. Hurriedly, she returned the papers to the file, with no time to straighten them before shoving the folder back into the cabinet. With a flash of worry, she hoped no one would think twice about the papers' haphazardness, or even notice it.

A shadow blocked the light from under the door as Jordan closed the cabinet drawer as quickly and noiselessly as possible. She had only just released the handle when the door opened. The nurse shuffled in, supporting Akira with an arm under his shoulder as he limped beside. The older woman gave Jordan a look of concern.

"Are you all right, Jordan-*sensei*? May I get you anything?" Mrs. Takahashi guided Akira to the only other bed, separated from Jordan's by a curtained partition. When the boy saw the nurse was looking in the other direction, he mouthed *Okay?* and gave a hopeful thumbs-up. Jordan nodded at Akira but answered the nurse.

"I think I'll get a drink of water and sit at my desk. I'm feeling much better now, thank you." She squinted and spoke quietly, as though trying to overcome the discomfort of her headache. Mrs. Takahashi protested a moment but acquiesced when Jordan insisted on returning to work.

Jordan was mindful not to rush to her seat, but her phone seemed to tug at her pocket with the weight of the photographs it held. When she came to her desk, Mr. Mori, Ms. Tatsuya, and a third teacher were in quiet but animated conversation. They gave her very little notice, for which she was grateful, allowing her to inspect the pictures. She shielded the screen of her phone, loaded a photograph, and resumed reading the small text.

"I suspect Emi may be pregnant. I recommended appointments with her regular physician and the visiting counselor next week."

The notes ended there. Jordan bit her bottom lip in thought. Had Mrs. Takahashi told anyone else, and if so, whom? Maybe she had kept tight-lipped on the subject because she was friends with Emi's mother, as evidenced at the wake. Though the information in Emi's file could broaden the sphere of suspects, Jordan felt that her suspicions of Ms. Nakamura were bolstered.

At least one staff member at the school knew, and any other of them could have easily accessed the students' files. Jordan felt almost happy, pulled ever closer to some truth. But like a ball tossed in the air, her lifted spirits swiftly sank as she thought of Toshihiko. He *knew* at least one other person within the school was aware of Emi's pregnancy. And yet, he had called her idea into question. No doubt another strategy to distance her from the case. Even knowing that she shouldn't, she composed a text message to the inspector.

Did the school nurse tell anyone else?

Jordan stabbed at the keyboard on her phone as she sent the message to Toshihiko. She doubted he would respond; if anything, he'd probably just admonish her and implore her to mind her own business. To stay safe. Still, she felt slightly better.

Her tablemates were still talking but her attention was drawn to the head table, namely, to Ms. Nakamura.

The woman sat so straight-backed that she seemed tied to her chair. A pair of reading glasses lay low on her nose, and she narrowed her eyes to read the paper held between her bony fingers. Everything about Ms. Nakamura, even the smallest mannerism, seemed detestable to Jordan, and she couldn't help but glare with cold contempt.

Seeming to sense eyes on her, Ms. Nakamura turned to glance at Jordan, expression severe. Jordan whipped her gaze to the announcement board behind Ms. Nakamura but guessed the gesture wasn't very convincing. As nonchalantly as possible, Jordan turned back to her own desk and tried to fold herself into the ongoing conversation among the other teachers. Ms. Tatsuya was speaking.

"But he stepped down from his office. Isn't that enough?" she said.

"Yeah, no one commits *seppuku* over a few embezzled yen anymore," a young male teacher said in agreement. With one foot propped on the desks, his body leaning into his knee, he looked like a vulture perched over a meal. Ms. Tatsuya gave a small gasp at the young man's comment, despite his support of her opinion, and shook her head in disapproval.

"He was a public official, and he disgraced himself and his position. He should be accountable for his actions," Mr. Mori said firmly, and a spark of heat glinted in his eyes. Jordan hadn't the slightest clue about whom they were talking. As she listened, she trawled her memory for any similar details she may have picked up from the newspaper or television but came up short. Mr. Mori pulled back his sleeve to look at his watch. "I would like to continue this conversation, but I have a meeting at the Board of Education to attend. If you'll please excuse me."

As he moved to leave, Jordan noticed her cell phone's screen blinking like a buoy in the sea of papers on her desk. An icon of an envelope greeted her and she was surprised to see a message from Toshihiko, which read:

What do your investigations suggest, Inspector?

She could have kicked herself for not thinking of it earlier, Jordan thought as she approached the staff parking lot. She had left a few minutes before the final period of the day, citing her feigned headache and the need to rest, but she still surveyed the entire lot to ensure that no one else was nearby.

About twenty small sedans and a handful of trucks and hatchbacks sat in the school's lot, shining in the low afternoon light. The yellow car was easy enough to spot, like a single dandelion yet to seed among a field of its feathery white siblings.

Jordan looked around her once more, and when convinced she was alone, approached the car casually. She cupped her hands to either side of her face and peered inside the driver's-side window. The interior was extremely tidy—no papers, no leftover drink bottles, no cigarette packs, and no indication of whom the vehicle belonged to. She sighed and pulled away.

Jordan was tempted to wait around on some pretense to see who drove away in which cars, but most of the teachers would continue to work for a few hours more. Plus, she'd have a hard time explaining why she was loitering around the parking lot after claiming her headache was severe enough to warrant going home early. Mind made up, Jordan headed for her bicycle and decided to return early the next day as everyone was arriving.

TWENTY-SIX

Jordan crouched further into her jacket and tried to flex her chilled fingers, feeling equal parts cold and ridiculous. She had arrived before everyone else, when the sky was still shifting from grey to pink in the early dawn, and had staked out a lookout spot behind some hedges near the ball field. She had even laid her bike down beside her on the hard ground, so no one would know she had arrived, feeling positively clever.

But after forty-five minutes crawled by and not a single person had yet arrived, she simply felt silly, huddled behind a bush to spy on her coworkers. She sincerely hoped no one would see her; not for the sake of the case, but rather her reputation.

As she fretted, the first vehicle finally arrived. The janitor's truck wheezed out huge plumes of exhaust, matching the breath that stuttered from between Jordan's chilled lips. Gradually, more cars arrived, until at last, she saw a patch of yellow coming up the road, moving like a ray of bright sunlight between the trees and buildings.

Jordan held her breath as the yellow car pulled up and slowed to a stop. She leaned forward anxiously, as though that extra few inches would allow her to peer into the car.

The door of the yellow sedan sprang open and the driver struggled out of the car, head down as she carefully placed her feet. Jordan's heartbeat thudded in her throat, her eyes scanning the figure's slim frame, rumpled skirt, and white hair. Slowly, the woman straightened and turned. It was the school lunch lady.

Surprise and disappointment battled inside Jordan. She noticed that the lunch lady was also quite short and hunched with age. The old woman did not match Junichi's sister's description of a tall stranger at all. Maybe the mysterious figure and the yellow car weren't related to the murder after all. Or perhaps one was a key clue while the other was not, and Jordan was just chasing flickering shadows of the truth. She felt suddenly hopeless and impossibly frustrated.

For the first time, she wondered whether she was grasping at straws. She had built her theories upon rumors and distrust of Ms. Nakamura, and now that foundation had begun to split with ever-growing fissures. Jordan felt a hot tear run down her cheek and scrubbed at it angrily as Ms. Nakamura pulled up in a white sedan. The vice principal collected her purse, closed her car door, and walked calmly to the front entrance, not seeming to feel the crisp touch of the morning air.

After Ms. Nakamura entered the building and no one else was nearby, Jordan righted her bike and locked it up in the bicycle lot. It was still much earlier than her usual arrival time, and the teachers' room was mostly empty when she reached her desk.

She half-heartedly thanked the lunch lady—silently cursing her yellow car—when the old woman brought her a cup of steaming instant coffee. Jordan pressed the mug to her lips, but a whisper of caution stilled her hand before she could take a sip. She lowered the untouched coffee to her desk, the cup rattling in her unsteady grip, and tuned a smile for the lunch lady.

"I just remembered something," Jordan said brightly, and the woman widened her eyes with attention. "You weren't at a symphony in Yamagata City on"—she searched her memory for the date Ryusuke had been killed—"January seventh, were you?"

"Oh, no, I don't believe so. I can't remember the last time I went to a concert," the lunch lady said, happily engaged. "Why do you ask?"

"Really? I could've sworn I saw you there! Oh, well, I'm sure you must've been up to something else exciting," Jordan said in a gently probing way. She knew it was odd of her to ask, especially over a month later, but she also guessed the lunch lady would simply be pleased for the conversation. Assuming she wasn't the murderer, that is.

"I really couldn't say, child. All these days start to look the same after a while." She chuckled warmly and made small talk for a moment more before returning to serving drinks.

With a defeated sigh, Jordan rolled the still-warm coffee cup between her palms. Of course, she couldn't really have expected the lunch lady to remember such a specific date *and* provide an alibi for Jordan to investigate. But perhaps she could try again later, armed with different questions and the dates of the other students' deaths.

She pushed aside the mug and began to arrange papers, when a low voice suddenly addressed her from behind.

"Jordan-*sensei*, good morning," Ms. Nakamura said. "You seem to be feeling better." What would otherwise seem like warm concern was chilled by the older woman's dry, monotone voice and downturned lips.

"P-pardon?" Jordan stammered, taken off guard.

"I saw you leave early yesterday. When I checked on Akira in Mrs. Takahashi's office, she said you had been complaining of a headache." Ms. Nakamura's expression was unreadable, and though she hadn't asked a question, she seemed to be waiting for Jordan to explain herself in some way.

Jordan felt the blood siphon from her face at the thought of the vice principal visiting the school nurse. Was she being too obvious in her prying? Had Akira said anything? Or more importantly, was he in danger, now that he had caught Ms. Nakamura's attention? She swallowed hard.

"Yes, that's right. But I'm feeling much better now, thank you." She attempted a smile. "How's Akira?"

"His injury was quite...superficial."

"That's good. I'm glad he's all right," Jordan said, feeling actually quite worried for Akira's well-being. Ms. Nakamura stared back implacably. "Well, I'd better—"

"You're here unusually early."

"I decided I should make up for going home early yesterday," Jordan said quickly. She felt rather proud of her fast thinking, knowing that Ms. Nakamura couldn't possibly argue against punctuality and a sense of duty. Ms. Nakamura nodded once, appeased, and Jordan was flooded with relief.

But just as quickly as the relief had come, it was replaced with a surge of revulsion. Jordan felt sick at her own actions—at how she was always scrambling to please the vice principal, to say just the right thing in her presence.

Jordan looked hard at Ms. Nakamura. The older woman met her gaze unflinchingly, and Jordan straightened, refusing to be the first to avert her eyes. As she faced Ms. Nakamura, Jordan reminded herself that *this* was the woman who was very likely responsible for Ryusuke's death. Responsible for all of Ogawa's empty spaces hollowed out by loss. Jordan's hands clenched at her sides.

Like Ms. Nakamura herself, the older woman's stare was stridently cold and unfeeling, and Jordan imagined she could see the woman's guilt rolling off her in icy waves. A few more tense seconds passed before the vice principal lifted an eyebrow and parted her withered lips.

"Very well, Jordan-*sensei*. Now if you'll—"

"Speaking of Akira," Jordan said, knowing the segue was tenuous at best but feeling emboldened enough to push forward. "Months ago, you confronted him about Yuki. About him stealing from the school?"

Ms. Nakamura said nothing for a long moment. Her face remained impassive. "Yes. Why do you ask?"

"How did you know something was missing from the storeroom?" Jordan's mouth had gone dry, but her voice was steady. She hadn't thought of any reasonable pretext for asking this and didn't offer further explanation.

Besides, whether Ms. Nakamura answered her or not was unimportant. What Jordan wanted was a reaction.

"Inventory," Ms. Nakamura bit out impatiently. The corner of her mouth twitched, and she pinned Jordan with a look one might give a cockroach on a kitchen counter. Then, Ms. Nakamura abruptly turned away and stalked to her desk.

With Ms. Nakamura's back to her, Jordan smiled triumphantly. The vice principal hadn't implicated herself, but neither had Jordan been cowed, and she would embrace that as a victory.

"Yes, you were perfect. Brilliant," Jordan said for what felt like the hundredth time, reassuring Akira that he had played his role to a tee the day before. She smiled. "Thanks again for your help."

"Sure! I would do anything for Yuki. A-and for you too, of course." He smiled sheepishly. "If you tell me your plan, I bet I could help even more. I know I could!"

"I'm sorry, Akira. I hope I can tell you soon," she said and shook her head, feeling doubly guilty for withholding information from Akira and for unwittingly putting him on Ms. Nakamura's radar. She tried to ignore his crestfallen look and convince herself that the less he knew about the murders, the better.

"Well, I'd better get going, *sensei*. Clubs already ended."

"Of course, sorry to keep you," she said. Akira nodded and shrugged in a casual way that suggested she hadn't really inconvenienced him. He shouldered his backpack and was just about to duck out the front door of the school when Jordan caught his sleeve. "Akira! Don't let Ms. Nakamura in your home if she comes by."

It all came out in a rush of breath, and Jordan wasn't surprised by the perplexed look Akira gave her.

"*Sensei?* What are you talking about?" He half-laughed.

"Don't let *any* faculty members inside, for that matter," she amended hastily. "Promise me."

"Not even you?" His laughter came fully this time. The kind that bubbles up to obscure a tenor of uncertainty.

"Not even me." Jordan forced a jocular smile to put him at ease. "Promise?"

"Sure, I promise," Akira said, more to humor her and be on his way than with deep sincerity. He was already halfway out the door before he had finished speaking, and he flung a wave over his shoulder before hurrying on. "Bye, *sensei!*"

"See you tomorrow." Jordan doubted Akira even heard her as he rushed away, and she sighed, not at all assured that he would heed her warning. As though her thoughts were literally weighing her down, she followed Akira out of the school with a certain dragging slowness.

Though she wanted to simply go home, she knew she'd arrive to an empty fridge, and an even emptier stomach. Instead, she pointed her bike toward the Ai-Yu grocery store and doggedly pedaled onward.

The small store wasn't busy, which Jordan was glad for, since she often had to make several circuits to find everything on her list. She had not fully adjusted to her food options, still unable to identify those dense orange fruits that resembled tomatoes, fish after fish with only subtle differences in stripes and fins, and rows of canned items of which there were no American equivalents, like rubbery *konnyaku* and pickled burdock root.

Jordan finished up in the frozen aisle, where desserts could be relied upon to be identifiable and unintimidating. She selected *matcha* ice cream and headed to the checkout cashiers.

One of her younger students waved to her from a rack of comic books near the checkout aisles; she waved back to him with a smile as she fished in her wallet for the store's point card. She paid in cash, bagged her own items, and exited to the darkened parking lot.

An open trailer with startling orange-red lights had moored itself in the small lot. Dark, aromatic smoke puffed out of its side, so thick that the flavor of savory charcoal and grease touched Jordan's tongue. A hand-painted sign reading *yakitori* slapped the side of the trailer in the evening breeze. Lit by the orange glow of the grill's coals and the trailer's lights, skewers of chicken glistened.

The fatty sizzle of grease and meat was tempting to Jordan, but she made up her mind to prepare her own dinner as she packed her grocery bags in the basket of her bike. She rolled up her pants to the knees, swung one long leg over the side of the bike, and pedaled into the night.

Though the sun was well down, most people were still at work, and Jordan found herself in the bubble of the early evening lull when salaried workers had yet to commute home, stay-at-home moms and grandparents had already finished their daily errands, and children were hunched over school books before dinner.

Jordan cursed her luck when she heard perhaps the only car on the road rumble close behind her, its headlights stretching her shadow in stark relief against the pock-marked pavement. The road was narrow, braced on either side by shoulder-high brick walls that hugged in nearby houses. Since she took the same route to and from her apartment nearly every day, Jordan knew the roadway would soon thin even more as it formed a small bridge over a man-made culvert.

Jordan was aware she was riding slowly, so she skirted the wall as close as she dared. She was careful not to sink the bike's tires in the long gaps between the sidewalk and roadway, which directed water from the surface to be diverted away underground. She motioned for the car to pass her, but it made no change in course or speed, its headlights staring ahead unblinkingly. Jordan shrugged and began to move closer to the center of the road as the bridge approached.

The rubber of her bike's front tire had only just whisked across the threshold of the bridge when the car gave a throaty roar and heaved forward. Jordan could barely begin to register or anticipate the car's movement as it crushed in on her in the space of a breath. She heard a crunching squeal and felt her body rush forward under a powerful force, like an enormous hand had swatted her.

In the next instant, Jordan was tumbling and panic gripped her, her heart beating so fast it ached. The headlights' glare swirled end-over-end, mixing in a looping spiral with the street lamps and pale moon. She finally landed with a wet smack and a painful heaviness that pressed her into the culvert's algae-slick stones.

She felt that never moving again would be too soon. Her arm, from shoulder to fingernails, complained of hurt after absorbing the brunt of the fall. Jordan groaned as she attempted to catch her breath and right herself with her free arm, though it slipped in the slow stream of water that slid along the culvert.

Over her anxious breaths, she could hear the sound of the car picking up speed, though it had already passed out of sight. The high wail of its engine soon diminished as it pulled away into the darkness. Jordan sat in the channel a minute longer, shaking with residual fear and cold as the creeping water soaked into her clothes.

Carefully, she moved her arm, wincing with pain. The elbow and shoulder ached, but she could move her arm with a little effort; it seemed unbroken. Jordan got unsteadily to her feet and climbed out by pulling at the coarse weeds at the top of the bank.

Once out of the water, she further assessed her condition. The wind had been knocked out of her and she swore at a gash across her knee, but she felt otherwise unhurt besides the possible injury to her arm. She shuffled with halting, nervous steps to the bridge and let out a gasp at the sight of her bike.

It was crumpled and grotesquely twisted, like a body in a crime scene photograph. The handlebars were wedged so high in the bridge's railing that the bike seemed to be rearing on its back wheel, or at least what was left of it. Both rims were bent beyond repair. A pedal and the seat were torn off and scattered on the ground amid other crushed debris.

She was struck by the violence of the encounter, overcome by a shudder that had nothing to do with the frigid water darkening her clothes. Judging by the scene, she had somehow been thrown over the railing instead of crushed between it and the car.

She took a few deep, calming breaths before grabbing the bike frame to wrest it from the bridge and clear the roadway. As her palms closed around the bony metal, a patch of brightness along the bridge's railing caught her eye: a gash of yellow paint.

TWENTY-SEVEN

"Do you have a moment, Inspector?" Jordan said and felt some small satisfaction when Toshihiko twitched in surprise. She hadn't intended to startle him, not really. But she *had* tucked herself behind a tree near his parked car so that she could catch him, without drawing attention, as he left the school.

"Jordan, as much as I enjoy being your sounding board, I'm afraid I must return to my office," Toshihiko said blandly and fished in his coat pocket for his keys. "I'll be returning to the school next week if you'd like to speak with me then."

"I won't take up much of your time, I promise. If you could just give me a quick lift home, and I'll say my piece on the way." She knew she was pushing her luck, but she suspected his patience would stretch far enough. "Please. You're headed that direction anyway."

"Don't you have a bike?"

"Actually, that's sort of why I wanted to talk to you," Jordan said, purposefully leaving out any other details. If she knew Toshihiko, which she felt she did at least a little, those few words would stoke the coals of his curiosity. And he couldn't ignore any information that could contribute to his case, even if she was the source.

He lifted an eyebrow and cast a wary glance around the parking lot. Jordan knew she almost had him, but her satisfaction was fleeting, sobered by the reason *why* she wanted to speak with him in the first place.

After limping home the night before, Jordan's first instinct had been to call Toshihiko. But her cell phone—like her bike—had not survived the accident. As she had stared at its ruined display, splintered into silvery webs, she had convinced herself it was best to speak with Toshihiko in person anyway. If he would just agree to give her a ride.

"Don't worry, there's no one around," she said to herself as much as to him. "Besides, if anyone does see us, it's not like it's that unusual for you to be talking to me, right?"

"Yet you felt the need to hide behind a tree so we wouldn't be seen together." Toshihiko's lips quirked in amusement.

"I wasn't *hiding*, exactly, just exercising reasonable caution." Jordan huffed and crossed her arms, wondering just how much of a hurry he was in, if he could find the time to needle her. "After all, the murderer is probably a faculty member."

"All right. Get in," Toshihiko said with a sigh. The car unlocked with a soft beep, and Jordan piled in the passenger's side. They drove away in silence.

Not until they reached the fire station at the end of the road did Jordan realize Toshihiko wasn't going to prompt her for her story. It irked her that the inspector would insist on pretending he wasn't interested, and she considered stubbornly refusing to share, but what she had to say was important this time. She knew she couldn't hold back, and she needed his help.

"Someone tried to kill me yesterday."

"What?" The car lurched when Toshihiko pressed on the brakes in surprise. He looked between Jordan and the road in quick succession, concern and confusion plain on his face. "What happened?"

"I was biking home from the grocery store when someone drove their car right into me," Jordan said and shuddered at the memory. Her shoulder still ached terribly, but it seemed to be improving. Though, the deep, purple bruises that stained her arms and legs where she had fallen would probably persist long after the gnawing pain faded. Absently, she ran her thumb against her forearm, feeling a whisper of hurt at the touch even through her sweater. "I'm lucky to be alive. If I hadn't been flung from my bike..."

"You're sure it wasn't an accident?" Toshihiko said carefully.

Jordan could tell he didn't entirely doubt her, and the question was a reasonable one, but she still bristled.

"Yes, I'm sure! As soon as I started crossing the bridge over the culvert...right there." Jordan pointed as they passed in front of the grocery store along the main road. "The car sped up, hit my bike, and kept going. They didn't slow down or honk or anything. If it was an accident, they probably would have stopped to see if I was okay, right?"

"One would hope so. Did you get a look at the car? Or the driver?" Toshihiko frowned as he scanned the road. From the way his eyes moved behind his glasses, Jordan suspected he was flipping through his mental catalog, making notes for later.

"No, it was totally dark, and it came at me from behind. All I saw was headlights," she said. "But here's the interesting part—there was yellow paint on the bridge's guardrails."

"Yellow paint?"

"It must have been a yellow car. Just like the one Junichi's sister described." The excitement in Jordan's voice took even her by surprise. But she felt they were close to something, like sensing a storm before the first drop of rain painted the ground. Now that she wasn't immediately in harm's way, her anxiety over the incident began to ebb, and the force that had galvanized her during the past months resurged. "Don't you see? It was definitely the murderer who tried to run me over."

"And you still believe the murderer is a member of the school's staff?"

"Yes," Jordan said firmly. "Don't you?"

"Only one person at Ogawa High School owns a yellow car." Toshihiko softened his voice, as though to blunt the effect of his words. "It's registered to—"

"The school lunch lady." She ignored the long-suffering look he directed at her. "Are you sure there's no one else?"

"Not according to our records."

"She could be a suspect, right?" Jordan was doubtful, not only because the lunch lady seemed so sweet and unassuming, but also because she couldn't shake her suspicion of Ms. Nakamura.

"No. She was in Hokkaido visiting her sister when Yuki was killed. She has an alibi for the night of Emi's death, as well." Toshihiko said matter-of-factly.

Jordan knew she shouldn't be surprised that he had already investigated the staff's vehicle records and followed the lead on the yellow car —he was nothing if not thorough. What did surprise her was that he was actually answering her questions, listening to her. Maybe the shock had lowered his defenses.

"The color of the car could be a coincidence," Toshihiko said thoughtfully. "Or the paint on the guardrail could be unrelated—"

"Or we could be on to something. It's obvious the murderer sees me as a threat. First the note warning me to stop nosing around, and when I didn't, they decided to get serious and—"

"This is exactly why I didn't want you to get involved in the case, Jordan," Toshihiko said, his voice rising with each word. The car skirted under a streetlamp, washing his face with enough light that Jordan could see a glare twisting his features.

"And what am I supposed to do? Just sit on my hands while some crazy person picks off my students one by one?"

"It's not your place. No—" Toshihiko's finger shot up from the steering wheel to silence her noise of protest. "If what you theorize is true—that the same person who murdered the students is now targeting you—you've placed yourself in danger."

"I can't believe this. You're blaming *me* for almost getting killed, instead of the person who did it." Jordan was near to shouting, her voice resounding through the car, but she was beyond caring.

"I don't know how else I can say this. Just stay out of it."

"I have more reason to be involved than you do. Sure, it's your job, but do you actually know these kids? Do you even *care*?" Jordan could feel the heat of her anger warming her face and neck. She steeled herself to lob back whatever rejoinder Toshihiko might try.

Instead of arguing, though, Toshihiko closed his mouth into a firm line and said nothing. Jordan could see his eyeglasses pulse as he clenched and unclenched his jaw, but soon even that movement stopped. With nowhere to vent, Jordan's ire fizzled out, like embers doused with a bucket of water. She huffed in annoyance and trained her attention out the window instead. Her apartment building was already in view and Toshihiko's car crunched into its gravel parking lot less than a minute later.

As soon as the car came to a stop, Jordan launched herself out the door.

"Thanks for the ride," she said dryly, looking away from him as she moved to close the door.

"Jordan." Toshihiko's voice was calm, imploring.

Jordan wanted to just leave, and she bounced her palm against the door's frame impatiently. After expelling a long sigh, she finally turned back and craned to look into the cabin, lifting her eyebrows in question.

"What?"

"Thank you for telling me about this. Your information could be important to the case, and I'd like to take it down properly," Toshihiko said. His expression had clearly softened. The car's dome light made shadowy lines across his forehead where it was creased with concern. "If you could go to Ogawa's police station tomorrow at noon, I'll take your statement then."

"S-sure." She was too surprised to feel much relief or satisfaction at being taken seriously. Toshihiko had certainly never humored her before, and she doubted he would start now. She narrowed her eyes in thought, letting a few breaths of silence pass between them.

"Please be careful, Jordan."

"I will. You be careful too."

"Good night," Toshihiko said and offered a small, closed-mouth smile.

Jordan nodded in return, allowing the car door to swing shut softly. She didn't watch him leave but listened until the hum of the engine disappeared into the torrent of cars speeding past on the highway.

TWENTY-EIGHT

DESPITE THE WARM BREEZE, THE AROMA OF *YAKISOBA* AND BEER, and the gentle notes springing from an acoustic guitar, Jordan couldn't relax. After the incident on the bridge, Jordan's investigations had ground to a halt. Even Toshihiko, with all his official know-how, was unable to unearth any leads or information related to the car "accident."

As promised, Toshihiko had recorded her statement at the police station the day after she had cornered him at his car. He even divulged that he had taken photos at the scene and a scraping of yellow paint from the bridge's railings.

Both the interview and evidence collection had encouraged Jordan, but Toshihiko was quick to point out they had no vehicle other than the lunch lady's to compare the paint sample against. Besides not matching the sample, the old woman's car was free of any scratches or dents that would indicate a collision. The scraping from the guardrail might be helpful when compiling evidence for a conviction, Toshihiko had said, but Jordan could tell he was not optimistic about that eventuality.

Neither the encounter with the car nor the fact that at least one other person knew of Emi's pregnancy pulled forward any new evidence. The well of information, once rippling with eddies, had smoothed into glassy stillness. Not even after over a month of poking at the edges of these incidents did Jordan have anything to show for her efforts.

She had continued to keep a wary eye on Ms. Nakamura, looking for any change or clue in her behavior. Toshihiko still frequented the school but had yet to make an arrest or unearth further evidence.

Jordan felt some grim satisfaction, knowing he had only as much to offer as she did. Unless he was playing his cards close to the chest, it didn't seem likely that he would resolve the investigation soon. At least, not as far as she knew. In the last couple of weeks, Toshihiko hadn't exchanged many words with her beyond mundane greetings.

More than once, she had considered reaching out to him just for an aimless chat. Especially in the lonely, dark hours of night when the doorknob rattled in the wind and every creak sounded like a heavy footstep. But if there was anything Toshihiko was less inclined to talk about than the case, it was the vaporous thread still entwining them.

Jordan realized she was fixating again and sighed with frustration.

"Jordan-*chan*, are you all right?" Mrs. Okubo asked with a smile. She bumped her shoulder against Jordan's as they sat hip-to-hip on a blanket spread across the ground. Jordan gawked for a moment at not being called "sensei" for perhaps the first time by Mrs. Okubo. The other woman's cheeks were blushed by alcohol, no doubt the cause of her more casual demeanor.

"I'm fine, Okubo-*sensei*. Thank you," Jordan said, though she didn't feel it.

Mrs. Okubo had invited Jordan to join her and her family for a *hanami*, or flower-viewing celebration. On the burgeoning cusp of spring, cherry trees across Japan had plumped up with succulent, tightly balled buds. Over the brief course of a few weeks, waves of these buds had burst open like popcorn kernels on a stove. Currents of downy pink blossoms unfurled and crept up the island like a spool of silk pulled by the warming breezes.

In these weeks, no one missed an opportunity to spend an afternoon under the cherry trees, enjoying the company of friends and a cup of sake. There were organized *hanami* events too, which took the form of bustling yet low-key festivals.

Jordan had traveled with Mrs. Okubo's family to Sagae's *hanami*, where there were more cherry trees than in Ogawa. They had laid out their blanket, folding chairs, and refreshments from the *konbini*, squeezed companionably between other viewers under a lattice of dark branches and pale flowers.

Only when Jordan stopped her thoughts from wandering down the muddy, over-trodden path of the homicide investigation did she feel cradled by the murmur of conversation surrounding her. Felt the warm air thaw the chill in her core still lingering from winter.

Blushing white blossoms flocked the branches above her head, joining with gauzy clouds and patches of sky that peeked through the trees. A petal fluttered into her face as she looked up and she laughed, remembering that she was there to enjoy herself.

"The blossoms are wonderful, aren't they?" Mrs. Okubo let out a contented sigh.

"Yes, definitely."

"You see, these sakura blossoms are like life: brief, but all the more beautiful for it," Mrs. Okubo said and smiled wistfully as she rolled a tender petal between her fingers. "That's the Japanese way of it."

Jordan nodded and took a sip of the beer that had grown warm in her hand, giving herself a moment to think. The acoustic guitar was now joined by bass and drums as a band warmed up in the nearby amphitheater.

From the other direction came the shouts of children at play as they ogled the food stands serving up *takoyaki* and *yakisoba*. Jordan's stomach rumbled, and as if on cue, Mrs. Okubo's nine-year-old daughter came bounding over with two candy apples clenched in her fists. Her lips were bright red and glistening from one apple's sugar shell. She thrust the other apple, still wrapped in crisp cellophane, toward Jordan.

"Here, Jordan-*sensei*!" The girl, Nanako, flashed a wide, gap-toothed smile and threw herself onto the blanket with a giggle. Jordan thanked her as the girl happily, and noisily, crunched away at her own treat.

Jordan was content to sink into her canvas chair, tilting her head back until only the white, blue, and pink splotches of the trees and sky filled her vision. She drifted, somewhere between a catnap and meditation and let all distractions roll off her like water. It wasn't until some minutes later that she surfaced from her doze at the sound of Nanako's shrill complaints and Mrs. Okubo chiding her.

"No, you've had enough of your candy apple. You practically gobbled it all up anyway," Mrs. Okubo was saying flatly. "Look, there's only the core left! You'll give yourself a stomachache if you eat the seeds."

Nanako pouted a moment but was soon distracted by her father handing her a sour plum *onigiri*. Jordan sat still in her chair, mouth falling open at the thought that alighted upon her.

Apple seeds and cherry seeds contain cyanide. The murderer doesn't have to buy cyanide itself at all, only harvest it.

Jordan's mind ballooned with possibilities. Ogawa was famous for its cherries. Anyone in town could acquire or grow large quantities without raising suspicions.

Jordan scrambled for her phone, only to remember that it had been dashed to pieces. She itched to have the internet at her fingertips so she could determine whether it was feasible for the murderer to extract the poison from fruit seeds. She perched on the edge of her seat as though waiting for a signal to spring into action. An anxious smile spread across her lips.

Mrs. Okubo chuckled and nudged her husband as she whispered to him.

"Look, she's finally having a good time."

———

After the sun settled low in the trees' branches and the air brought chill eddies, the Okubo family decided to pack up and leave. Jordan told them she had some shopping to do while in the city and finally assured Mrs. Okubo she could find her way home, despite the woman's many protests.

It was true that Jordan planned to buy a new cell phone and bicycle, but more than that, she didn't think she could wait the hour it would take to return to Ogawa before researching her theory.

She picked her way through the many people still enjoying the *sakura* blossoms, which were now lit by red paper lanterns that dyed the petals with crimson light. The park was in the heart of the city, and though she didn't know Sagae well, Jordan soon found a *mangakissen—* an internet and comic book cafe.

When she walked in, the man at the counter masked his surprise and greeted her politely when she asked for an hour's time. Likely few Westerners, much less women, frequented the place, she surmised from his reaction.

The cafe was quiet, filled with low, discordant hums from rows of computers that stretched through the middle of the room. A few hulking vending machines added to the deep electric thrum and cast their cold light on the walls.

She walked to her computer station, taking in the large bookshelves packed with an astounding number of paperbacks from countless comic book series. She recognized a few of the titles—discussed animatedly between her students—and felt a squeeze at her heart when she recognized a series Kenji and Ryusuke used to chat about.

Jordan wondered again how Kenji was faring at his new school without his best friend. Also, she felt certain that Kenji could shed some light on why Ryusuke was targeted, if only she could find a way to contact him. She was still convinced of her theory that the victims were being brought to justice in the murderer's eyes, but she had yet to unearth Ryusuke's wrongs.

She hurried the last few steps to the computer, entered the password the clerk had given her, and pulled a set of headphones off a hook alongside the monitor. There were quite a few patrons at the other stations, and the air hung heavy with cigarette smoke and the musky, mushroomy scent of books. The image on her monitor was glazed yellow with the thin sheaf of smoke that hung in the air, like it had been steeped in strong tea.

No one seemed to be looking at her, and she doubted the store monitored its customers' activity too closely, but she still felt nervous as she typed in, "fatal dose of cyanide," "how much cyanide is in a cherry seed," and other similar criteria into Google. She couldn't help but glance over her shoulder with each new search.

Less than half an hour passed before she felt vindicated in her theory that the murderer could extract sufficient cyanide from cherries, or from apples and pears, all of which were abundant in Yamagata Prefecture. The seeds had a coating that could not be penetrated by stomach acid, so swallowing a seed or two was harmless. But if the seeds were pulverized or refined, the cyanide contained within could certainly be toxic.

Though she was satisfied that her suspicion had been correct, she realized the information didn't prove Ms. Nakamura's guilt. If anything, the possibility of deriving cyanide from seeds only widened the net to cast.

Countless orchards splayed across the fringes of Ogawa, creating a skirt of white and pink blossoms that frothed against its foothills. Fruit containing cyanide certainly wasn't in short supply. Jordan even supposed that the murderer could eventually amass enough seeds with a little patience, several trips to the store, and an unsuspecting grocer.

Still, she wondered whether Ms. Nakamura had her own private orchard and how exactly she could track one's fruit purchases. Jordan even considered suggesting to Toshihiko that he check orchard records against the school staff but decided he would not appreciate her direction.

With an additional thirty minutes of internet use already paid for, Jordan idly surfed. She sifted through a few news stories, and while waiting for one to load, let her eyes wander. They landed again on the comic series that had been Ryusuke and Kenji's favorite, as though drawn to any whisper of a connection with the boys.

Jordan felt a caress of guilt when she realized she had not followed up with Kenji since the last failed phone call to his mother, but then, she had also been understandably distracted. Slowly, an idea rose up about how she could possibly contact Kenji.

Jordan typed mixi.jp into the browser's URL bar and was greeted by a cheery website with a friendly orange word bubble. She knew from reading a recent article that Mixi was among Japan's more popular social networks.

She had also heard it mentioned by Mrs. Okubo anytime she talked about her niece, who apparently spent "too much time online." Mrs. Okubo had even given Jordan an invitation to the website and encouraged her to contact her niece, who was the same age as Jordan. She hadn't really considered using the invitation before but was now very thankful to have it. She made an account and username under a pseudonym and searched for "Kenji Ito."

The results were staggering and none of the profile pictures helped to narrow the search—there was an image of a duck for one user, Doraemon for another, a teapot, a plate of *takoyaki*, a smiling edamame bean, and on and on. The only image she found of an actual person was a popular singer in a J-Pop band.

Jordan sighed. There was no feasible way she could determine if any of those users were the Kenji she was looking for. It was unlikely that he even registered with his real name, as most people on Mixi didn't. Not even she had, too worried about the repercussions of messaging a student online, even a former one.

A message popped up on her screen warning her that she only had two minutes of internet access remaining and would she like to pay for more? Feeling vindicated about the possibility of cyanide poisoning through fruit seeds, yet defeated in her search for Kenji, Jordan decided to call it a night and collected her things to leave.

She gulped at the fresh night air gratefully as she left the cafe. The streets were busy with pedestrians leaving the *hanami*, mostly couples and groups of men, their voices amplified by alcohol. Jordan wove herself into the crowd and made her way to the train station. Stray cherry blossom petals that had been carried on the breeze dotted the dark pavement, pressed and flattened underfoot by the steady flow of passersby.

TWENTY-NINE

THE MORNING AIR WAS PERFUMED WITH BLOSSOMING FLOWERS uncoiling under the warm sunlight. The students who rushed past Jordan out the front entrance whispered excitedly, but she felt mired to the floor, reluctant to cross the walkway to the auditorium.

It was graduation day. Already, Jordan knew she would miss the graduating upperclassmen. She would miss the between-class times spent chatting. The quiet camaraderie in the classroom. The paper flowers given to her in moments when the older students' practiced maturity was eclipsed by glimpses of eager adolescence.

Jordan told herself it was silly to be melancholy. She would soon have the pleasure of meeting new first-graders and watching the remaining students move forward. Still, emotion grabbed her as she remembered the parting messages left on chalkboards and the farewell notes that had piled on her desk.

She entered the full gym and realized it could very well be the last time she saw some of her pupils.

The students wore their usual school uniforms and were flanked by their teachers and parents. All of the adults were smartly dressed, and some held elegant bouquets. The blossoms flared with bright colors, visible through the plastic wrappers that encased them like ice. Jordan noticed that Toshihiko was seated in a corner among the parents, looking as neat and serious as ever.

Principal Kikuchi took the stage, his bald head and glasses shining. He began a speech praising the students' hard work and commitment to education. It wasn't so dissimilar from other presentations given throughout the school year, and Jordan allowed her thoughts and gaze to wander.

Near the front of the stage was Nanami, who had slowly begun to make new friends after Emi's death five months before. Her hair was pulled back for once, held away from her round face by barrettes in the school's colors. Nanami maintained a somber expression, like all the students, but her eyes were red-rimmed and puffy from crying.

As Jordan took in the assembled crowd, a tall man standing among the students caught her eye and she felt all the air sucked from her lungs. The young man looked remarkably, impossibly like Ryusuke. He was older but bore the same tanned skin, strong nose, and small mouth that always seemed to be holding back a laugh. His face looked like it had been molded by someone trying to recreate Ryusuke from memory —uncannily similar and different at the same time.

Based on the young man's age and resemblance to Ryusuke, Jordan could only assume he was his brother, accepting the honor of graduating on his younger sibling's behalf. In his hands, he held a framed portrait of Ryusuke. A black ribbon slashed across one corner of the photo like a crack in the glass. The picture captured every familiar detail of Ryusuke, despite the thin-lipped expression that replaced his usual grin.

Jordan pried her eyes from the evocative photo to find Toshihiko, wondering whether he was any closer to uncovering Ryusuke's killer. The principal concluded his speech, the students bowed, and all Jordan could think about was those who were conspicuously, painfully absent.

The graduation ceremony had ended a while ago, and Jordan was among the last few people still about. She had mingled and chatted, hoping to say goodbye to as many graduates as possible, until the crowd had finally thinned.

Just as she turned toward the school house to collect her belongings and leave, Jordan was once again arrested by the sight of Ryusuke's brother as he walked past. A short, round woman—no doubt his mother—held Ryusuke's framed photograph, cradling it gently against her chest. They exchanged no words as they both made their way toward the parking lot.

Jordan considered letting them go, but her affection for Ryusuke lassoed her to the mother and brother, pulling her along by an unseen rope until she closed the distance between them. At the sound of her brisk footsteps approaching, the young man paused and turned to greet her. He only looked at her for a moment, but his features softened as though he recognized her.

"Hello. Ms. Howard?" he said in clear English.

"Yes, I'm Jordan Howard. You must be Ryusuke's brother," she said and offered a quick bow.

"Yes, my name is Hisao Suzuki. Nice to meet you." He returned her bow and she smiled at their instant recognition of each other despite never having met before. The warm, familiar look behind his eyes made her expression falter but she recovered herself before she replied.

"I wanted to say how sorry I am for your loss. I was very close to Ryusuke, and I...I miss him." She took in Mrs. Suzuki as she spoke, offering a sympathetic look and repeating her sentiment in Japanese. The woman thanked her politely but then withdrew from the conversation, directing her sullen gaze to the ground.

"I'm glad to know that so many people will keep Ryusuke's memory," Hisao said and smiled with only a flicker of sadness, expression carefully controlled. "Ryusuke spoke a lot about you. He said you were his favorite teacher."

"Well, he was certainly one of my favorite students," Jordan said and wondered whether Ryusuke's efforts in English class, though fruit-less, had been spurred by his elder brother's easy control of the language. "Ogawa High School isn't the same without him—and without his friend Kenji. The two of them were really the heart of the class."

"If only Kenji had left sooner," Hisao said in a low voice, and his face darkened.

"I don't—I thought Kenji and Ryusuke were good friends? They were practically inseparable..." Jordan shook her head in confusion.

"That's certainly true." Hisao snorted disapprovingly. "That boy was too close to Ryusuke." He cut himself off with a concerned look at his mother, but she was watching a bird peck at the ground and showed no regard for the conversation she clearly couldn't understand. "Well, none of that matters now anyway. Thank you for speaking with me, Ms. Howard. It really was a pleasure to meet you." He seemed suddenly anxious to go.

"You, too." Jordan bowed in parting as Hisao said something quietly to his mother and they both turned to leave. As Jordan watched them depart, the slow-healing wound left by Ryusuke's death reopened, allowing a fresh flow of melancholy to seep through.

Jordan sighed and frowned, replaying what Hisao had said about Kenji. She was baffled that Hisao had somehow disapproved of his little brother's closest friend. Ryusuke had obviously cared deeply about Kenji—his worry over Kenji's tussle with Tadao had been just one drop in the deep pool of their friendship.

And as far as Jordan could tell, Kenji had always reached back for the hand Ryusuke extended. The two had seldom been apart, but Jordan didn't consider them "too close," as Hisao apparently had. If anything, one added to and improved the other.

Jordan recalled the only time the boys' behavior had been strange: when she had stumbled upon them late after school in the washroom. They had acted almost guilty somehow, caught like a couple under the bleachers. She exhaled a sniff of a laugh at the image, but then her breath froze. She let the thought slowly approach, fearing that the idea would flee like a wild animal if she looked it in the eye.

The washroom. Tadao's slur against Kenji. Ryusuke's question to Jordan about concealed feelings. Kenji's withdrawal after Ryusuke's death. Hisao's reservations over the boys' relationship.

Were they...together?

As the idea finally assumed form, it seemed more possible than not. Her stomach plummeted. Had she really known Ryusuke at all?

A few moments passed, her thoughts simmering, before Jordan released a wobbly sigh. She would have to consider the revelation more, and what it meant to the investigation.

She had only just entered the school's lobby, still ruminating, when raised voices and the echoing trod of footsteps diverted her attention. At the top of the stairs, several figures began to descend.

There, Ms. Nakamura was joined by two men at her sides, neither of whom Jordan recognized. As they came closer to Jordan, she saw that the men were guiding the vice principal—their grip tight on her arms, her wrists in handcuffs.

Jordan gasped at the procession. Surprise, vindication, and a strange mixture of disappointment and anger tumbled over one another like boiling water. She knew her mouth was hanging open, but she couldn't be bothered to care as she took in Ms. Nakamura and her handlers.

The older woman was as stone-faced as ever, her features chiseled and unmoved. Her eyes remained straight ahead as though she were completely uncaring, or unaware, of the serious men pressing against her. Jordan thought Ms. Nakamura's chin may have even been raised, in defiance or pride, and she looked more like a powerful woman being escorted by bodyguards than a criminal who needed to be corralled.

As though she could feel the intensity of Jordan's gaze, Ms. Nakamura swiveled her head toward her. Their eyes locked, and Ms. Nakamura's narrowed. Jordan anticipated the familiar chill of Ms. Nakamura's icy, unfeeling stare, yet the coldness did not touch her. Jordan was too hot with triumph—burning with it. Her lips curled into a victorious smirk, which only broadened when Ms. Nakamura broke eye contact.

Then, she and the police officers swept through the bright, open doorway without a word.

Everything seemed to speed up after they passed from view, as though Jordan had been watching a recording of a long-past event replayed in silent slow motion. She heard animated voices from the top of the stairs and realized a conversation had been going on all along— she had been too shocked by the scene to pay attention before.

At the stairs' peak, Toshihiko was joined by Principal Kikuchi, Mr. Mori, the school lunch lady, and the boys' gym teacher. The principal looked confused, and his hands moved frantically as he spoke— clutching at his bald scalp, adjusting his glasses, pulling at his lapels. Toshihiko replied patiently and opened his palms in a sort of placating gesture. Mr. Mori nodded, arms crossed, and seemed to agree with whatever the inspector was saying.

Jordan had just made up her mind to join them, to sate the curiosity tripping along her every tingling nerve, when Toshihiko bowed and then descended the stairs. She had to draw upon all her willpower to resist running up as he walked toward her.

"I was right," Jordan said in a low voice, suddenly without breath. "She did it."

"Ms. Umiko Nakamura has been arrested under suspicion of murder in the deaths of Emi Hirata and Ryusuke Suzuki. Further evidence pending, more charges may be brought," Toshihiko said, carefully professional. "It gives me little satisfaction to say so, but it appears you may have been correct."

"Has she confessed to anything?" Jordan asked hurriedly, several more questions already piling up.

"Ms. Nakamura has not said a word, yet, but she's being taken to the station for further questioning," Toshihiko said flatly.

"I thought you'd be happier—closing the lid on your big case." Jordan wanted to say more—about how her suspicions had been justified all along and how he should have accepted her help—but it felt wrong to gloat when, at the end of the day, there were still several people dead.

"I do my job for duty, not for pleasure," he said with a small quirk of his lips. Jordan thought she knew him well enough to detect pride gilding his voice. She almost smiled too, relieved.

"I think I know why she went after Ryusuke," Jordan said but didn't feel fully convinced, hoping the inspector would fill in the details.

"Even now, you are relentless." Toshihiko gave her an appraising look over the top of his glasses. "His relationship with Kenji? Ryusuke kept a journal of sorts." He supplied the last few words at Jordan's questioning look.

"So you *did* establish motive as Ms. Nakamura's twisted sense of vigilantism? Morality policing?"

"That's still just a theory..." Toshihiko said and glanced toward the teachers mingling at the top of the stairway. He dropped his voice and led Jordan a few steps away. "*Your* theory. Not necessarily one my department shares."

"You must have considerable evidence, then." Jordan followed suit, speaking quietly.

"Traces of cyanide were found in her home. Hairs matched to her were also found at the scene of the last victim's murder. There are other, more circumstantial, pieces of evidence of course. A tin of hibiscus tea in her cupboard, for one," he said, and Jordan nodded with satisfaction.

"And you can compare that tea to what was put in my jacket!" She had wanted to ask about the tea and the yellow car earlier but had decided it would be too selfish to ask so soon. Now, though, she couldn't hold back.

"Yes, we can." Toshihiko actually smiled for a moment, pleased and a little caught off-guard at her reaction.

"Did you find anything in the school's storeroom?"

"We recovered a pestle and mortar with residual cyanide. Of course, more people than just Ms. Nakamura had access to the storeroom, which is probably the exact reason why it was kept there—so she wouldn't be found in possession of it." Toshihiko slipped into his outdoor shoes as he spoke and retrieved his folded jacket from a cubby. "I apologize, but I really must be going now. We can talk more about this later."

"Of course! Don't let me keep you." She was disappointed that her remaining questions would go unanswered in the meantime, but she was even more eager for Toshihiko to finally, completely close the case. Maybe even coax a confession from Ms. Nakamura.

"Goodbye," Toshihiko said simply and bowed, to Jordan and to those still at the top of the stairs, before leaving in a rush.

Mr. Mori and Principal Kikuchi both gave Jordan a hard look, likely wondering what had passed between her and the inspector, and resumed talking to each other in low voices. Jordan left then, too. She watched Toshihiko's white sedan pull out of the parking lot, the back of Ms. Nakamura's head visible through the rear windshield.

THIRTY

THEY HAD ALREADY BEEN IN THE CAFE FOR A WHILE, BUT JORDAN was still getting used to the unreality of sitting with Toshihiko for a casual chat. Or, at least, as casual as discussing a murder investigation could be.

She had contacted him frequently from the time of Ms. Nakamura's arrest, suggesting they meet. He had put her off, though with apologies, citing such pressing duties as Ms. Nakamura's interviews, her arraignment, and even the introduction of new cases.

Jordan had waited, kept an ear out for any talk of the case, and read the papers, from which inky photos of Ms. Nakamura sneered up from the pages. The "Red Tea Murderer."

Finally, weeks later, Toshihiko had agreed to meet her at a cafe in Yamagata City, where they had settled into opposite ends of a small booth.

"She still maintains her innocence," Toshihiko was saying. "When she says anything at all. But she hasn't even attempted to provide an alibi for the nights of any of the deaths."

"The DNA evidence from the hairs at the crime scene—surely that will be enough to convict her, on top of everything else. Like the tea and traces of cyanide at her home."

"That's what the prosecution is hoping, yes." He paused to sip at his coffee.

"I still can't believe the tea didn't match what was sent to me," Jordan said, her anger and disbelief resurging once more. Toshihiko had broken that news to Jordan days before, but her ire felt as fresh as ever.

"It's not that the teas are absolutely different, just that the results of the comparison were inconclusive. The tea from Ms. Nakamura's home and what was in the envelope may very well be one and the same," Toshihiko said in a placating tone.

"'*Inconclusive*' can't be used as evidence against her though." Jordan huffed.

"True enough," Toshihiko conceded with a sigh.

"Did she ever explain where the cyanide came from? Or the yellow car?"

"No. She denies any knowledge whatsoever. But, there were traces of organic matter in the mortar from the storeroom as well—fruit, the lab technicians tell me. So we can conclude that the cyanide was likely derived from fruit seeds."

"That's really possible?" Jordan said, amazed that her theory had been borne out.

"Yes. Strange, isn't it?" Toshihiko had interpreted her reaction as surprise that such a thing could be done, and she wasn't about to correct him. She had to know how her primary theory was faring.

"Do agree with me, about her motive?" Jordan had built her personal investigation on the foundation that Ms. Nakamura had punished Yuki for his wrongdoing, however small, and all the other victims who had followed—or preceded. The deaths of the students in Sagae years before might be on her hands as well.

Jordan now realized how silly she must have seemed, rushing forward with only a whiff of suspicion to fuel her efforts, when Toshihiko had DNA catalogs, ion chromatography, search warrants, honed interviewing techniques...

Again, she felt a tide of embarrassment and looked down to hide the rising flush in her cheeks. Still, if she was right, she had managed to architect the same conclusion about Ms. Nakamura *without* Toshihiko's resources.

"Moral vigilantism seems to be a good theory. Ms. Nakamura has been known to take a...severe tack with misbehaved students," the inspector said. Jordan raised her eyebrows and he elaborated. "Her former school, Sagae Middle School, appealed to the prefectural school board for her transfer after she continually humiliated students. She even struck some with switches, apparently. Her supervisors said they were unaware of her actions until parents raised concerns about their children's mistreatment."

"So I heard," Jordan said. She continued, undeterred by Toshihiko's exasperated sigh. His protests meant little now that the investigation had been concluded. "I had a conversation with Sadako Kudo from Sagae. Her younger brother was one of the students Ms. Nakamura abused."

"You spoke with Sadako Kudo?" Toshihiko sounded surprised, but his expression seemed to say, *of course she did*. He shook his head. Jordan suspected all sorts of thoughts about the poisonings in Sagae were bounding through his skull, as they were in hers.

"Speaking of what happened in Sagae—do you think you'll be able to level any more charges against Nakamura? Yuki's and Junichi's murders? Hajime, Haruka..."

"Doubtful. Finding any additional physical evidence for Yuki's or Junichi's case would be nearly impossible now, much less for supposed suicides that happened years ago," Toshihiko said. "But they certainly follow a similar pattern."

"The deaths in Sagae and Ogawa were all relatively recent. Is there anything suspicious further back in her history?"

"Not deaths, no. But there have been complaints about Ms. Nakamura's treatment of students throughout her career, as far back as the schools' records go. She was even questioned on accusations of child neglect against her own son nearly thirty years ago. Details on that are scant, however."

"Can't you ask the son yourself?" Jordan wondered.

"He has proven rather difficult to find. And he appears to be Ms. Nakamura's only surviving relative, so there's no one else to provide information on those old allegations," Toshihiko said with a touch of disappointment. "Ms. Nakamura seems to have cut off all ties with anyone close to her. There's not even a single family photograph in her entire house."

"Wow. That's just creepy."

Toshihiko smartly disguised his snort of a laugh with a cough. "At any rate, her apparent dislike of children is something of a long-standing secret."

"Yet she has been in schools this whole time. And she's a mother," Jordan said in disbelief.

"Unfortunately," Toshihiko said, regaining his aura of profession-alism despite the topic. "So it seems your theories stand for the moment."

"You really didn't need my help at all," Jordan blurted and ran a hand through her hair. "I thought I was doing something. I thought I could…" She stopped and sighed loudly, wondering whether she would ever shake that feeling of uselessness, of never doing enough.

Toshihiko's eyebrows crept above his glasses with a questioning look, but he said nothing. After a moment, Jordan wrangled her expression into something resembling calm, though she couldn't keep from tapping at the handle of her coffee cup as she spoke.

"There's something I've been thinking about. If I'm right about Ms. Nakamura's motive, why didn't she target Kenji too? Did she only know about Ryusuke?"

"I don't know."

"What did Kenji have to say?"

"I haven't interviewed him," Toshihiko said, then elaborated quickly when Jordan's mouth fell open in surprise. "He ran away after Ryusuke's death. Even his parents don't seem to know where he is."

"He ran away?" Jordan gasped, her stomach sinking. Except for his fight with Tadao, Kenji had been the perfect student, upstanding and conscientious. Kenji abandoning his community and family seemed so out of character, Jordan could hardly believe it, which only concerned her more. "Was he running from Ms. Nakamura? Or maybe something happened to him? Before Ms. Nakamura was arrested, she could've—"

"Jordan. Don't let yourself get caught up in that line of thinking," Toshihiko said gently and placed his hand over hers. Her hand remained tense, and he withdrew his touch a moment later, ducking his eyes. "I'm sure Kenji is fine."

"Come on, now. It's not like you to draw conclusions without any evidence," Jordan said with a twitch of a smile, knowing he had said it for her benefit.

"There's also no evidence to suggest he is in immediate danger."

Jordan nodded and bit her lip as she thought, far from mollified.

"Principal Kikuchi said Kenji's parents had enrolled him at a different school. Did he lie for them?" Jordan wondered.

"No, Mr. and Mrs. Ito admitted they had fed a story to the principal. They are very embarrassed by their son's actions. I'm not sure if they would speak to Kenji, or if they would inform me of his whereabouts, even if they did know."

The fact that Kenji hadn't been in contact with anyone for so long —not even his parents—was worrisome, to say the least. Despite Toshihiko's attempt to placate her fears, Jordan felt her thoughts spiraling and had to force herself to breathe calmly.

"Are you still trying to find him?"

"I'm doing everything possible to locate Kenji, and to ensure that he's safe. He could bring very important testimony to the case," Toshihiko said, and Jordan nodded, her gaze drifting over and far beyond the inspector's shoulder. Toshihiko sighed, recognizing the signs of her plotting. "You think you can find him."

"I'm not sure, but I might have an idea." Rather, she had the inspiration to once again try to track down Kenji online. To really dig into possible social networks.

For a few minutes, neither of them spoke. Either Toshihiko was uninterested in Jordan's idea or thought it best not to encourage her. Or there was something else on his mind.

As Jordan added more sugar to her coffee, she spied Toshihiko glancing at her surreptitiously. He then cleaned his glasses, twice, and cleared his throat as many times. Just as Jordan geared up to dispel the strained atmosphere, or maybe simply to excuse herself to the restroom, the inspector finally spoke.

"I apologize for cutting off communication so abruptly when the case resumed. I could have handled that better," Toshihiko said and looked squarely at Jordan. The collar of his dress shirt rose and fell against his neck in time with his quickened pulse. "I hope you will forgive me."

"I forgive you," she said but felt her stomach heave, feeling nervous without entirely knowing why.

"I know you understand why I acted as I did," Toshihiko said with an uncertainty that belied his words.

"Professional integrity—I get it."

"If I had let my judgment become clouded, I might have never closed this case. My behavior was more for the sake of the victims than myself."

"I understand," Jordan said, hoping the same could be said of her visit to Junichi's mother, her faked illness in the nurse's office, her phone calls to the Itos, her acquisition of Ms. Tatsuya's keys. She had to swallow hard to push the coffee down her throat.

"Good." The inspector smiled and his shoulders relaxed, noticeably more at ease. "Perhaps we could meet again soon... Not to talk about murders or the case."

Jordan didn't immediately respond, allowing the waitress to refill her mug, and took a slow sip through the ribbons of steam. She had suspected this was the destination of the conversation as soon as Toshihiko had gone down the path of apology.

It was a conversation she had anticipated—rehearsed even—several times before. But each time, her imagined responses grew weaker and thinner, as though her energy for it was draining away as time passed.

Had Toshihiko sought reconciliation sooner, she probably would have accepted. But now...

Jordan knew more surely than ever that Toshihiko's priorities lay with his work. What was to stop him from snipping another romantic entanglement with her as soon as the tendrils of a case curled around him?

She even had to admit that part of her resented Toshihiko for breaking away in the first place, and for assuming that she would readily pick up where they had left off. Not that she would refuse his proposal out of spite, but it roused the old ache.

Besides, her contract would expire in just a few months' time, and she doubted she would seek to renew her employment. Not after everything that had happened. Even if she did remain in Japan, for she also couldn't bear the thought of returning home, she'd likely move on from Ogawa, and away from Toshihiko.

Jordan felt a pang of sadness and regret when she realized what her answer would be.

"I've grown used to my own company, to tell the truth," she said finally and tried to ignore the way Toshihiko's lips pressed into a tense line.

"I understand." Toshihiko nodded, and Jordan wondered if he truly could.

It wasn't just an excuse. From the moment Jordan had set foot in Japan, it was as though a bubble had sprung up around her. Even when she tried to move closer to people, she could approach only so far—never quite touching—before being pushed back.

Jordan once thought that Toshihiko had glided through the barrier. But then she wondered whether he had just pushed so close, so gradually, that the bubble had stretched yet never broken.

Toshihiko looked at her silently from across the booth in the cafe, his eyebrows drawn and his coffee pushed aside, but he made no protest to her noncommittal reply. She felt a flicker of warm gratitude.

"I could always use a friend," she said and grimaced at hearing the classic brushoff come from her own lips.

"All right. Just text me if you have the time," Toshihiko said with forced cheerfulness.

Jordan nodded and stood up to leave, but the inspector made a small noise to catch her attention. He smiled wryly as he spoke.

"And let me know if you hear from Kenji."

———

"This is pointless," Jordan said to her computer, sighing as she tossed away a bottle of oolong tea after taking one last tepid gulp. She had been searching the Mixi network for any sign of Kenji for the past two hours, with little success.

She pressed her fingers against her closed eyes and rubbed until blossoms of muted, writhing light spouted against her eyelids. Her hands were numb from perching over her laptop, and she felt just about ready to give up.

After searching for Kenji by name had led nowhere, she had begun exploring communities where users with common interests congregated and shared stories. Even though Kenji had run away, Jordan had little doubt that he knew of the murder investigation and Ms. Nakamura's arrest. The Red Tea Murderer was all over the internet and news outlets, after all.

And because homicides were relatively rare in Japan—about 0.4 per 100,000 people, according to an article she had just read—Jordan felt she would have luck in tracking down related communities and their members.

After a bit of searching, she had found both the "Families of Victims of Violence" and "Friends of Victims" communities, which seemed promising. But hours and hundreds of posts later, Jordan felt emotionally exhausted, choked by countless expressions of grief that all began to adopt the same grey cast.

Because of the general anonymity of the website, she harbored no delusions of stumbling upon a post entitled, "My boyfriend at Ogawa High School was fatally poisoned," but still, she held out hope.

With another sigh, Jordan stood up, stretched until her shoulder gave a dull pop, then settled back with mildly stoked enthusiasm. She continued scrolling until her eyes settled on a post halfway down the page.

A suspect was arrested for my friend's murder, but...

The entry was dated a few days after Ms. Nakamura's arrest. She clicked on the link with renewed interest.

...I can't come forward with the information I have against them. If I go to the police, I might expose myself too. But his killer has to be brought to justice. What should I do?

Jordan's brow knitted. It was an odd, vague message. The responses to it were few, encouraging the poster to trust in law enforcement and offering their sympathy.

Somehow, Jordan felt the post was promising, if only for its timeliness, and clicked on the poster's name: Yakyuubi. The poster's profile had no information besides a short welcome message, but Jordan's pulse quickened when she explored the other communities he belonged to: the Rakuten Eagles Fan Club and the Ōfuri Hangout. Groups related to Kenji's favorite baseball team and comic book, respectively.

She navigated to the private messaging system and composed a brief note, reading:

Hello. Are you Kenji Ito? This is Jordan Howard from Ogawa High School. Please reply.

Jordan wondered whether it sounded too cagey, but she didn't want to allude to the murders, lest she scare him off. Finally, she decided it would have to suffice. She clicked the send button and closed her laptop with a satisfying click.

THIRTY-ONE

AT THAT MOMENT, IT WAS IMPOSSIBLE TO BELIEVE THAT THE people surrounding Jordan had been touched by murder so few months ago, much less unknowingly harbored the culprit in their midst.

Principal Kikuchi literally hooted with laughter as the head teacher performed a mumbled rendition of "Living on a Prayer" while wearing a blonde wig. Everyone was hollering or giggling behind their hands. Ms. Tatsuya, Mrs. Takahashi, and even Mr. Mori were grinning openly. Jordan had taken a spin on the microphone herself, minus the wig but plus a few beers.

She remembered how, just a few days ago, many of them had argued against the two-day staff retreat to the mountain *ryokan* resort. They had suggested it was unbecoming in light of the arrest of one of their senior members.

Eventually, Principal Kikuchi had appealed to tradition and insisted that they congratulate the head teacher on his retirement during the yearly retreat. His tactic had worked, and earlier that evening, Jordan had found herself squeezed three to the back seat of a hatchback that twisted at a startling pace along the mountainous, cork-screwing roads.

Nearly every one of Ogawa High School's teachers—besides the few who had wandered off to play ping pong—were piled in the resort's karaoke room. Its dark interior became celestial with dots of rotating lights and the milky glow of captioned screens in the smoky air.

Ms. Tatsuya leaned across the table to shout at Jordan, but even then, she couldn't hear the math instructor's words and just nodded amicably.

Jordan smiled, enjoying this uncharacteristic glimpse of her coworkers that she was unlikely to see again. If she was being honest, she was enjoying letting her hair down, too. Everyone seemed to converge into one swaying, multi-limbed entity—touching shoulders, grasping elbows—that pulsed in time with the music.

Jordan shook her head and wondered bemusedly if it was the alcohol inflating the scene in her own mind. Not caring much to examine the answer, she took another drink of beer and cheered as the head teacher relinquished his microphone to the principal.

One person, however, did sit apart from their cluster of camaraderie: Toshihiko. Unsurprising, considering he was the only one not affiliated with Ogawa High School.

Such staff retreats were usually very insular, extending only to the employees—excluding even their spouses. But Principal Kikuchi had insisted upon inviting Toshihiko as a way to express the school's gratitude for the inspector's successful work on the homicide investigation. Privately, Jordan also thought it was a way for the principal to demonstrate that there was no love lost between him and Ms. Nakamura.

Perhaps more surprising was that Toshihiko had accepted the invitation. Jordan wondered, with admitted suspicion, whether he was trying to gather more information while everyone's guard was down. It seemed unlikely that Toshihiko viewed the retreat as a social opportunity. He had driven himself to the mountain resort separately and booked a single room. Everyone else in the party was sharing rooms, with up to five futons to a suite.

Toshihiko had been at his most social during dinner, when they had all knelt together at low tables throughout the dining room. By that time, they had all changed into casual *yukata* robes and were admiring the food laid before them: ramekins of wobbly egg *potaaju*, bowls of broth for *shabu-shabu* kept warm by Sterno, and large shrimp curled in ice bowls, their antennae and black eyes glistening.

Jordan had occasionally heard Toshihiko's voice as it mingled with laughter and the clinking of glasses. The two of them hadn't spoken beyond exchanging pleasantries, but Jordan had sometimes seen him looking her way. They would smile if their eyes met, and Jordan was relieved that Toshihiko seemed unsoured by their last conversation in the cafe.

Again, in the karaoke room, Toshihiko sensed her scrutiny and looked up from his sake. He raised his cup as though toasting her and grinned in a goofy way that was very unlike the staunch inspector. Perhaps he, too, was allowing himself to relax for once. Jordan picked up her drink, spilling a bit as she fumbled for it, and made to join him.

Her world gone fuzzy around the edges, Jordan miscalculated the seat and stumbled on top of the inspector. By the time she settled, they were pushed hip to hip. She laughed. He did too, and neither moved. The music and laughter were loud, making conversation next to impossible. After a minute, Toshihiko leaned down close enough that his lips could have brushed her ear.

"Nice to see you." His warm breath swept over Jordan's cheek, making her shiver pleasantly, like she had walked into a tongue of sunlight on a chilly morning.

"You too," she said loudly and gulped the rest of her drink, which made her grimace at the dry sweep of alcohol down her throat. Toshihiko smiled at her with no small amount of amusement and fondness. Under the thin frame of his glasses, his cheeks were flushed and his dark eyes held a bright intensity.

Jordan's breath caught. She felt drawn to him in a way she never quite had before, as though she had to stop her fingers from reaching for him. As though her skin were burning where their legs and elbows touched. Before she could talk herself out of it, she rested her hand on his robed knee.

Toshihiko took a languid sip of his sake with impressive nonchalance and placed his hand over hers under the table. Slowly, he moved his hand, pressing his fingertips against the bones along the back of her hand, brushing her knuckles, and then lacing his fingers between hers. His palm was warm and soft, and he simply held her hand in his. Even such a small embrace sent tingles to Jordan's fingertips.

After a moment, Toshihiko let go, but instead of withdrawing, he slid his hand across folds of fabric until it came to rest on the exposed skin of her thigh. Jordan jumped, then let out a low exhalation when his fingers traced the inside of her leg. She knew no one could hear but felt herself flush nonetheless.

"That *yukata* doesn't fit you very well," Toshihiko said with a teasing smirk, face close to hers. Jordan knew it was in his nature—and was his job—to observe, but she felt indignant.

She had been self-conscious about the robe all night. It was thin and worn only with undergarments, tailored for the average, petite Japanese woman. She had often caught flashes of her pale legs in the gap where the robe fastened, like paper between the folds of an envelope, no matter how many times she had gathered the fabric.

Jordan drew another slow breath and tensed her thigh under his hand.

"I could just ditch the *yukata* altogether," she said with enough force to be heard, and to get her point across. Toshihiko's fingers paused on her leg, his breath catching. She laughed, emboldened and heady. "You have a single room, don't you?"

He managed to nod and moved his grip to her wrist, laid bare by a too-short sleeve, pulling her after him as he rose from his seat. Jordan tugged her robe together as they exited, she slightly behind him. No one seemed to notice, or if they did, they said nothing.

Compared to the raucous karaoke room, the hallway was like a library—quiet, empty, and infused with the brittle smell of paper and wood. Jordan couldn't help but giggle as they shuffled away, socked feet thumping on the floor like books dropped one upon the other.

They scurried quietly through the sprawling lobby, which

displayed an arresting collision of aesthetic sensibilities. Rustic wood-work met chic modern accents; a sheath of water trickled down a floor-to-ceiling monolith of black marble that evoked a waterfall in the woods despite its stark minimalism.

When they reached his room, Toshihiko fumbled in his billowy sleeves for the pocket that contained the entry card. Jordan had never seen him so impatient and had to bite her lip to keep from laughing.

"I'll help you find it," she said in a low voice and ran a hand over his backside, feeling the muscle tighten under her palm.

"Jordan!" Toshihiko yelped but managed to rein in his voice on the last syllable. "You're not helping." He smiled and leaned in to kiss her.

It was tentative at first, a simple press of closed lips, before they pulled away to take open-mouthed, shallow breaths. Jordan drew closer and guided Toshihiko's mouth to hers with a hand on the back of his head, deepening the kiss.

From where his hands pulled her hips against his, currents of heat fanned out, curling tightly across her skin and pooling in hollows. When their lips rejoined, their teeth bumped and Toshihiko's glasses pushed into her cheek with the urgency of their grasping embrace. Jordan laughed breathlessly, but then stopped at a noise.

Over the furious rushing of her heart in her ears, Jordan had heard the thud of footfalls nearby. Her breath thickened in her throat as she whipped her head to see down the hallway.

Before she and the inspector could disengage, Mr. Mori rounded the corner and stopped. Jordan jumped away from Toshihiko, though it was far too late. But if Mr. Mori were shocked or appalled, he didn't show it beyond the almost imperceptible raising of a single eyebrow.

"Excuse me," he said with an admirable lack of sarcasm and bowed before entering the men's restroom a few feet away from the pair.

For a moment, Jordan was concerned that the interruption would jolt new life into Toshihiko's sense of propriety, raising an instant and unscalable wall. But before the worry could take hold, Toshihiko laughed and grinned at her.

"Find that key?" Jordan smiled wolfishly.

He answered with a kiss to her temple and pulled her through the open door.

They got dressed in companionable silence, each allowing the other to their thoughts. But as Jordan pulled on her *yukata* and the warmth of their encounter began to cool, her giddiness deflated.

She didn't regret what they had done—had quite enjoyed it, in fact. But she was niggled by guilt nonetheless. While she had followed Toshihiko to his room as a romp—a pleasant distraction, thrilling and fleeting—she hadn't told him she had no intention of resuming their relationship.

Actually, she hadn't given much thought at all to what would follow that moment. And she couldn't even guess as to what Toshihiko had thought, or was thinking.

Jordan turned her back to him, afraid one kind look would dissuade her from what she had to say. She swallowed hard.

"Toshihiko...This doesn't mean we're back together," Jordan said softly. Even though she wasn't facing him, she ducked her head and fiddled with the ties of her robe.

There was a beat of silence. A slow exhalation.

"You're going about this the wrong way." Toshihiko's voice came from behind her.

"Excuse me?" Jordan pivoted and gave him a sharp, questioning look.

"Your *yukata*—you're tying it all wrong. Here." He walked over from where he had been leaning against the wall and gently began to undo the tied belt at her waist. "Fold the left side over the right side. It's never worn the other way. Only the deceased are dressed for burial with right over left, you see?"

"You saved me from quite the fashion faux pas, then," Jordan said, still feeling a bit silly from drink and wanting to overwrite the morbid image Toshihiko had created.

"Quite." He let out a sniff of a laugh, focused on righting the *yukata*.

Toshihiko rearranged the folds of the robe, cast in blue moonlight from the window. His hands glided over and smoothed the *yukata*, and Jordan could feel the warmth of his palms through the fabric along her stomach and hips.

"Thank you." She offered a small smile. A brittle, bittersweet thing.

"Of course," Toshihiko said warmly, but his tone was at odds with the sadness in his eyes.

"Well, I'd better..." Jordan motioned at the door instead of saying more, unable to muster the right words.

Toshihiko gave a knowing nod and reached past her to open the door, his hand brushing against her arm.

"Goodnight, Jordan."

"Goodnight," she said as she stepped into the hall, and he shut the door with one last tender look.

She didn't move for a long time, staring at Toshihiko's room and wrestling with the urge to knock. Finally, a cool breeze swept across her skin and she shuddered back to herself.

She had been away from the rest of her group for well over an hour, but it was still early in the evening, and people were bound to be about. Not wanting to be caught by one of her colleagues again, she made to slip around the corner. She could probably rejoin the other teachers unnoticed and without comment. As long as Mr. Mori hadn't said anything.

That thought chilled her, yet, somehow, she doubted Mr. Mori would share what he had seen. Gossip just didn't seem to coincide with her image of the taciturn instructor.

Now on edge, Jordan paused where the hallways met, casting a quick look one way before turning the other. She gasped, startled, when she was suddenly face-to-face with Ms. Tatsuya.

"Oh! Jordan-*sensei*, where have you been?" The small woman's owl-like eyes grew even larger with surprise.

"I thought I might check out the *onsen*. I guess I got a little lost."

Jordan gave a short laugh that sounded nervous to her own ears, but she congratulated herself for not fumbling for an answer.

"You came from the hallway to the men's wing." Ms. Tatsuya's lips drew back from her large front teeth in an odd sort of smile, her tone dipping between questioning and incredulous.

"I must have been *really* lost." Jordan offered no more, even as the silence began to grow thick.

"Well, I'm glad I found you, then! I happen to be going to the *onsen* myself. You'd like to join me?"

Jordan agreed and followed Ms. Tatsuya through the narrow corridors until they arrived at the entrance to the hot springs. The *onsen* was denoted by a canvas flap at the doorway, which bore a symbol of a pool with three swishing lines rising above it like steam.

As soon as Jordan stepped through, a sheet of freezing air pressed against her and almost drove her back inside. The resort was high in the mountains and the night held a sharp edge, making the prospect of slipping into the hot springs all the more appealing.

The air sagged with humidity, despite the cold, and a sulfuric odor crept to Jordan's nose. They rounded a corner onto a wide, open-air porch where wooden walkways led to the women's changing room on one side and the men's on the other.

The separation struck Jordan as perfunctory at best, seeing as the hot springs were co-gender and no one was permitted in the pool unless completely bare, but she was grateful nonetheless. Already, there were a handful of people in the pool beyond the porch, though it was difficult to make them out through the plumes of steam and the dim evening light.

The pool cut a bright shape out of the darkness, shrinking and swelling as its steam heaved into the cold air. Water trickled out of the far end of the pool and ran down stepped rocks that dropped off the ledge of the hillside a hundred feet away. Only the sky and the crests of nearby mountains, jagged with pines and aspens, could be seen past the plunging lip of rock.

"This way, Jordan-*sensei*," Ms. Tatsuya said and motioned her toward the changing room. Though open to the air, the inside was soupy and stagnant. Jordan saw three stalls with shower heads at waist height, drooping over short plastic stools. "Please wash off—your hair too—and then we can go in."

Without offering further instruction or even turning her back, Ms. Tatsuya undid her robe and began to remove her bra. Jordan looked away and tried to disrobe as discreetly as possible—which was not at all. Jordan's thoughts were still soft around the edges from alcohol, and she contemplated whether she would have proceeded any further if not for the pleasant numbness.

Eyes down, she folded and stored her clothes, then sat on a stool in front of a showerhead, rolling a cracked, grey-veined bar of soap in her hands. The water was tepid and the air cold. She shivered, eager to clothe herself in the silky waves of the pool.

Finally, Ms. Tatsuya signaled that they could go. She gave Jordan a folded hand towel soaked in cold water, instructing her to put it on her head once in the *onsen* to keep from overheating.

Jordan had to restrain herself from running to the pool and was immensely grateful for the shroud of steam that rose up to block her view of the other bathers, and, hopefully, theirs of her. She dropped herself in with an inelegant, sloshing splash and a gasp of surprise at the remarkable heat. The prickled goosebumps along her skin instantly smoothed and she felt as though she had melted into the water, like an ice cube dropped into soup.

A slight breeze, not cold enough to penetrate the pervasive heat, brushed away the steam damask to reveal the head teacher, Mr. Mori, and Mrs. Okubo. All were flushed and wearing hand towels draped across their crowns.

"Jordan! Tatsuya-*sensei* found you," Mrs. Okubo said with a chirpy lilt and a wide smile. Jordan guessed Mrs. Okubo was at least as tipsy as she.

"Poor thing, she was wandering the halls like a *yuurei*. All the way on the east side of the building." Ms. Tatsuya tutted. Mr. Mori's gaze swept from her to Jordan, lingering for just a moment.

"Oh well, we're having fun now right? First time in an *onsen*?" the head teacher asked, his words slurred.

"Yes." Jordan grinned and ducked her head, once again self-conscious of the fact that only the milky water was dividing their nude bodies.

She felt not only embarrassed but also vulnerable. The instinct she had developed to be watchful and on-guard while around her coworkers came alive again with a start. She reminded herself that Ms. Nakamura wasn't a threat anymore, and she coaxed the wariness back to sleep.

When the other teachers resumed talking among themselves, Jordan was finally able to relax. The water, the air, her body—everything was enshrouded in heat that seeped through the skin to the marrow. When Jordan's hands moved through the water, she felt no resistance—no push where the water began and her fingertips ended. In the breath-like fog of steam, it was impossible to distinguish between the water and the creamy shadows of limbs.

Jordan sighed and closed her eyes, the others' voices dispersing among the droplets of steam and rising away before they could reach her ears.

The next morning was a subdued affair. The teachers quietly ate their breakfasts in the dining room, chirps of birdsong and waxing sunbeams filtering through the open *shoji* doors.

Jordan didn't so much eat her breakfast as poke at it—stringy fermented soybeans over rice wasn't exactly her idea of a hangover remedy. She slurped at the miso soup instead, at least enjoying its warmth. The pleasant quietude was jostled by a knock at the threshold.

"Pardon the interruption," Toshihiko said from the doorway, and Jordan looked up in unison with her colleagues. The inspector was already fully dressed, the *ryokan*'s *yukata* given over for a suit and tie.

He didn't look the least bit worse for wear after the night's carousing, and, for once, Jordan envied his imperturbability.

"Ah, good morning, Inspector Sakurai," Principal Kikuchi said, bowing without rising from his seat at the floor. "Will you be joining us?"

"My apologies, but no. I have to return to Yamagata City earlier than expected."

"Is it something to do with..." The principal didn't complete his question, but it was obvious he was thinking of Ms. Nakamura. His eyes darted for just a moment and a few teachers suddenly found something very interesting in their bowls of rice.

"No. I have other cases I must attend," Toshihiko said with a placating smile. "So if you'll excuse me, I'll be going now. Thank you for your hard work." The inspector bowed deeply as the room returned their thanks.

Before Toshihiko left, he caught Jordan's eye. She gave a little wave, keeping her hand below the table so only he could see, and mouthed, "bye." A private smile curved his lips before he could hide it, then he nodded once and left.

THIRTY-TWO

JORDAN TRIED TO TAKE AT LEAST SOME SATISFACTION IN THE inane errand Ms. Tatsuya had given her.

Perhaps the math instructor was simply too overwhelmed to do it herself, now that the new term was in full swing. After all, the task did only entail retrieving some items from the school greenhouse. Ms. Tatsuya had somehow felt the need to create a list: large pot, watering can.

Jordan shook her head wryly as she shoved the list into her pocket, wondering if Ms. Tatsuya really thought her incapable of remembering two things.

After Jordan exited the main school building, she turned and was faced by the empty baseball field. For a fleeting moment, she saw the specters of Ryusuke and Kenji running across the green grass. Saw a baseball arc through the sky before pegging a certain inspector...

She realized then that she had paused just feet away from where she and Toshihiko had first met. Ripples of fondness and regret trailed behind that memory, and then in the eddies of their other shared moments that floated to mind. Jordan thought of the mountain *ryokan* and smiled.

Perhaps it had been for the best that Toshihiko had rushed off without a proper farewell. They had at least avoided any awkwardness, or the temptation to continue where they had left off. The two of them had texted every few days since: casual, friendly messages that ghosted past anything serious, aside from the case. Jordan's smile wilted and she shook her head, reminding herself that she had things to do beyond navel-gazing.

"One large pot and a watering can, coming up."

She strode forward toward the greenhouse, which stood tucked behind the baseball field at the schoolyard's outer boundary. Though much of the school had been refurbished, the greenhouse was obviously old and seldom used. Panels of plastic film made opaque by grime pulled away from the building's ribs, like battered sails straining in the wind. Jordan almost couldn't distinguish its footpath amid the clumps of weeds that bullied its edges.

As Jordan arrived at the door, she took a quick step back, surprised to hear voices coming from within. She knocked as she entered.

The three boys standing in the greenhouse whipped their heads toward Jordan so quickly that she thought they would spin right off their necks. Their eyes went wide and two of them became a flurry of movement, grabbing some items off a table and thrusting them into their pockets. Jordan thought she glimpsed a thousand-yen bill before it disappeared into one boy's slacks.

"J-Jordan-*sensei*, what are you doing here?" the boy at the back said, his voice pitched high. Jordan spent a moment taking in their faces. Of course, she recognized them—the school was too small not to, and she taught every student there—but she couldn't recall any of their names. They were newly minted third-graders; she had remembered that much, at least, and their nametags confirmed it.

"I think the better question is what are you boys doing here?" Jordan knew the students seldom took her reprimands seriously, so she made an effort to sound imposing and crossed her arms for good measure.

"Nothing. Just hanging out." This came from the boy who had ferreted the money into his pocket. He had succeeded in wiping away the look of abject guilt from his face, replacing it with a veneer of nonchalance. A few beads of sweat rose at his temples like blisters.

"Well, you should either be at your club meeting or be headed home by now," Jordan said firmly.

The boys exchanged furtive glances, heads lowered.

"Okay, let's go." She propped open the door and gestured for them to leave.

Grudgingly, the boy who had last spoken came forward, shuffling toward the door at an unhurried pace. As he approached, Jordan scrutinized his nametag: *Nao Ka*-something. Nao's eyes were shaded by his mussed hair, but standing so close, Jordan could see that they were bloodshot—a lacework of thready, red veins. His shoulder jostled hers as he stepped outside and he mumbled something that couldn't even be mistaken for an apology.

The other two boys followed him, almost comical in their haste to scramble out of the greenhouse.

"Thank you, boys," Jordan drawled, hoping the sarcasm wouldn't be lost in translation. They didn't turn toward her voice or further acknowledge her in any way. As they ambled toward the bike racks, Jordan wondered if maybe she should have followed them. Or marched them straight to the new vice principal. She didn't know exactly what to accuse them of besides slacking off, though they had obviously been caught red-handed at something.

Jordan sighed and let the door squeal shut behind her. Tugged by curiosity, she moved to look at the table the boys had been crowded around. Nothing seemed out of the ordinary. There were only swipes in the dirt covering the table—vague shapes of fingers and hands where the boys had hurried to retrieve whatever had laid there.

She looked a minute more, scanning the floor and shelves. Everything was washed a sickly green color by the sunlight filtered through the plastic walls, but the empty seed trays, rusty trowels, and assorted gardening tools were not otherwise notable. Jordan shrugged and widened her scope to take in the whole room.

"Large pot. Watering can."

THIRTY-THREE

"Excuse me. Is this your change?" Jordan asked with careful enunciation and held a few yen coins in her open palm toward Mrs. Okubo.

"Oh! My change! Thank you!" the English instructor said with a touch of melodrama. Jordan smiled, and some students chuckled, while others diligently followed the dialogue in the textbook.

As with many previous lessons, Jordan protested to Mrs. Okubo that the sample conversations sounded unnatural and that the students would be ill-served by memorizing such stilted lines. Mrs. Okubo agreed to an extent but said that if they deviated from the curriculum, the students would not pass their college entrance exams.

Jordan was tempted to ask whether they were trying to teach English or merely prepare the students for a single test, but she knew it'd be like pushing against a large stone sunk deep into the ground. Instead, the two of them mimed along with the lost change conversation once more and instructed the students to then practice in pairs.

Jordan strolled through the classroom, listening and offering tips over a background chorus of, "Oh! My change!" that rippled like a song in round through the pairs. Over the noise, Jordan heard the sliding rattle of the door being opened. She had to shield her eyes against the morning sunlight slanting through the windows to see who entered. The new vice principal stepped inside. He tempered his expression, but his cheeks were flushed and sweat stippled his brow.

He went straight to Mrs. Okubo without offering the customary apology for the intrusion or even bothering to close the door behind him. He spoke urgently in her ear, standing so close that each puff of his breath lifted the hair at her temple. The students' practiced conversations quieted at his entrance, but Jordan still could not hear a thing. Mrs. Okubo nodded wordlessly, straight-faced, and the vice principal turned on his heel and left.

"Class, can I please have your attention? Everyone, return to your seats."

The students rushed to obey and exchanged questioning, tight-lipped glances. Jordan joined Mrs. Okubo by the chalkboard and would have asked what was going on, except the other woman seemed completely unaware of Jordan's presence at her side as she addressed the class.

"This morning, Nao Kazuki of *san-nensei, san-kumi* was found dead in his home."

Gasps and incredulous exclamations burst from the students. Jordan had to strain to listen over their murmurs and the thrashing of her heart in her throat as Mrs. Okubo spoke.

"School is dismissed for today. Please return home if you are able. If you must wait for a parent to pick you up, please remain here in your homeroom. There will also be a counselor available in the afternoon."

"Okubo-*sensei*?" A boy in the front row raised his hand and continued without being called upon. "Was Nao murdered?"

"I really can't say, Eiji. I'm sorry, class, but Jordan-*sensei* and I must go to a teachers' meeting. Hopefully we will have answers for you soon, but in the meantime, please return home or wait here until you are able. Thank you." She nodded grimly and left, Jordan right on her heels.

"Do you know more than what you told the students?" Jordan said as soon as they were out of earshot of the class, itching to get to her cell phone and text Toshihiko.

"Nao was found just like the others. The police don't know for certain yet but—"

It wasn't possible. It couldn't be.

Jordan's stomach dropped to the floor and she staggered as though tripped by it. Already pounding, her heartbeat throbbed even harder in her ears.

"But Ms. Nakamura is in jail awaiting trial..." Jordan said with effort, her breath strangled. She didn't expect any sort of answer from Mrs. Okubo but had to give outlet to her over-spilling thoughts. She shook her head, but it did nothing to clear the fog of disbelief clouding around her. "How can this be possible?"

"I don't know." The instructor's words were clipped, reined between grief and uncertainty.

"What if it wasn't Ms. Nakamura?" Jordan said, rejecting her own words even as she spoke them, refusing to give the thought purchase. Mrs. Okubo didn't respond and instead hurried forward, leaving Jordan behind in the hall.

She slowed to a stop and simply stood there. Unable to move, Jordan felt her thoughts hurtle themselves in all directions and slam into the walls of her skull, only to slide back down and churn.

Jordan leaned against her kitchen counter and rocked on her feet impatiently, waiting for the kettle to come to a boil while she stared out the window. There was only a thin glaze of yellow light still remaining along the horizon. She could see little beyond the silhouettes of spiders rappelling across their webs under the building's eaves.

She had remained at the school for what had felt like an interminable amount of time, waiting for news. Principal Kikuchi had reported that Inspector Sakurai was at Nao's home and would be relaying information to the school, and Jordan had texted Toshihiko numerous times herself. But hours later, no word had come, and Jordan was eventually ushered home.

Jordan looked away from the kitchen window to fish her cell phone out of her pocket, checking it with a sigh. No new messages.

She texted Toshihiko yet again, pleading for details. Not expecting a response, she put down her phone to tend to the rattling teapot that gargled and hissed like a broken pipe on the stovetop. She nearly dropped the spitting kettle in surprise when her phone dinged at a new message.

Toshihiko had responded.

I'm still at the crime scene. Talk later.

Jordan's stomach clenched. For its few words, Toshiko's text conveyed quite clearly that Nao's death was indeed a murder. Numbly, she keyed a quick reply and stirred some instant coffee into a mug of hot water, her mouth gone dry.

For a while, she sat at the kitchen table, sipping her coffee and listening to the whoosh of vehicles that passed along the highway. She had no idea where to start. Was it a copycat killer? Was Ms. Nakamura truly innocent? How could they have been so wrong?

Jordan knew nothing of Nao Kazuki, either. She thought perhaps she could track down and speak to his friends, ask questions like she had before. She could inquire after Nao's shady behavior in the greenhouse, for one.

But instead of being flooded with determination and curiosity, she felt only a weak pulse of energy that had already begun to stutter to a stop. Jordan remained sitting long after her mug had emptied, letting thoughts float by, unable to latch onto a single one.

Only when the ten o'clock chime tripped from the town's PA system through her open window did she move. She wasn't sleepy and doubted she would be anytime soon. She opted instead to turn on the television and her laptop.

As she browsed the internet and checked her email, she was reminded of Mixi and her private messages to the user whom she assumed was Kenji. Though Jordan's first message had gone unanswered, she had not been deterred, following up with three more requests for him to reply—each more insistent than the last. She had also messaged a few other promising users.

Still, she had not heard a word in close to two months, not from "Yakyuubi" or anyone else. Yakyuubi had posted nothing new to the community, either.

She suspected that she had scared him away, or at least pushed him to adopt a new pseudonym. So it was without much expectation that Jordan logged in to her Mixi account. She was unsurprised to find no new messages. With a nagging sense of finality, Jordan composed another private message to Yakyuubi:

Kenji, if this is you, please contact me right away. There has been another murder. What do you know about Ryusuke's death? Please respond, or better yet, contact the police. –Jordan-sensei.

She pressed the send button, which made a sound like a drop in a shallow puddle. Unconvinced that she would ever receive a reply, Jordan closed the laptop and sprawled as best she could on the small couch, her long, bare legs sliding on the faux leather.

Slowly, the television newscaster's gentle voice and the wave-like rushing of passing cars lulled her. She pushed aside thoughts of Nao, Kenji, and eventually, even Ryusuke, until only the blankness of sleep tugged at her.

Jordan awoke some hours later, her neck sore and tight from sleeping against the couch, ear to shoulder. She let her exhaustion-heavy eyelids flutter and nearly drifted back to sleep when a blinking light on the table drew her attention, as bright as a moon orbiting the television's blue face.

The tiny beacon issued from her cell phone. She was greeted by the image of an envelope in the corner of the screen. Jordan opened her inbox and squinted as the bright light assailed her eyes. As soon as she saw that the message was a forwarded notification from Mixi, she sat straight up, fully awake.

Yakyuubi had replied:

Hello, Jordan-sensei. Please do not tell my parents or the police. I trust you will not. Let's meet in person to discuss this...

Jordan reread the entire message twice over, writing down the address and time when Kenji—or Yakyuubi—instructed her to meet.

THIRTY-FOUR

Risshaku-ji Temple looked as ancient as the dense cedars and twisting rocks that surrounded it, as though the temple had sprouted from the earth centuries ago. It was mid-afternoon and the temple grounds were teeming with tourists armed with umbrellas and wide hats to repel the sun. Most look tired but pleased, having just ascended the hundreds of steps that zippered up the mountainside.

Jordan watched the crowd carefully for any sign of Kenji, though her eye was constantly drawn to the hall's swooping roof and colorful banners. They undulated in a languorous breeze she couldn't feel.

She was more than happy to visit the picturesque mountain temple of Risshaku-ji, but it seemed an odd place for Kenji to choose—not really a hotspot for runaway teenagers. Then again, she wondered if that was exactly why he wanted to meet here. His message had been cagey to the point of downright distrusting, and he was obviously hesitant to communicate over the computer. A lively destination like Risshaku-ji was probably the last place anyone would expect him to be, and a safe, public place.

Just as Jordan started to suspect she had been put on, twenty minutes past their agreed time, she saw a familiar figure emerge from behind a cluster of people. Jordan's heart jumped, relieved to see Kenji safe—happy just to see his face again. Though, that was tempered by his forlorn look.

Kenji noticed her immediately and nodded when he caught her eye. Instead of walking toward her, however, he veered to the side until he reached an outcropping off the main path. Jordan followed.

"Hello, Kenji." Jordan found a smile. "It's good to see you again."

"Jordan-*sensei*," Kenji said, his expression solemn. The young man's eyes only stayed on Jordan for a moment before flicking to the side nervously. He cast his gaze at anyone who came close, though the other visitors didn't even look in their direction. "Did you come here alone?"

"Yes, just as you asked me—"

"And you haven't told the inspector?"

"No, I haven't," Jordan said hesitantly, taken aback by both Kenji's demeanor and her guilt over hiding the meeting from Toshihiko.

She had spent restless nights wrangling with whether or not to tell the inspector. Kenji had insisted that Jordan come by herself and threatened to bail on the meeting if he had even the slightest suspicion that she wouldn't comply.

Plus, until the moment Jordan actually laid eyes on Kenji, she had harbored strong doubts about Yakyuubi's identity. She couldn't imagine Toshihiko's frustration if she had dragged him to the temple for some internet troll's prank.

Yet there was no denying Kenji was pivotal to the case. She couldn't risk losing his testimony, but asking to record him would only scare him off. Another layer of guilt had heaped upon her when she decided she would have to record Kenji in secret.

As nonchalantly as possible, she took a step closer to him and tapped her phone in her pocket to start an audio recording app. She cleared her throat and attempted to reengage him.

"How have you been, Kenji?"

Jordan had a good idea of his answer but thought it would seem odd not to ask. Even if she didn't already know the circumstances behind

Kenji fleeing Ogawa, his appearance clearly spoke to his state of mind. His clothes were wrinkled and stained with sweat, looking quite slept-in. His hair wasn't exactly dirty, but it was wildly tousled, and not artfully. Despite his disheveled look and the dark circles under his eyes, his handsome, sharp features couldn't be entirely disguised.

Instead of answering, Kenji merely shrugged. Jordan tried again.

"Thank you for meeting with me. I'm sure you can shed some light on what happened to Ryusuke...and the others." She paused when Kenji grimaced at Ryusuke's name. "You think you know who killed them?"

"It was Ms. Nakamura." Kenji's eyes fully met hers for the first time, dark and unyielding. "I'm sure of it."

Jordan felt a current gallop through her body and vibrate every bone.

She knew it. All along.

Yet, the longer she weighed Kenij's words, the more her vindication loosened its grip and backed away. Kenji had bolstered her long-held belief in the vice principal's guilt, but Jordan also realized that she had hoped he would provide different information. A new lead perhaps.

"But Nao was murdered after Ms. Nakamura was arrested. It couldn't have been her," Jordan pressed.

"No. Whoever killed Nao must be a copycat murderer." Kenji became more animated with each word and a fierce look suffused his eyes.

"A copycat murderer?" She had considered that explanation herself, even bounced the idea off of Toshihiko. He had said it was a possibility but was characteristically close-lipped about the likelihood. The newspapers had divulged almost as much information about the case as Jordan knew herself. Parts of the police report had also been made public—more than enough fuel for another killer to stoke a new fire. "Why are you so sure that Ms. Nakamura—"

"The night before Ryusuke was murdered, Vice Principal Naka-mura came to my house," Kenji said, voice trembling around his friend's name. "She said we needed to talk about my grades."

"But you were at the top of your class."

"At the time, I didn't even think about that. I was too worried about pleasing her—you know how she makes people feel." His eyes narrowed as he continued. "I told her my parents weren't home, but invited her in. What else could I do?"

"So she came inside?" Jordan felt her chest constrict with worry for Kenji, though he was standing before her unharmed.

"She was about to, but our neighbor, Mr. Tanaka, saw her and said hello. He worked with Ms. Nakamura for years when they both taught at Ogawa Elementary School, so he knew her pretty well. They talked for a minute or two, but I could tell Ms. Nakamura wanted to leave."

"How do you mean?"

"She kept trying to end the conversation and was sort of fidgety. I don't know, she just seemed nervous—not like how she usually is. As soon as she was able to, she excused herself and left without another word to me," Kenji said. His next words formed with eerie calm. "I think she planned to kill me that night."

"Kenji..."

He looked not at all like a young man then, only a child. Jordan wanted to reach out and fold her arms over his shoulders. It would be easy to do—the space between them was so short and thin—but she clutched her hands to her sides and didn't move.

"I have no doubt that she murdered Ryusuke and would have done the same to me. She knew Mr. Tanaka could place her at the scene; otherwise, she would have gone through with it. Maybe she even came back to try again, but I left right after I heard about..." Kenji's voice died away, his expression distant. Several seconds passed before he spoke again. "Ms. Nakamura has to be held responsible for what she did to Ryusuke. She *has* to."

"She will be. Especially if you go to the police with your story—it would help the case a lot."

Kenji nodded but looked unconvinced, shuffling his feet in the dirt. "No one would believe me."

"I believe you, Kenji. And so will Inspector Sakurai," Jordan said firmly. If anything, Kenji looked even more doubtful, or maybe it was fear molding his expression.

"What good would the police do? Where was that inspector when Ryusuke was killed?" He spat out the words, and Jordan felt a pang of remorse on Toshihiko's behalf. After a few deep breaths, Kenji calmed, but he still looked torn. "Besides, if I go to the police, I would have to tell them everything, wouldn't I?"

"Everything? What do you mean?"

"About me and Ryusuke. About how we..." He dropped his eyes. "My parents would never have me back if they found out."

"I don't think the police have to know about that, if you don't want them to," Jordan tried reassuringly.

Kenji's only response was to fix his gaze at the ground and shake his head in refusal.

Jordan struggled to reconcile the image of the gregarious young man she once knew with the listless, vengeful person before her. But, as she pictured Kenji with his easy smile, Ryusuke appeared right beside him, throwing an arm over his shoulders. A part of Kenji must have passed along with him.

A long silence followed, fissured by the tinkling of coins tossed against stones as visitors made their prayers.

"Will you come back to Ogawa? I'm not the only one who misses you," Jordan said with a small smile. She considered saying his parents missed him, too, but didn't know how Kenji would take it, or whether he'd be able to read her uncertainty. No matter what she said, words seemed too frail to even begin to penetrate the barrier he had raised.

"I don't think so, Jordan-*sensei*. But thank you." Kenji's lips twisted in an attempt at a smile that fell away. He cast his eyes toward the path down the hillside. "I should go now."

"Wait! Do you need a place to stay? Or some money?" Jordan reached into her purse, but Kenji began to protest before she even touched her wallet.

"No—no, that won't be necessary. I should go." He took a step back and shot another longing look at the path.

"Okay, Kenji," Jordan said, reluctant, and felt her eyes flood. "Thank you again, for speaking with me."

"Sure." He shrugged, already walking away. "Goodbye, *sensei*."

"Goodbye," Jordan said, too quietly for anyone else to hear. She watched Kenji as he made his way down the mountain, disappearing among the thick trees.

THIRTY-FIVE

"ARE YOU SURE THERE'S NOTHING ELSE YOU CAN TELL ME about Nao?"

Nao's friend Tomo shrugged at Jordan, his meaty arms rising and falling listlessly. Tomo had met every one of Jordan's questions with a sullen, mumbled reply of no more than a few words. Soon, even those scant remarks had been replaced by grunts and nods that could be interpreted to mean any number of things.

Jordan wanted to give Tomo the benefit of the doubt; after all, his good friend had just been murdered. But she felt his resistance stemmed from more than grief. Perhaps he was still wary of her since she had stumbled upon him and Nao in the greenhouse. Jordan sighed with frustration, deciding the boy needed a little extra push to be more forthcoming.

"Come on, Tomo. I know Nao was up to something." She whispered and leaned in. "He was selling drugs in the greenhouse that day, right? Or were you going out there to smoke? What was it—pot?"

It wasn't exactly a stab in the dark. Jordan could think of few other reasons why the boys would have met in secret to exchange money. Their skittish behavior and Nao's bloodshot eyes had only made her more certain. Still, Jordan was surprised when Tomo looked to her with abject fear.

"I—I don't know what you're talking about," he said, casting his wide eyes about nervously. His reaction offered all the confirmation she needed, and Jordan tried not to feel too satisfied as Tomo began to back away. "I have to go."

"Okay. Thank you, Tomo," Jordan said with no small amount of sardonic sweetness.

The large boy nodded jerkily, pushing together the pillowy band of flesh beneath his chin, and walked away from her down the hall. Tomo swung a wary look over his shoulder as he navigated through the milling students, and seeing Jordan watching him, shuffled away faster.

Tomo wedged past the boys' gym teacher—Mr. Seki—and Mr. Mori as they came from the other direction. Mr. Seki watched the student's back as he passed and shook his head.

"Is Tomo doing all right, Jordan-*sensei*?" he said. "I saw you talking to him, poor kid."

"As well as can be expected, I suppose," Jordan said and felt guilty about only perfunctorily asking how Tomo was before plumbing the depths of Nao's life.

The small success she had felt at guessing Nao's indiscretion was already being eroded by gusts of doubt. If Nao had in fact been breaking the law, he matched Ms. Nakamura's other victims. But with Ms. Nakamura in jail, perhaps Jordan's theory of the killer—and his or her motive—had been wrong all along. It was possible that the thefts and trysts committed by the other victims had merely been unrelated events—ones that had created the semblance of a pattern only to those hoping to find one.

"Any word from Inspector Sakurai?" Mr. Mori said, jolting Jordan away from her thoughts.

Despite what Mr. Mori had seen at the *ryokan*, Jordan felt a spike of indignation at the question. Yes, she had exchanged words with Toshihiko when she had sent him the audio recording of her meeting with Kenji, but he had no progress on the case to report. At least, not to her.

"I only know what the principal has relayed to us," Jordan said truthfully.

Mr. Mori looked at her, eyes scanning from her mouth to her eyes, before he nodded once in acquiescence.

"Perhaps Ms. Nakamura will be released from custody soon," Mr. Seki said, almost hopefully. "She couldn't possibly have hurt Nao."

Jordan's stomach twisted at his tone, and though he was right about Ms. Nakamura and Nao, she couldn't help but bite out her next words.

"I hope she's ready to make herself comfortable in prison. She has to be involved with at least some of the deaths. Kenji said that—"

"You've seen Kenji?" Mr. Mori said, eyes sharp behind his glasses. "When was this?"

"Uh, the day we all found out about Ryusuke, I think. Before he transferred schools." Jordan settled on the lie to avoid any discussion about why or how she had been in touch with Kenji long after he had stopped attending school in Ogawa. She thought she had covered her hesitation well enough, but Mr. Mori continued to scrutinize her. She gulped at the intensity of his gaze.

"And? What did Kenji say, Jordan-*sensei*?" Mr. Seki asked. He, too, funneled his full concentration toward Jordan, caught up by curiosity.

"Never mind. It was just gossip."

"More rumors than facts flying around, that's for sure," Mr. Seki said. "I know anyone would agree, though, it'd be impossible for Ms. Nakamura to kill anyone from a jail cell." He nodded decidedly at his own logic.

Nao's death was indeed a murder. That much had been confirmed to the general public, as had the manner of death—identical to the others. At this news, murmurs about Ms. Nakamura's guilt had gradually transformed into proclamations of her innocence. Mr. Seki was apparently one of her supporters, and not the first Jordan had encountered.

Speculation about the murders, which had originally been confined to Ogawa, had now galloped across the prefecture. Even some national media outlets had picked up the story.

News reporters, with their hulking cameras and microphones, had appeared overnight like mushrooms. Most were pretty, soft-spoken women in immaculate dress suits who looked like generations of the same-model doll. Jordan had avoided one near the school the day before, though the reporter didn't seem to be taking interviews, merely using the building as a backdrop.

As if reading Jordan's mind, Mr. Seki continued. "Did you see the reporters? I heard they're calling this the Red Tea Murders—"

"It's almost time for the after-school meeting," Mr. Mori interjected, taking in both Jordan and the gym teacher. "Let's head on."

Mr. Seki quickly apologized to Mr. Mori for delaying him, and Jordan followed them toward the teachers' room. Mr. Seki was still eager to talk, though his focus had shifted.

"I'm glad it's finally Friday! Are you doing anything this weekend, Jordan-*sensei*?"

"I'm taking the train to Yamagata City tonight for dinner, but no other plans," Jordan said. She asked in turn about Mr. Seki's weekend, making small talk until the three of them reached the teachers' lounge.

Jordan spared a look at what was formerly Ms. Nakamura's desk and frowned, conflicted, as she passed.

Jordan blinked sleepily as she disembarked from the train and exited Ogawa's station. Despite dozing on the ride home from Yamagata City, she wasn't rested, but rather in a detached state hovering below full wakefulness. She yawned, checked her watch—just before midnight— and headed to the poorly lit bike lot covered by a corrugated roof.

Before Jordan even reached her new bike, she could see it was listing badly, and closer inspection revealed a woefully flat front tire. Jordan cursed, but admittedly, she hadn't been relishing a long ride home through the dark streets anyway.

She walked to the pay phone outside the station and picked up its bright green receiver, preparing to dial the cab company whose advertisements mottled every surface of the booth. Before she could slip any yen into the machine, a voice called to her.

"Jordan-*sensei?*"

A sedan rolled up beside Jordan, its headlights blinding her. Because of the dark and the lingering after images, Jordan needed a moment to recognize the man behind the wheel.

"Oh! Good evening, Mori-*sensei.*"

"How are you doing? Everything all right?" Mr. Mori's car pulled to a stop, gravel crunching under its tires, and he leaned an elbow out the window. He didn't appear overly concerned, probably only asking out of politeness.

"I'm fine. My bike has a flat, though. I was just about to call a cab."

"Please, let me give you a ride. Your apartment is on my way home."

It didn't surprise her any more that so many people knew where she lived, seeing as every foreign teacher before her for the past fifteen years had been housed in the same apartment. Before she could answer, Mr. Mori leaned across the car to unlock the passenger's side door.

Jordan hesitated, feeling uncomfortable about taking advantage of his kindness when she still wouldn't consider him more than a tenuous acquaintance, despite sitting across from him and watching him grade papers and sip his tea every day.

A wave of tiredness made up her mind for her, and she couldn't stifle a yawn as she stepped toward the car. She climbed in and closed the door with a heavy rattle that made her reflection quiver in the rearview mirror.

She didn't bother to latch the seat belt, as she was often chided for wearing one, told time and again that only children needed such precautions. Even though it was almost too dark to see Mr. Mori, Jordan turned to address him.

"Thank you for the ride. Are you sure it's not too much trouble?"

"Not at all," he said. The car pulled from the parking lot and slipped into the street, which was awash with red light from an izakaya's neon sign. Its glow gave some semblance of life to the abandoned stores that slumped against the izakaya on either side. Even if there were more light to see by, there was little beyond the car's windows besides a few houses opening up to stretches of rice fields.

Jordan glanced around the car's cabin. It was fastidiously clean and perhaps the first car she'd been in during her time in Ogawa that wasn't pervaded by the smell of cigarette smoke. Mr. Mori continued to drive in silence for a minute more before Jordan felt obliged to make conversation.

"I didn't see you on the train. Did you go to Yamagata City too?"

"Sagae, actually. I was visiting some former colleagues."

"Oh, yes. You said you worked at Sagae High School before being transferred here last year, right?" Jordan said with a smile, glad that she had remembered at least one of their few, undoubtedly brief, conversations.

"That's right."

"Do you miss Sagae much?"

"Not really," he said and smiled without any real pleasure. He took a sharp turn, and Jordan grabbed the door to keep from sliding into the center console. "Ogawa is much the same, I find."

"Maybe too much the same. First those deaths in Sagae, and now here, too," Jordan said, drawing without a second thought upon the well of information she'd filled over the past months.

"Those students died years ago. You know about that?"

"Yes. I—"

Jordan froze, every muscle in her body seizing up. She stopped herself from exclaiming when a cascade of thoughts hurtled against her like an avalanche.

Slowly, she turned her head to look at Mr. Mori. He was already peering in her direction. His mouth was closed in a tight line, eyes obliterated by the sheen of a passing streetlamp over his glasses. She had to scramble for breath before she could speak again. "I overheard something the inspector said once," she finished quietly.

"You certainly do know more than you let on." Mr. Mori returned his gaze to the road.

Jordan said nothing, devoting all her power to inhaling and exhaling around the fist of apprehension that stoppered her throat. All of her thoughts surrounding the case rushed to the front of her mind and tumbled end over end.

Ms. Nakamura wasn't the only one who had lived in Sagae when Sadako Kudo was first poisoned and the suspicious deaths had followed —Mr. Mori had been there at the same time.

Any one of Ogawa High School's staff could have accessed Emi's medical file, and the storeroom.

Mr. Mori's car was... She didn't have to look to know the answer, yet she slid her gaze to the side-view mirror, which reflected a coin of yellow paint against the backdrop of the roadway.

Jordan wondered whether the car still bore a scratch from when it had ground against the bridge's railing instead of her body—whether she would have noticed, if only she had paused for another moment outside the phone booth.

And it wasn't the only time that she had been oblivious to what had laid before her. Jordan had been so single-mindedly focused on Ms. Nakamura that she had been blind to everything else in the periphery.

Jordan swallowed thickly and contemplated fishing her phone from her purse to alert Toshihiko, but she couldn't risk revealing just how much she knew. Not until the car trundled past the turnoff to Jordan's apartment without even a moment's pause did she feel a spike of panic plunge between her ribs.

"Mori-*sensei*, we passed my apartment," she said, and with great effort, leveled her voice to a casual tone. "If we could just turn around here?"

"You know I can't do that now," he said, his utter lack of emotion seeping coldly into Jordan. "You never belonged here in the first place."

"I'm not that easy to get rid of. But you knew that already," Jordan said with more bravado than she felt, speaking loud enough to cover up the slide of her purse's zipper as she thrust her hand inside to retrieve her phone.

"Stop."

Jordan gasped, both at the abrupt command and the firm pressure of something touching her side. She looked down to see a knife pressed against her, its edge disappearing among the folds of her shirt but not penetrating her skin. Blood rushed to her head with a sweep of nausea, but she stayed stock-still.

Mr. Mori glanced at her impassively for just a moment before returning his eyes to the road. He accelerated the vehicle despite driving with only one hand on the wheel, the knife in the other. He spoke again in a low voice.

"Put that behind you in the back seat. Move slowly."

Jordan did as she was told, wrenching her arm behind her to deposit the purse without aggravating the knife. Swells of desperation, hopelessness, and incongruous curiosity collided in Jordan's chest.

"Why did you do it?" Jordan infused her voice with enough anger and accusation to keep her words from trembling.

"Oh, you were right. I heard you talking with that inspector more than once," Mr. Mori said. His eyes glittered in the dim light as they flicked to her face. "They were all too dishonorable—too immoral—to realize their own shame. They were blind to their transgressions."

Mr. Mori let out a long breath through his nose and continued.

"Would you like to know what Nao did?"

"He sold drugs to the other students." Jordan floundered to breathe, and her voice came as a weak, gasping noise. With considerable effort, she managed not to be sick in her lap after she parted her lips to speak.

"How can you say that so carelessly?" Mr. Mori spat out the words, as though they were bitter on his tongue. "Do you really think that kind of person has a place in our community? In society?"

"I don't—"

"They have no place," Mr. Mori said, his voice rising and filling the car. Jordan shrank against the door as the knife poked harder with each word. For a minute, they drove in silence. Jordan took quick, shallow breaths to avoid touching the weapon's sharp edge.

She noticed they were traveling farther away from any semblance of town, down a dirt road without streetlamps. Only the occasional dot of a home's lights floated over the surrounding rice fields like foxfire. In the dark, she could barely make out the road as it swept by in a dusky stream.

Sheer disbelief began to climb above her panic and fear. She felt as though she were watching her predicament from just outside the car, running alongside the vehicle and peering in its windows as it skipped between the watery fields.

"Why didn't you kill Kenji?" The question fell from her lips before she even realized she was speaking aloud.

"Kenji was gone before I could get to him." Mr. Mori let out a snort, or maybe a bark of laughter. Then, his voice became almost wistful as he looked to the road. "Yuki was easy. So desperate to please his teachers, after he had been caught, that he let me in without question. And Ryusuke. Too dumb to even—"

"Ryusuke was a better person than you could ever hope to be," Jordan said, unwilling to let the insult stand, despite how it paled against everything else. Despite how Mr. Mori might retaliate. But he simply continued undeterred.

"Emi was surprisingly cooperative. She drank the tea freely...just like the rest of them. And she was so kind as to leave a picture of Junichi for me to find in her diary. By the end, they all knew what they had done wrong." He paused. "I don't expect you to understand."

"I understand enough to know that you're nothing but a hypocrite," Jordan said in a wave of anger that grew too quickly to be stemmed. "You're the shameful one. A murderer! Don't you see that what you're doing is far worse than any of their mistakes?"

Mr. Mori only smiled to himself in private amusement as she railed on.

"Emi was pregnant. You took her child's life along with hers."

Jordan's words rushed out breathlessly. "And you framed Ms. Naka-mura. Sent an innocent woman to jail—"

"I did not!" The car swerved as Mr. Mori's hand jerked the wheel with the force of his exclamation. "Cleansing the students was her idea."

"What..." Jordan's mind raced. So Ms. Nakamura *had* been involved, just as Jordan had always suspected. But why would Mr. Mori go along with her plot? And why would she recruit him, of all people? They hadn't even met before working at Ogawa High School together...or so Jordan had been led to believe.

They must have some deeper connection, or relationship.

Jordan rifled through all she knew. Ms. Nakamura was consider-ably older than Mr. Mori, and Toshihiko had said she had an estranged son. Jordan had rarely seen them interact, but when they did, Mr. Mori was eager to please the older woman. Now that she thought of it, they even looked similar, with their height and pinched features.

Every small piece finally resolved to form a complete image, like pixels on a screen. The two of them had hidden the secret well, but Jordan felt certain when she spoke.

"She's your mother."

Mr. Mori nodded, not looking at Jordan, and his voice quavered when he collected himself enough to resume his story.

"She taught me what it means to be upstanding, and honorable. Loyal. Like any dutiful son, I obeyed her when she explained why we had to cull the students. Trim away the infected limbs so the body—so we all—could live."

"But she disowned you! You don't even share the same name."

"Oh, we've had our...disagreements. That's why I had to help when she told me about her plan, to please her. But she never, *never* got her hands dirty, did she?"

He jerked the wheel violently to round a corner, and Jordan had to brace against the momentum to keep from impaling herself.

"She prepared the tea, but it was always up to me to get them to drink it. How she chastised me when I failed to properly poison that first girl in Sagae. After my failure with Sadako, it was too risky to target her again. She got away... But I never made that mistake again."

Even in the poor light, Jordan could see Mr. Mori reddening in agitation, his birthmark livid against his neck. Every other word became strangled.

"I never failed after that. Yet she wasn't satisfied. Always finding fault with the littlest thing I did or didn't do. If it was as simple as she said, why couldn't she do it herself? I couldn't stand her criticisms any more. That's why I made her take care of the Ito boy."

"Kenji?"

"It was her fault he got away, you see? She was weak. She couldn't go through with it. For all her words, she was too weak." Mr. Mori paused for a long moment, and though his expression remained fixed, his dark eyes shuttled with thought. "I did place her hair with Ryusuke's body. I needed her out of the way, and I knew she wouldn't reveal me. She never will."

"You—"

"She knows the work I do is too important. Necessary. She started it, after all." He spoke slowly, as though he hadn't heard Jordan. She saw a change sweep over his face, pushing his lips and eyebrows into a pained look. "I do regret leaving her to the police like that, but she failed me first. I'll be more effective without her."

"Would a loyal son leave his own mother in prison? You can free her, if only you turn yourself in." Jordan doubted appealing to his filial affections would work, but a wild flash of hope blinded her for an instant. "You can help her right now, if you just let me go."

"No." The cold finality of the word hit Jordan like a blow. "I gave you the chance to walk away from all this. But you ignored my warnings—the tea, and at the bridge—and you kept sticking your nose where it didn't belong."

"You're right. I should've listened. If you let me go now, I promise I won't tell a soul what I know. I'll go back to America and..."

"Oh, no, it's too late for that." He actually chuckled. "You're a blight in the garden. I see that now."

"Me?" Jordan's voice cracked, but she was beyond caring. "I haven't done anything wrong. I don't even know the first thing about Japanese honor. If I've somehow—"

"But that's exactly it. You willfully know nothing." Mr. Mori's veneer of emotion was supplanted by an eerie calm. "You insinuated yourself into our school, among our children, never once showing the proper behavior befitting a teacher."

"I didn't—"

"You and the inspector," Mr. Mori said and sneered. "He at least should have known to show restraint. Shameful. I will see to him next."

His emotionless voice chilled Jordan to her spine, and her immediate fear compounded with worry for Toshihiko.

Then, the car began to slow. Mr. Mori leaned closer to the windshield, squinting into the dark. He seemed to be looking for a place to pull over—a fact that churned the blood through Jordan's veins even faster. The vehicle had only lessened its pace a little, the road slipping by quickly. When the knife pressed against Jordan, as the car lurched over a bump, she knew she had to take a chance.

Mr. Mori was still straining over the wheel, and his grip on the knife loosened with distraction. Jordan took one more look out the window and grasped the door's handle.

With only a beat of hesitation, Jordan wrenched at the door and pushed all her weight against it, straining against the current of momentum just long enough for her body to slip through the opening.

The shock of the landing was even greater than she had imagined. Her shoulder and arm melded into a wedge of pain that shot tendrils from her toes to the crown of her head. As she lay in the road, hobbled by pain and shock, she felt as though she would never move again. She briefly welcomed the thought of sinking into the soft, pungent mud beneath her.

Then, Jordan heard the raspy shudder of the car as it skidded in the road, followed by the groan of its door being thrown open. She screamed at her limbs to move. On her first attempt to stand, her arm and leg folded under her like a sheet of paper set on its edge, but the sound of Mr. Mori's footsteps approaching pushed her to stagger to her feet.

In the distance, Jordan saw the porch light of a small home. The belly of the moon was just bright enough to reveal a footpath stretching through the rice fields toward the home. With no other options, Jordan surged in that direction, spurred by each footfall close on her heels.

Jordan ran as best she could along the path, though she limped and faltered often, each step sending a relay of pain through her body. She could hear Mr. Mori's heavy breaths behind her, wheezy with the strain of exertion. The sound was like a physical force that pushed against her and gave her legs the strength to hurtle forward just a bit faster.

She concentrated on the house, wishing she could simply *be* there and breach the distance instantly, like closing a book to join two pages. But as Mr. Mori neared, she knew running would not be enough. She wrenched her head to peer over her shoulder.

Mr. Mori was only a few strides away, and closing fast. His face was flushed from running and he wore a twisted grin, as though he had caught a whiff of victory at hand and was running to meet it. The knife reflected slices of moonlight as it swung with each arc of his arm.

With a deep breath that did little to buoy Jordan's sinking hope, she instantly dropped to her knees and curled into a tight crouch, her face pressed against her arms and her hands on her head.

Mr. Mori, caught unaware, slammed into her huddled side and vaulted over her back. Though the impact of his foot against Jordan's ribs sent sparks shooting across her eyes, she let out a gasp of relief that her gamble had worked.

Jordan stumbled to her feet. Mr. Mori laid sprawled partly off the path, his legs and torso disappearing into the water of the shallow rice field. She noticed then that both of his hands were empty—he wasn't holding the knife. He clawed for purchase in the slick mud as he began to right himself with a groan.

Jordan cast her gaze along the road frantically until she saw a shiny sliver not far off. She hobbled toward the knife and was nearly in arm's reach when a force slammed into the back of her knees.

She fell. Her head bounced against the hard-packed dirt, and her teeth snapped together with a clack. Mr. Mori had tackled her and his arms were still wrapped around her legs. Jordan twisted in his grip, turning until she faced skyward, and heaved her pinioned legs like a fish's tail.

One leg broke free and she kicked at him, using the other foot to push against the ground and leverage herself toward the knife. Mr. Mori growled low in his throat and yanked at her jeans to pull her away from the weapon. With a yell, she thrashed with renewed vigor. One kick hit her attacker in the shoulder and another glanced across his face, hard enough to send his glasses flying into the water.

His hold loosened just enough for Jordan to scramble free and swoop upon the knife. Her fingers closed around it and she swiveled to face Mr. Mori, brandishing the knife in front of her.

Mr. Mori had also gotten to his feet. His face was red from running and had already begun to swell where her foot had connected with his cheek. His whole body heaved with deep, shuddering breaths, his muddied shirt clinging to him. A sneering look of anger contorted his features and Jordan had to tamp down a ludicrous urge to laugh. Mr. Mori took a single step forward, prompting Jordan to jump back a pace.

"Don't come any closer," Jordan said, trying urgently to look imposing. She flicked the knife to remind him of that small advantage weighing on her side of the scales. His expression changed little and he offered no response. The air between them filled with his labored breaths and the soft chirps and splashes of frogs in the paddies.

Jordan bit at her lip and considered resuming her sprint for the house, but he could tackle her again and wrest away the knife. Instead, she flooded her lungs with the night air and yelled.

"Help! Somebody, help! Please—"

Her words transformed into a sharp cry of surprise as Mr. Mori lunged at her with startling speed. Jordan was only able to take two steps backward before he was upon her, his large hands pawing at her arm that held the knife.

Jordan thrust the weapon toward his belly in what she thought was a quick motion, but he batted her wrist away with enough strength to almost knock the knife from her hand. Before she could recover, his fist struck her squarely on the nose.

Her face blossomed with pain that burrowed between her eyes and straight to the back of her skull, like a hatchet halving a log. As her head rocked, so did her body, and Jordan began to topple backward.

She was overcome by a wave of panic as she tumbled, feeling Mr. Mori's hands on her. In the flurry of motion, Jordan was unable to make sense of what was happening, much less protect herself. Instinctively, one hand shot out to prevent her fall, but it instead caught in Mr. Mori's shirt, and he cried out with surprise as she pulled him with her. Her other arm flailed for balance.

What seemed like minutes later, though it had only been a matter of seconds, Jordan's back met the ground, followed by the crushing weight of Mr. Mori atop her, which pushed her into the soil. The air fled from her lungs and she struggled to breathe, caught under the body that blanketed her from shoulder to torso.

She pushed at Mr. Mori's stomach with her knee that was trapped between them, but he was unresponsive. Only his breath moved, whispering across her cheek in a disturbing imitation of intimacy.

Finally, slowly, Mr. Mori stirred. He planted his palms against the dirt and raised himself up, his head lolling as though hanging from a thread between his shoulders. As his head righted, Jordan flinched and shrank against the road, willing herself to be swallowed up by the dirt rather than face the sight before her.

A slender red path ran below Mr. Mori's jaw and across his neck, bisecting his birthmark. When his head moved, the gash opened like parting lips, revealing flesh that shone brackish in the night. Jordan drew in a sharp breath as blood spurted from the wound and dotted her arm and cheek.

A look of confusion suffused Mr. Mori's face. Jordan knew she was wearing a similar expression, not fully understanding what had happened.

His eyes trailed from the spray of blood across her face, raking down her arm to the knife that shook in her grip, its blade lacquered in red. Still staring at the knife, he wrapped his hand against his throat as if he were choking. The wound issued another surge of blood that soaked into his shirt in a widening circle of crimson.

He pulled away his reddened hand and held it before him. As though the sight itself were injurious, he let out a long, low groan from his slackened mouth, his lungs rolling up to squeeze out every last bit of air. His eyes went glassy.

Without warning, his body crumpled and pitched forward, like every joint was removed. Jordan managed to thrust her arm in front of her protectively, just as Mr. Mori's weight fell into her. His head landed with a thump above her shoulder, and she felt wet warmth paint her chest. She yelped, shoving against his limp form, until she was able to struggle free.

Jordan leaped to her feet despite the screams of protest that issued from every inch of her body. With unsure, shaking movements, she held the knife pointed at Mr. Mori, one hand wrapped around the other to steady the blade. The tall man didn't move. His already pale skin looked like white ash, made all the starker by the wet, dark halo spreading into the earth about his head.

A flutter of relief as feeble as moth wings patted in Jordan's chest, but her fear and panic had yet to abate. More seconds crawled past, and Mr. Mori still did not stir.

After one last look at his body slumped on the ground, Jordan turned toward the light of the house and ran.

THIRTY-SIX

THE CLOCK ON THE WALL READ 4:03 A.M. JORDAN WAS EXHAUSTED —physically, emotionally—but she couldn't imagine falling asleep. Every time she closed her eyes, she saw Mr. Mori...the Red Tea Murderer. His cold, black stare, the knife in his hands, his body on the ground. Again, he surfaced in her mind, floating over her turbulent thoughts.

She shuddered and forced herself back to the present, though her current position wasn't very heartening. The white hospital room stared back bleakly, sterile and silent. At least she had a single room. She couldn't bear the thought of being left alone with a stranger. Having only her thoughts for company wasn't much better, though.

With an unhappy groan, she wondered when she would be released. The doctors had cleared her of any major injuries, though the throbbing of her broken nose begged to differ, so she guessed they were keeping her for observation. Or waiting for the police to interview her, since she had been whisked away by paramedics before any investigators had arrived.

Just as she prepared to press the call button to summon a nurse and get some answers, the door opened after a perfunctory knock. Jordan startled at the sound, and at the alarming sight of a man rushing toward her. Fear seized her body.

Just as she raised her hands to push him away, she could finally, really see him and instead wrapped her arms around his neck, like a drowning woman grasping at the shore. His embrace squeezed at her bruised ribs painfully, but she didn't protest.

"Jordan." Toshihiko's voice was like a balm on her nerves, smoothing the frayed sensation she felt all over. Reluctantly, she loosened her hold as she felt him pull away. "Are you all right?" he asked urgently.

Toshihiko's hands moved to cup either side of her head. His eyes searched hers, then roamed her face, darting over every feature as though memorizing her. One hand stroked her cheek; the other slipped through her hair. He paused his survey of her and winced sympathetically at the bruises across her nose and under her eyes.

Jordan leaned into his touch, relieved yet regretful that it had taken this to provoke such emotion. She set that thought aside and focused on the warmth of Toshihiko's palm against her skin, on the steady, solid presence of his touch. The room suddenly seemed much brighter. If not for the late hour, she would've sworn the sun had dawned.

"I'm okay," she finally said with a long sigh. Toshihiko didn't argue, but his look was doubtful, and she amended quietly. "I'll live, at least."

Toshihiko slid onto the hospital bed beside her, his hand never lifting as it glided from her shoulder, down her arm, and then entwined in hers.

"I'm so sorry," he said and mumbled something in Japanese that Jordan couldn't make out, though it sounded reproachful. "If only I had put it all together sooner. Just a few minutes sooner and none of this would have happened."

"What do you mean?" Jordan sat straighter, some of her weariness giving way to a need to know the answers to the questions that still gnawed at her.

"I'm sorry; I shouldn't have said anything. We can go over all this later, Jordan." Toshihiko shook his head, and with and apologetic look, squeezed her hand. "You should just take some time to recover now."

"No," Jordan said with enough force that Toshihiko was visibly taken aback. "I haven't come this far—all these months—and gone through everything that happened tonight only to wait longer."

Jordan's voice quavered, and she barely managed to blink back threatening tears. For a moment, neither of them said anything, allowing Jordan to take a few shaky breaths.

"I deserve to know," Jordan said, more calmly now. She tried to muster a smile. "Besides, I could use the distraction."

With a thoughtful, soft look, Toshihiko nodded in agreement. He didn't insist on any more apologies or protests before proceeding with his explanation, for which Jordan was silently grateful.

"I had been trying to locate Ms. Nakamura's son for weeks, but finding any record of his whereabouts was...difficult. However, just a few days ago, I discovered a trace. An old car title registered in his name."

"For a yellow car," Jordan said, feeling that familiar spark of adrenaline. This time the excitement was chased by whispers of remembered fear, but she tamped them down.

"Precisely," Toshihiko said, encouraged by Jordan's usual willingness to jump in. "At first, I had simply wanted to interview the son about Ms. Nakamura. Until Nao's death, there hadn't been any evidence to suggest she had accomplices, much less that her estranged son was involved. After discovering the car title, however, I knew that it was imperative to find him. But there were no leases, no employment contracts, no bank loans, nothing under the name Makoto Nakamura in recent years."

"So that's Mr. Mori's real name? Makoto Nakamura?" Jordan tripped over the syllables, afraid that it would somehow summon him.

"Yes," Toshihiko said, speaking more quickly as he explained, as though he were closing in on the Red Tea Murderer all over again. "It became clear to me that he had deliberately left no paper trail for the last twenty years, and had likely adopted an alias. But determining his new identity proved harder than expected. Frankly, Mr. Nakamura covered his tracks well."

"Yet you found him somehow," Jordan said with encouragement. Toshihiko nodded.

"I decided to try a different tack, to find a photograph of Makoto Nakamura and hope he could be positively identified."

"But Ms. Nakamura didn't keep any family photographs..."

"Yet another reason why it took so long to solve the case." Toshihiko frowned, drawn again to regret. "I asked myself: where could I find a photograph from before Mr. Nakamura assumed another identity? When and where do young people have their pictures taken?"

"At school. School photos, yearbooks," Jordan offered.

"Exactly so. I found record of three Makoto Nakamuras in the region where he grew up and contacted their high schools for photographs." Toshihiko began to explain but then stopped mid-thought, adopting a faraway look. He deflated, as if he had been siphoned of all energy, and he failed to continue after a long pause.

"Toshihiko?" Jordan squeezed his hand in hers.

Still looking away, he gathered himself back up, his voice now low and deliberate.

"The first two were dead ends. The last school's archived records had been misplaced in the prefectural office. Only a few hours ago did I locate them, and his photograph." Toshihiko took a deep breath, and Jordan felt her own catch in suspense, despite knowing the outcome. "As soon as I saw the birthmark, I knew. It was Norio Mori."

Jordan could only imagine how Toshihiko must have felt at that moment, especially since he showed no desire to speak of it now. He slipped into a silent stupor, but Jordan could see echoes of emotion flit across his features: shock, anger, even fleeting triumph.

She had felt it all too. She felt it again, amazed that the thin membrane keeping her emotions from spilling over could stretch to accommodate more. The last piece had finally slid into place, yet it somehow felt more like a wedge driven between her and Toshihiko.

Just as Jordan opened her mouth to fill the ever-deepening quiet, Toshihiko breached it first.

"Jordan, please know that this..." He turned to face her fully, taking her in with a penetrating look. "This is not how the investigation should have ended. You getting hurt, targeted by the murderer—"

"Is this the part where you scold me for getting myself into trouble again?" Jordan said with as much humor as she could wring out, mostly to stop Toshihiko from painting the grim tableau she had faced and forcing her to recall it.

"No, I would never...I don't know what I would have done if you hadn't saved yourself tonight." Toshihiko's hand tightened around hers and he reached again for her face. He brushed his thumb across her cheek, his eyes not leaving hers. "If only I had discovered him in time, none of this would have happened to you."

"It's not your fault," Jordan said, feeling a tear spill onto her cheek. "It's over now. That's all that matters. It's finally over."

Toshihiko seemed to want to say more, but he nodded in silent acceptance. A minute passed with only the steady hum of the air conditioner and Jordan's heartbeat in her own ears to disrupt the quiet.

Tentatively, she leaned into Toshihiko, wrapping one arm across his back and then the other. He returned the embrace, holding her as one might cradle a baby bird, as if she were liable to break.

For an instant, the weight and heat of Toshihiko conjured up memories of Mr. Mori. His tackling her to the hard ground. His breath against her ear. His heavy body trapping her. Jordan shook her head, as though she could shake the images loose from their hold in her mind, and she buried her face in the crook of Toshihiko's neck.

She hugged him to her, hard. Toshihiko instantly acted in kind, intensifying his hold, pressing his hands against her back as desperately as a climber grasping a ledge. He let out a shuddering sigh, grateful to no longer hold back.

Their embrace hurt, but Jordan didn't care. If anything, she welcomed the pain radiating from her jostled bones and bruised skin. It anchored her there, with Toshihiko, and his every minute move alighted her nerves.

Jordan tried to cleave even closer, to leave no room for even thought to insinuate itself between them. She felt the steady, blunt throb of Toshihiko's heartbeat resonate in her chest, harmonizing with her own pulse. Slowly, her breathing calmed as the quiet stillness of the room enfolded them.

THIRTY-SEVEN

EVEN THE SMALLEST SIP OF COFFEE MADE JORDAN'S STOMACH turn. She set down the mug on her table and took slow breaths, willing herself to be calm despite the day's events to come. She was tired and nervous, and she looked it.

In the mirror across from where she sat on her couch, a weary, darkened face stared back at her. A line of faint purplish bruises swiped across her nose and under one eye. Her nose was healed, but the bruising had yet to disappear, looking as though she had brushed a sooty hand over her face.

Not for the first time that morning, Jordan felt self-conscious and looked away, only to be greeted once again by her own face, on the television this time. All the news agencies had latched onto the same photograph: a smiling picture of her taken two years before at her sister's wedding, her blonde hair long and curled. In stark contrast to her own cheerful, static expression in the corner of the screen, the news reporter's stoic voice droned on.

"Jordan Howard, a visiting English instructor from America, is due to provide testimony in court today in the trial of Umiko Nakamura. Ms. Nakamura is accused of assisting in the homicides of at least two of her former high school students. Only last week, Ms. Howard was absolved of any charges in the death of Makoto Nakamura, also known as Norio Mori, the Red Tea Murderer. Prefectural police ruled Ms. Howard's act as self-defense. After this harrowing encounter with the Red Tea Murderer, some are calling Ms. Howard a hero—"

Jordan jabbed the power button on the remote. *Hero.* She had also seen such words as *brave* and *inspiring* pinned near images of her in the newspapers. She shook her head and stood to make her way from her apartment to Yamagata City's courthouse.

As she picked up her purse, she spared a glance at the framed photograph beside it and touched her fingers to Aiden's indelibly smiling face. She imagined she could feel warmth radiating from the picture, and an echo of her brother's smile ghosted across her lips. When at last she walked out the door, it felt like moving toward something, not running away.

―――――――――

"You claim in your statement to the police that Mr. Makoto Nakamura said, 'It was her idea.' Can you please elaborate?" the prosecutor said to Jordan in an unaffected manner that bordered on blasé.

Jordan spared a quick look at Ms. Nakamura. The woman might as well have been presiding over Ogawa High School for all the emotion she showed. Seemingly unfazed by being on trial for multiple homicides, her expression was one of rigid stone. Her hands lay still in her lap like the pale, folded wings of a bird.

She looked so innocuous sitting there, just an old woman letting the world flow around her. Jordan was staggered by a wave of disgust and disbelief, still baffled that Ms. Nakamura had concealed her darkness so well, and for so long.

Though Ms. Nakamura didn't look her way, Jordan felt her stomach twist with fear and had to take a sip of water before she could speak. She managed to keep her hand still as she returned the glass to the desk.

"Yes. I accused Mr. Mo...Mr. Nakamura of framing Ms. Naka-mura, which made him furious, and he insisted that targeting the students had been her idea."

At first, Jordan directed her answer to the prosecutor, but then she let her eyes come to rest coldly on the defendant. Jordan willed Ms. Nakamura to face her, to lay bare the evil that had trickled through her to her son, but she didn't even bat an eye.

"What happened next?" the prosecutor asked, glancing at the judge as though to make sure he was paying attention.

"Mr. Nakamura revealed that Ms. Nakamura was his mother and that her intention had been to murder Kenji Ito."

The defense lawyer shot to his feet with an exclamation. Jordan didn't catch every word of the attorney's quick statements, peppered with Japanese legalese, but it was obvious he was protesting her testimony.

The lawyers held a brief exchange before the judge's resounding voice interjected and the defense counsel returned to his seat. The prosecutor calmly continued. Instead of directing another query to Jordan, he presented evidence of birth records and household census data that established the murderers' familial connection, plus Mr. Nakamura's theft of the deceased Norio Mori's identity.

This eventually segued to evidence of Mr. Nakamura's vehicle ownership. Namely, of the yellow car he had kept under yet another false name at a rented parking unit in Sagae City.

As Jordan waited to either be addressed or dismissed, she wrestled with the urge to scan the rows of spectators. Toshihiko had been a witness for the prosecution himself and was somewhere among those seated.

When Toshihiko had coached Jordan for her court appearance earlier that day, she had detected a current of nervous energy just below the surface of his professionalism. He had even spilled tea over his hands as he had poured a cup—anxious about the case, right as it was reaching its crescendo and the baton was in someone else's hands.

She wondered whether his nervousness had been due to worry over

her and what she would say, how she would handle herself. At one
moment, when he had thought she wasn't looking, Jordan had seen him
slide his gaze over the dusky bruises still mottling the bridge of her
nose. His expression of solemn regret had been unmistakable. But in
the next instance, he had recovered himself and had even smiled
mildly.

Jordan felt lighter just thinking of Toshihiko and tried to replay
their entire conversation over the prosecutor describing the events of
the night she was attacked: the laundry list of injuries, Mr. Mori's fatal
wound.

Jordan concentrated on the sound of the court reporter's fingers
striking the stenograph until it was all she could hear.

A bailiff escorted Jordan to an adjoining waiting room at the conclusion
of her testimony. The judge had advised her that it was unlikely she
would be called back, but she would have to wait close at hand just
in case.

Jordan's curiosity needled her. The course of Ms. Nakamura's fate
was being charted just beyond the wall, yet she was relegated outside.
She thought about pressing her ear to the door but decided it would be
worse to hear snippets than nothing at all.

After almost two hours passed, though, she strongly reconsidered.
She wondered whose testimony they were hearing now. Occasionally, a
muffled voice would intersect the quiet of the waiting room, ebbing
before she could glean anything. More minutes dragged by before
Jordan heard murmurs and shuffling movement inside the courtroom.
She jumped when the bailiff swung open the door.

"Ms. Howard, the court is taking a short recess, and you are
dismissed for today," the burly man said, his gruff voice at odds with his
formal words. "Thank you for your testimony."

The bailiff exited as quickly as he had appeared, and Jordan was left to show herself out. Just as she shouldered her purse and stood to leave, the bailiff reentered, this time with someone in tow.

"Please wait here until the session resumes," the bailiff rumbled to the young man and once again ducked out before anyone could respond, leaving him and Jordan alone in the room. The boy looked up from his feet, and Jordan gasped with surprise and relief.

"Kenji!"

He looked much improved since she had last seen him at the mountain temple. His hair was in place, his dress clothes tidy and ironed, his tie straight and shoes polished. Even his demeanor seemed restored. Life glittered behind his dark eyes, and he ventured a half-smile so familiar that the sight of it touched Jordan like a warm caress.

"Jordan-*sensei*."

Neither spoke, both unsure of what to say, but it was a comfortable silence. There was an opaqueness between them too, though—a knowledge that they were both reaching the end of something once shared.

Jordan didn't intend to break the silence so suddenly, but she was capsized by a wave of guilt when she realized that Kenji wouldn't be here if not for what she had done. She had betrayed Kenji, and his trust.

"I'm sorry I told the inspector how to contact you," she said in a rush. "I know I promised that I wouldn't, but when I—"

"You did what you had to do," Kenji interjected quickly. Then, more subdued: "I should have come forward sooner, on my own."

The guilt in his voice was obvious. He made to run a hand through his hair but stopped upon second thought, dropping his arm to his side and shaking his head. Jordan piped up again before the silence could resurge.

"But you're here now. That's what matters," she said with conviction. "You're ensuring that Ryusuke's murderer sees justice, just like you said you would."

Kenji winced upon mention of Ryusuke but then nodded, seeming more sure with each bob of his head.

"You're right, *sensei*. I just hope that Ryusuke..." he choked on the name. "I hope Ryusuke can finally rest now."

Saying as much obviously pained Kenji, but his discomfort was slowly overtaken by a fond look. His expression lightened as some feeling suffused him, illuminating his features inch by inch, like sunlight sweeping across the face of the earth. Kenji's shining eyes focused on the empty space beside him, and Jordan wondered what he saw there, as a lopsided smile creased his lips.

The quietude only lasted a breath longer, interrupted by the bailiff's reappearance.

"The court is preparing to reconvene, Mr. Ito." The bailiff opened the door just enough to relay the message before closing it again.

"Well..." Kenji let the word hang, uncertain of what to say and reluctant to do so.

"Do your best in there," Jordan offered with a wavering smile.

"Sure." Her smile had fed his, and Kenji grinned openly, teeth glinting. He took a step toward the courtroom and raised his hand in a sort of salute. "Bye, *sensei*."

"Bye, Kenji." Jordan watched him walk through the door and disappear, though it seemed more like sinking, her vision gone wavy with welling tears. But her smile stayed in place as she wiped at her eyes and heard the courtroom come back to life. A gavel resounded like the crack of a bat sending a ball sailing into an open, green field.

Toshihiko was already waiting in the hallway when Jordan exited. He stopped mid-stride upon seeing her, and if she didn't know him better, she would've guessed he had been pacing.

"There you are," Toshihiko said with relief. As he stepped toward her, his look became concerned, no doubt noticing her wet, reddened eyes. "Are you all right?"

"I'm okay. I just ran into Kenji."

"Between your and Kenji's testimony, the defense doesn't have a leg to stand on. You did just fine in there, Jordan." He spoke with confidence but she grimaced, still skeptical. Toshihiko looked insistent. "Really."

"How many more days do you think the trial will last?"

"Three, possibly a bit longer, and then deliberations." He began to walk away, motioning for Jordan to follow. Their shoes echoed from the tiled floor to the high ceiling.

"Do you think they'll find her guilty? Tell me honestly." Jordan had to hurry to keep abreast of Toshihiko's long strides. Her still-recovering ribs pinched as she tried to speak and quicken her pace at the same time.

"A not-guilty verdict wouldn't say much for my police work." Toshihiko didn't smile when he said it, but Jordan wondered if it was an odd attempt to be funny. She had never seen him so nervous, and her expression morphed into one of displeasure. Toshihiko caught her look and appended his statement quickly. "I'm sure Ms. Nakamura will be found guilty. There is considerable evidence against her."

"Where are you going in such a hurry, anyway?" Jordan said in an effort to change the subject.

"Walking you to a cab, and then I really must return to the courtroom. They've already resumed testimony."

"Why are you walking me—" Her words fell short when she rounded the corner and saw reporters lining the doors to the courthouse entrance like mannequins in a shop window. "Oh."

"I would advise against saying anything," Toshihiko said and straightened his suit jacket. Jordan also adjusted her blouse and dabbed at her eyes before nodding in agreement. "Stay close."

His fingers closed above her elbow, pressing a bit too firmly against still-tender, bruised skin concealed below, and he shouldered through the door. Immediately, he had to shield her as the reporters closed in. Black microphones, cameras, and digital audio recorders jutted from the reporters like antennae, but both Jordan and the inspector said nothing in response to the tide of questions.

"How did you escape the Red Tea Murderer?" one shrill voice demanded.

"When did you first suspect Norio Mori?"

"What's it feel like to be a hero?" This question was shouted in poorly enunciated English and Jordan blinked in surprise.

"What was Umiko Nakamura like in court today?"

The barrage of questions soon fused together—many directed at Toshihiko—as the reporters all raised their voices and crowded in. Just as Jordan contemplated shoving the nearest reporter away and running through the breach, she saw the waiting taxi that Toshihiko was steering her toward.

They both hurried their steps and Jordan lunged through the taxi's open door, falling inelegantly on the back seat. With no time for a farewell, Toshihiko shut the door behind her and spread his fingers in a small wave.

Jordan waved back, but the inspector had already turned away and was fording the crush of reporters pressing against him from all sides. She directed the driver to the train station, watching Toshihiko fade into the teeming bodies as the car pulled away.

THIRTY-EIGHT

As soon as she took her phone from her pocket, Jordan knew something had happened. The notification light on her cell phone faded from green, to red, to white, signifying voice, text, and email messages. The cell phone shook in her hand, both from her clenching grip and the humming vibrations that accompanied each new message pouring in.

Jordan dropped the magazine she had been flipping through and bounded toward the escalator that led to the store's main showroom. She took the steps two at a time until the escalator spit her out before a wall of televisions.

Jordan scanned them quickly, her eyes drawn to the NHK logo in the corner of one large screen. In the opposite corner was a photograph of Ms. Nakamura, hovering over the shoulder of a straight-faced reporter. Jordan's breath caught. She swallowed and drew close enough to hear the newscaster's soft voice.

"...the town of Ogawa in Yamagata Prefecture. After deliberations, Yamagata's District Court found Ms. Umiko Nakamura guilty on all charges. You may remember earlier reports of the death of Mr. Makoto

Nakamura, aka Norio Mori, otherwise known as the Red Tea Murderer..."

The sound of the newscast thinned into the air, overtaken by a gasping sob that swung into a laugh as it sprang from Jordan's throat. It was all over.

THIRTY-NINE

JORDAN PAUSED AFTER SHE FILLED HER BICYCLE'S BASKET WITH notes and flowers that commemorated her last day at Ogawa High School. No students were to be seen as she stood outside the school's main entrance. Still, the sounds of laughter, chatting, and clashing kendo sticks hung in the warm air to show they were not far off.

It was just as well that Jordan was alone as she made to leave. She had somehow managed to dam up the tears clinging at her eyes all day, from one goodbye to the next, but she didn't know how much longer her resolve would hold.

Jordan shielded her hand against the sun to take in the school one last time. It glinted with bright squares of golden light reflecting off its high windows.

"Goodbye," she said with a small smile. She then strapped on her helmet, swung her feet into the bike's stirrups, and began to pedal away.

Cicadas seemed to hug every branch—every leaf—for the volume of their droning that buzzed like powerful electrical lines. There were few cars on the roadways, and Jordan thrilled at zipping through an underpass and onto a street shaded by overhanging trees.

The road gently curved as it ran alongside an irrigation channel, from which some boys were fishing. Jordan heard a familiar laugh and recognized Akira as she neared. She slowed the bike and hopped off, holding it upright by the handlebars.

"Shouldn't you be at your club meeting?" she asked and smiled.

"Oh, Jordan-*sensei*!" Akira grinned broadly as soon as he recognized her. He began to splash and clamber up the culvert toward her, his rolled-up pants exposing thin legs soaked with muddy water. He sloshed close enough to be heard without yelling. "Kanazawa-*sensei* had to cover for Mori-*sen*...uh, for *his* club because of their upcoming tournament. So ours was canceled."

"I see." Jordan had asked teasingly, not really looking for an answer, and felt guilty for allowing the shadow of the Red Tea Murderer to fall over them yet again. She changed the subject.

"I just wanted to say, before I left, that it was great knowing you. I'm really glad we met." Her words sounded stiffer than she had hoped, and even after a year, she felt like she was still grasping at the edges of how to express herself in Japanese.

"Thank you, Jordan-*sensei*." Akira looked embarrassed and ducked his head to stare at the fishing pole that he rolled between his fingers. The sharp tinkling of wind chimes rushed to fill the space between them as he thought and chewed his lip. Finally, he met her eyes with a serious expression. "And thank you for what you did—for Yuki and the others."

He looked older than Jordan remembered, his face longer and his eyes keener.

"I didn't do anything really," Jordan said, embarrassment reddening her face more than the pressing heat already had. An uncomfortable tightness squeezed her stomach—all she had done was turn over the wrong rocks and then flee, until the murderer had literally fallen on his own sword. She forced her lips to smile. "I'm just glad everyone is safe now."

"I'll miss you, Jordan-*sensei*. We all will." He indicated the boys who had paused their fishing to watch Akira's exchange. Jordan noticed then that Yuki's younger brother, Shun, was among them. When their eyes met, he bowed shyly.

Jordan and Shun had shared only one real conversation after that day on the rooftop—a brief moment when he had mustered up the courage to speak and to give her a crudely folded paper crane. He was teaching himself origami from his brother's books, he had explained.

"Goodbye, Shun," she said gently.

The young boy mumbled a quick farewell, eyes to the ground. Jordan spied tears shining at the corners of his eyes and had to blink back the emotion welling in her own. She took a steadying breath and turned back to Akira.

"Keep practicing your English, Akira. I'll miss you." She held the boy's gaze, memorizing how he looked in that moment. How the sun lightened his hair and caught in the flecks of muddy water that dotted one cheek. Finally, she pulled away to climb onto her bike. "Goodbye."

Akira waved and smiled as she began to pedal back toward the road, her legs pumping to power her down the slope. Momentum soon caught up, and she willed herself to be still, to allow the invisible push to carry her.

Just like Ryusuke, Akira would, in all likelihood, never cross paths with her again. Jordan felt a tear trail down her cheek and then disappear into the warm air flowing over her.

FORTY

THE PARADE'S *TAIKO* DRUMS ROARED THROUGH THE EVENING AIR, each beat resonating deep within Jordan's bones. The drummers passing on the street were all young women. Their tan arms streaked across their sash-bound chests with each fierce strike of the drumsticks.

In clear, high voices, they shouted, *"Yassho, makkasho!"* as their stage drifted along. Its railings were strung with large paper lanterns, drooping like glowing berries that illuminated the night.

Jordan grinned as the drummers passed, but their chant remained strong, picked up and carried in one long, continuous thread by the hundreds of other performers who stretched down the street.

A group of older women followed behind the drummers, taking bird-like steps and twirling as they danced. Their teeth made smiling white crescents against the blushed makeup that covered their faces, and each wore identical robes.

As one, they maneuvered wide-brimmed straw hats ornamented with yellow safflower blossoms. The sedge hats were whirled, tipped, and touched to knees and elbows in intricate patterns as the dancers advanced in unison. Through the waves of drumbeats and mingling chants, a distinct voice surfaced to reach Jordan.

"You'll miss this, I can tell," Toshihiko said, only barely heard because he was standing so close. Jordan was surprised by the sudden voice, having been so entranced by the swaying dancers that she had nearly forgotten she was not alone. She turned to look at Toshihiko, who shot her a warm smile.

His shoulders were turned more toward her than the parade, and she wondered whether he had been watching her or was squeezed into that position by the crowd. Instead of the tailored business suit that had become something of a uniform of his, Toshihiko wore sandals, loose pants of navy cotton, and a matching shirt that fastened at the front like a robe.

Many other male spectators wore such traditional clothes, their girl-friends in floral *yukata* tied with stiff sashes. Toshihiko looked unchar-acteristically at home, and Jordan smiled back as she answered him.

"You're right. I'll miss plenty of things," Jordan said, and he grinned slyly. She hadn't exactly said that he would be missed, but it was true, and she left it at that.

"I know your teaching contract has expired, but you don't have to go." He said it so casually that the effort was obvious. Toshihiko directed his gaze at the dancers, eyes flicking side to side behind his glasses as he watched the procession. "Ogawa High School is still looking for your replacement—you could renew your contract. Or find another job. Your Japanese is good enough."

"I've already stayed longer than I meant to." Though her contract had just ended at the conclusion of the academic term, the days following Makoto Nakamura's death had piled on her like stones.

Between the doctor's visits, the police department's questions, her family's insistence that she return home, the constant requests for inter-views... Jordan sighed and looked away from the new set of performers to catch Toshihiko's expression. He was engrossed in the parade, or pretended to be, so his reaction to her response was impossible to gauge.

Toshihiko hadn't asked her to stay because of him—hadn't really asked her to stay at all. He had toed at the idea with innocuous suggestions before retreating to more solid ground. For weeks, it had been this way.

Jordan had considered asking him what, exactly, *he* wanted. Why it was so important to him that she remain in Japan. She would have liked to hear him say it. But, in the end, she decided it would be cruel to poke at him to see if he jumped when she knew his answer wouldn't change hers.

The thought of leaving Japan, leaving Toshihiko, hollowed her out with a deep ache. Yet she also felt relief. Everything reminded her of the Red Tea Murders. She couldn't see uniformed high-schoolers without thinking about everyone who had died. Apprehension would sometimes grip her without warning when a car approached, or even when she reached for a kitchen knife. Not that different surroundings would cure her of this, but maybe they would. Hopefully.

And then there was Toshihiko. Sometimes she would look at him and see the snow-covered trees of Zao, or feel his hands glide along her skin. Other times, she saw tea dashed onto her floor like blood, or heard footsteps pounding behind her and lost all breath. Jordan shook herself out of it and spared another glance at Toshihiko.

His expression slipped for just a moment, darkening as though a cloud had passed over the bright moon above. Jordan's throat clenched, but she forced her words around the tightness.

"I'm sorry."

"You don't have to apologize to me." He held her gaze, his dark eyes shining and sharp.

Their eyes remained locked for a long moment. For perhaps the first time, Jordan could feel Toshihiko's emotion like a physical thing. So tangible that it drew tears to her eyes. She ducked her head before they could fall and managed a wobbly smile by the time she looked back up.

"Thank you," she said, grateful. Toshihiko returned the smile, small though it was.

"Do you want a closer look? I know you're not one to stay on the sidelines." He indicated the procession with a tilt of his head. Before

Jordan could ask what he meant, Toshihiko grabbed her hand and began threading through the crowd, his tall figure splitting the onlookers like a rock jutting in a creek.

They continued down the street for a minute, shouldering past men and women who were too jovial to mind the jostling, until they arrived at the front of City Hall. Sprinkled among the costumed performers were festival-goers, adults and children, dancing and laughing when they misstepped or fumbled their sedge hats.

"Come on!" Toshihiko accepted a pair of flowered hats from a dancer as they passed, pulling Jordan along when she hesitated to join in. She followed Toshihiko to a pocket of empty space and giggled when he took up the hopping, swishing movements of the instructor.

The steps were simple enough, and it wasn't long before Jordan was dancing in unison with the revelers enveloping her on all sides. She caught Toshihiko's eye mid-twirl and they laughed. All around, golden flowers tumbled like jewels in a kaleidoscope. Jordan moved without thought amid the pulse of drums and voices in the night air.

THE END

Thank you for reading!

For more about Meg Mezeske find her across social media.

Twitter: @MegWritesWords

Website: www.megmezeske.com

ACKNOWLEDGMENTS

Dear reader (yes, you!), I thank you very sincerely for choosing my novel, reading it, and arriving at the end.

Thank you to my editor, Amanda, who Liked my Tweet one fateful day, and now here we are! I'm honored that you found something special in my story that I always believed was there, too.

Big thanks also to Tina, Yelena, and everyone at City Owl Press. You made Red Tea the best, most beautiful book it could be.

Of course, thank you to my parents, Mary and Reed. Thanks for leading—or should I say "reading"?—by example. You've always nurtured, supported, and inspired my love of words. From enrolling me in the library's summer reading program to helping me redeem those Personal Pan Pizzas. From encouraging me to learn a new word every day to treating me at the Scholastic Book Fairs. From funding my college education to believing in Red Tea since its very first, very rough draft. From being voracious readers yourselves to always having a book recommendation ready. The list goes on. All my gratitude and love.

Evan, thanks for being cool when I ignored you for hours on end to do my creative work. Sorry for the sacrificed co-op game time. I love you.

Thank you to my critique group: Heidi, Alan, Miles, Colleen, and Joan. Your talent and honesty helped shape Red Tea in a way I couldn't have done alone. I'm glad that I took a chance on a few strangers who became friends.

To everyone in Yamamoto-cho, Japan, my sincere thanks. You welcomed me as family, and I hope my story conveys how much I cherished my time there.

Thank you, Grant and Jessica, for your support and for equipping me with a legit Author pen. I can't wait for the boys to be old enough for mysteries.

Thanks to all my friends for cheering me on, especially Mel and Jen. BFFs make the best beta readers.

And finally, thanks to Jerry Seinfeld for his advice to all creatives. I didn't break the chain.

SSDGM!

ABOUT THE AUTHOR

MEG MEZESKE is a copywriter, podcaster, and dilettante who's happy to finally call herself an author.

Meg likes to put her characters in her favorite places—like Japan. Meg lived and worked in Japan as the only Westerner in a small town. From teaching English to being an impromptu interpreter when a Russian ship ran ashore, Meg fell in love with both the ordinary and extraordinary of Japanese life.

Author photograph by Phil Shen

Now, she retells that experience through her fiction, with mystery, murder, and romance thrown in for good measure.

Twitter: @MegWritesWords

Website: www.megmezeske.com

ABOUT THE PUBLISHER

Please sign up for the City Owl Press newsletter for chances to win special subscriber-only contests and giveaways as well as receiving information on upcoming releases and special excerpts.

All reviews are **welcome** and **appreciated**. Please consider leaving one on your favorite social media and book buying sites.

For books in the world of romance and speculative fiction that embody Innovation, Creativity, and Affordability, check out City Owl Press.

www.cityowlpress.com